Brent watched her walk away.

He felt a rush of humiliation. This was rejection, and it wasn't pretty. Well, he could have bungled it even worse. He could have grabbed her roughly and smothered her with kisses. Marla didn't look like the type who appreciated brute force....

Unable to sleep that night, he turned on the TV and watched an old movie. Clark Gable, a rough and rugged guy, was falling for a cool-as-a-cucumber dame who wouldn't tumble. Gable grabbed the woman roughly and smothered her with kisses. She fell madly in love with him on the spot....

Dear Reader,

Welcome to the Silhouette **Special Edition** experience! With your search for consistently satisfying reading in mind, every month the authors and editors of Silhouette **Special Edition** aim to offer you a stimulating blend of deep emotions and high romance.

The name Silhouette **Special Edition** and the distinctive arch on the cover represent a commitment—a commitment to bring you six sensitive, substantial novels each month. In the pages of a Silhouette **Special Edition**, compelling true-to-life characters face riveting emotional issues—and come out winners. All the authors in the series strive for depth, vividness and warmth in writing these stories of living and loving in today's world.

The result, we hope, is romance you can believe in. Deeply emotional, richly romantic, infinitely rewarding—that's the Silhouette **Special Edition** experience. Come share it with us—six times a month!

From all the authors and editors of Silhouette **Special Edition**,

Best wishes,

Leslie Kazanjian,
Senior Editor

LAURA LEONE
A Woman's Work

Silhouette Special Edition

Published by Silhouette Books New York

America's Publisher of Contemporary Romance

For my buddy Betty Brown,
who knows advertising, men, and Italian—
and not necessarily in that order

SILHOUETTE BOOKS
300 East 42nd St., New York, N.Y. 10017

Copyright © 1990 by Laura Resnick

ISBN: 0-373-09608-9

First Silhouette Books printing July 1990

Printed in the U.S.A.

Books by Laura Leone

Silhouette Desire

One Sultry Summer #478
A Wilder Name #507
Ulterior Motives #531
Guilty Secrets #560

Silhouette Special Edition

A Woman's Work #608

LAURA LEONE

grew up in the Midwest and has been on the move,
traveling throughout the world, since she was nine-
teen. Back in the United States for the time being,
Laura teaches French, Italian and English to adults
and "drifts a lot."

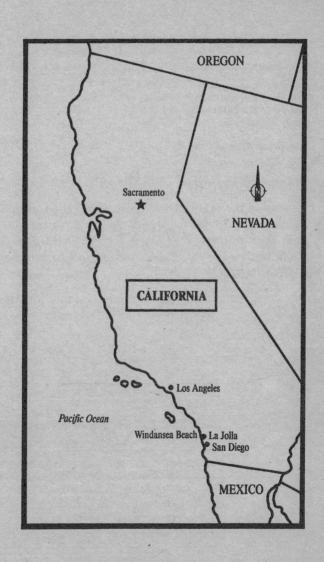

Chapter One

"Brent Ventura just arrived."

Marla Foster glanced up at the clock and then looked at Yvonne, the secretary she shared with three other account executives. "He's here already?"

"Hmm. And he's got the look, mama," said Yvonne with obvious relish.

Marla smiled as she started gathering together the information on her desk about Ventura. "What's that supposed to mean?"

"You'll see," Yvonne answered in a promising tone of voice. "I *really* hope he signs with the agency. That's one client I definitely wouldn't mind having around."

Marla stood up, straightened her peach-colored blouse and ran a comb through her long, straight, dark blond hair. "I hope he signs, too," she said earnestly. Her eyes met Yvonne's. It was no secret that Marla's career at the advertising agency had suffered some severe blows recently. In a highly competitive business where a dozen people could be laid off on any given day, her job was hanging by a thread.

"If he does sign, they'll give you the account, won't they?" Yvonne asked.

"No one has said anything definite. I have the related experience, but a couple of the guys are sitting in on today's presentation, too. It's possible that Ventura won't want a woman to handle his account. Or that he won't like me personally," she added.

Since the account executive was responsible for working with the client, developing a personal relationship with him and keeping in daily contact with him, personal compatibility was essential. A personality conflict between the account executive and the client could be disastrous, as Marla had discovered to her detriment.

"Marla?" said a male voice irritably. "We're waiting for you."

Marla lowered her eyes to hide the flash of exasperation there as Warren Tallman stuck his head through her doorway. Warren glared at Yvonne, who slunk back to her desk outside of Marla's colorful office.

"I'm coming," Marla said evenly.

There was no use in pointing out that Brent Ventura was twenty minutes early, that the senior vice president slated to participate in the meeting would be tied up until the scheduled time anyhow, and that she personally wasn't late, at fault or holding up the meeting.

Warren Tallman was a nervous, tense, inflexibly sexist account supervisor who considered Marla, like all other women, incapable of performing her duties with professional competence. In her three years at the agency, she had only worked with him once, but that one experience had had disastrous repercussions. He was part of the reason she was currently not the favored rising star that she had been since her arrival at the agency.

However, Marla recognized that the bulk of the responsibility for her current professional problems rested on her own shoulders. And she was determined to salvage her career at Freemont, Fox and Linsford Associates.

Warren was still standing in her doorway as Marla finished sorting through the papers she wanted to bring into the meeting with her. It annoyed her to see him standing there like a stern schoolmaster who didn't trust her to get to her classroom unless he watched her every step of the way.

I need this account, but I do *not* need to work with him again, she thought fervently.

She faced him with an impassive expression. "I'll be there in a few minutes." Her polite but unwavering stare was a clear dismissal. Warren tried to stare her down, but he flushed after a moment and walked away.

She was about to leave the room when the phone rang. She picked it up, and the switchboard operator informed her that her mother was calling long-distance from Chicago.

"Hello, Mom. How are things?" Marla had a feeling she already knew. Her mother only called when "things" were going badly.

"Oh—" her mother gave a slight sniffle "—John and I are attempting a reconciliation."

Marla suspected that the situation between her mother and her fourth husband was irreparable, but she tried to sound optimistic as she said, "Really? I hope it's working out."

"I just don't know," her mother wailed. "I really thought this time it would last. I don't have the strength for another divorce. But how can I live with that man?"

Marla kept an eye on the clock as she listened patiently to a familiar litany of John's faults, sins and general unreliability.

"And, of course, I lost my alimony when I married John, and he insists he'll fight any alimony claim I try to make on *him*. I just can't manage on what I earn as a receptionist at the beauty parlor, Marla!"

"Mom..." Marla glanced at the clock again, feeling guilty but aware that she had no choice but to end the conversation. "I'm sorry, but I have an important meeting right now. I've got to go. I'll call you tonight and we can talk then, all right?"

There was a pause before her mother said, "All right, dear. I guess I shouldn't have called you at work, but I'm so—"

"We'll talk tonight, Mom."

"You're so lucky to have a good job, Marla, to be so independent."

Marla thought fleetingly that hard work and determination had a lot more to do with it than luck, but she, after all, had grown up with a prime example of what she didn't want her life to become.

She hung up the telephone after saying goodbye, picked up her neat bundle of papers and notes and walked down the hallway toward the conference room.

The ad agency occupied four floors of a plush office building in downtown San Diego. Freemont, Fox and Linsford Associates employed more than one hundred people, most of whom Marla at least knew by sight. On her way to the conference room, she was joined by Vernon McConnell. He was one of the agency's associate creative directors. Marla had worked with him in the past, and she allowed herself to hope that they would work together on Ventura's account—if the Freemont agency got the account.

"I should have guessed Ventura would show up early," Vernon said in a low voice.

"Oh?" Marla said.

"He's an early bird. Up at the crack of dawn." Vernon groaned theatrically. "It's uncivilized to do business before ten o'clock in the morning!"

Marla smiled as they entered the conference room. Her eyes swept the elegant room, which was dominated by a long, well-polished table. Posters from some of the agency's most successful ad campaigns decorated the walls.

She spotted Brent Ventura instantly. She had never seen a photo of him, but there was only one man in the room who could possibly be the Renaissance man she had been reading about ever since she had learned she would be participating in this meeting.

Ventura shouldn't have looked particularly prepossessing. He sat slouched in a chair with his legs stretched out before him and a cup of coffee dangling from one hand. He clearly hadn't dressed up for the meeting. He wore khaki trousers, a cotton shirt and a light denim jacket.

Instead of looking out of place, his presence commanded the room. He was unmistakably tall, even when sitting down. Marla guessed he was several inches over six feet. His dark brown hair curled crisply around his head. When he turned slightly to listen to a comment addressed to him, the sunlight pouring through the windows touched his hair and brought out the tarnished red highlights it had burned there during his many hours in the great outdoors.

He was very tan and muscular, as she would have expected. What Marla hadn't expected was the strength of character in his ruggedly handsome face and the intelligence in the green eyes that suddenly met hers.

She was unusual. That was the first thought that entered Brent Ventura's mind when he suddenly, unexpectedly locked eyes with the woman who had just entered the room.

A nervous agency man—Warren something—was still bending his ear, but Brent had already lost track of what the man was saying.

She had lovely eyes. Big, hazel, slightly slanted rather than round.

He stood up as she and another man approached him. She was a little taller than average, slim and femininely rounded. She moved gracefully, holding his eyes with friendly curiosity as she crossed the room. Interesting face, too. High cheekbones, a strong chin, very smooth skin. She would get better looking as she got older, he thought. Then he wondered why he had thought that.

The nervous man next to Brent introduced him to Vernon McConnell, a plump, grinning man in bright clothes. Brent shook his hand absently, aware of the woman's subtle perfume.

"And this is Marla Foster, one of our account executives."

"Mr. Ventura." She smiled and took his hand. Her hand was slender and fine boned, with tapering fingers and long, unpolished nails. Her voice was just a shade lower than he had expected.

"Miss Foster."

"I thought Marla would be a welcome addition to this meeting," said one of the senior executives, joining them. "She worked on our campaign for the California State Park System, and she currently handles the account for Rawlins Pocketknives."

Brent caught the eager tone in the man's voice as he continued extolling Marla Foster's virtues; he nearly dismissed it as typical businessman's hype until he noticed the watchfulness in her eyes.

He had visited five other ad agencies recently, and Marla Foster was only the second female account executive he had been introduced to. Apparently the agencies assumed that a company like Ventura, which made rugged outdoor equipment and apparel, would not put their faith in a female account executive.

Katie, he thought with fond memory, would have set them straight without delay. And without much tact, either. He tried to be more subtle when he said, "You certainly sound experienced, Miss Foster."

That seemed to relieve everyone. Marla Foster let her eyes warm up a bit, and he was pleased with the effect. She was personable but reserved. After suffering through two weeks of overeager friendliness and insincere admiration from agencies anxious to have his business, Brent liked the quality of dignity that seemed to surround her.

Someone suggested they all sit down and start the meeting. Marla Foster smiled at Brent again and then moved away to apparently prearranged seating with three other account executives.

Nigel McBain, vice president of Ventura, slid into a chair next to Brent and winked at him. An agency man introduced Brent and his lanky, blond Australian associate to the room at large and then began the presentation.

Brent tried hard to keep his eyes from glazing over as he heard the usual patter about why *this* ad agency was the very *best* agency and the only one that could meet Ventura's needs.

Brent loathed businessmen. He detested the atmosphere of stuffy offices, status symbols, pecking orders and rigid rules. He didn't trust or like men who wore three-piece suits and had soft hands and soft middles. He hated the whole insincere, money-hungry atmosphere of the business world. He was only here out of necessity. Ventura needed a big ad agency. It was also the only way to get Nigel to stop nagging him.

Marla studied Brent Ventura across the room. He looked like a man trying unsuccessfully to hide his boredom. His associate, the blond Australian, seemed to be much more absorbed in the presentation as Vernon McConnell, Warren Tallman and the director of new business each in turn showed examples of past ad campaigns, explained how the agency had approached various problems and emphasized the agency's extensive experience and resources.

Yes, Nigel McBain seemed interested. What would it take to get through to Ventura? she wondered.

He was an outdoorsman, a renowned mountaineer, archer, cross-country skier, kayaker, diver, sailor and surfer. What little she had been able to read about his company so far intrigued her. Ventura Incorporated, manufacturers and suppliers of sporting equipment, camping gear and outdoor apparel, had been developed out of and around Brent Ventura's interests. When he couldn't find equipment good enough to suit his needs, he had started making and designing his own. From that small beginning, he now had a company that did more than twenty-five million dollars of business a year. And the man was only in his late thirties.

The research department had provided Marla with a copy of an interview Ventura had given several months earlier. An irreverent, tongue-in-cheek sense of humor had come through in that interview. He had said that at Ventura, M.B.A. meant Management By Absence. His greatest professional priority was to have plenty of free time to play with his toys. Important business decisions took place at the volleyball net.

So here he sat, a sportsman who ran a successful business by unconventional means. What could make Ventura want to do business with Freemont, Fox and Linsford above all other agencies?

When the presentation was finally, mercifully over, Brent realized it was his turn to say something. He leaned forward and placed his folded hands in front of him, elbows resting on the table. The agency employees all looked carnivorous, except for Marla Foster, who tilted her head sideways and studied him speculatively with intelligent hazel eyes. She crossed her legs, and her skirt molded to the smooth length of her thigh. She looked as firm and as graceful as a Thoroughbred mare.

"You're on," Nigel muttered, bringing Brent back to reality after his short silence.

"We have, till now, assiduously avoided all but the most necessary advertising," Brent began, chiding himself for his distraction. "Therefore, we've been using a very small agency. Marketing at Ventura is handled jointly by Nigel here and by the director of our mail-order business, who, unfortunately, can't be with us today because she's busy showing the company off to some visiting Japanese executives. She and Nigel agree that our budget, our expanded production capacity and the increasing demands for our products both here and abroad have put us in a position where we need to consider a more thorough and long-range approach to our advertising needs."

This was the sixth time he had repeated this speech, and he hoped it would be the last time. "We've decided we want a nationwide campaign with high-profile advertising. We want to establish an image that will exemplify our products. Above all," he added emphatically, "we want to maintain the company's integrity."

That was the key issue for Brent, who didn't believe anyone in business, particularly in advertising, had integrity or would understand the image his company deserved. Advertising seemed to rely on gimmicks, catchphrases and cute symbols—none of which struck him as right for the company he had nurtured from its inception.

There was more back-and-forth dialogue with the ad agency's senior representatives. Nigel discussed the budget Ventura was considering. Brent could see that the others were disappointed that he wasn't immediately interested in radio or television advertising and that they hoped he would reconsider after a couple of years of successful advertising with them.

"If I may..." began Marla, whom Brent had noticed taking notes. In fact, he had noticed everything about her: the way her thick, glossy hair fell over her right shoulder as she leaned forward to get everyone's attention; the subtle shape of her breasts beneath her blouse; the elegant length of her hand as she rested it on the conference table.

"Yes?" said the director of new business, who seemed to like her. Brent noticed that the nervous one—Warren something—didn't seem pleased she had spoken up.

"It seems to me, Mr. Ventura, that what your company needs, both to project the right image and to separate you from other suppliers of sports gear, is a strategy that focuses on what makes Ventura Incorporated special and unique."

"Thank you, Marla," said the nervous one quickly.

Brent really started to like Marla a lot when she smoothly covered over her superior's blatant rudeness without batting an eyelash. She nodded as if being complimented rather than cut off, then continued speaking.

"Ventura is privately owned, by you. It's named after you. You founded it. It's the child of your hobbies and passions. The small amount of advertising I've looked at from your company emphasizes the undeniable quality of your products. What's missing, however, is the character of the company itself. You have interesting, humanistic management policies. An interview I've studied shows that you have an articulate philosophy about the outdoors and therefore about the equipment you started producing to enjoy the outdoors. I think that what you may want—and need—is a strategy that utilizes the individuality, the humor and the daring that characterize Ventura."

"Well said," Nigel responded amiably.

One of the agency's senior vice presidents continued with Marla's point now that Nigel had complimented her. Brent listened politely as the man more or less repeated what she had already said.

Brent glanced at Marla again. She was looking at him, and he could see she wanted his business. She wasn't the first to make such an appraisal of his advertising needs, but he liked what she said and the way she said it. He liked the simple self-confidence in her bearing. He liked her steady gaze. His feelings were based more on instinct than on evidence, but then, his instincts had kept him alive on more than one occasion.

The meeting was over at last, Nigel having satisfied himself that he'd gotten enough information and Brent having decided he had taken all he could stand for one day.

Everyone stood up to leave. After receiving a few hearty handshakes, Brent slipped around the table, inexplicably compelled to seize a brief moment with Marla Foster.

"I liked what you said," he told her honestly.

"I liked what you said in the interview I read," she countered. "Your advertising should capitalize on your personality."

He felt himself sinking into her eyes, absorbed by her subtle beauty. He couldn't think of anything to say. Certainly no insightful business questions came to mind. She started to smile, a friendly, nonprofessional smile that suddenly brought the sun into this oppressively formal conference room. He smiled, too, and shrugged.

Somebody jarred her arm roughly, and she dropped her pen. She and Brent stooped to retrieve it at the same time. He didn't think her simple peach silk blouse was meant to be sexy, but somehow on her it was. The modest neckline fell away as she bent, and he had a tantalizing glimpse of a swelling breast and the lacy edge of her bra. He stood up casually, pretending he hadn't noticed, pretending he wasn't intrigued. He handed her the pen.

"Thanks," she said softly.

"Do you—"

"Ready to go, mate?" said Nigel, directly behind him.

Brent suppressed an unexpected sense of frustration. Come on, he thought, it's not as if you can't interview her again if you need to. But he had a vague suspicion that *interview* wasn't quite the right word.

"Well, Miss Foster, we'll go think over your agency's proposal," Brent said.

"Yes. I imagine you'll need your volleyball net now." She raised her slanting brows inquisitively.

He grinned, flattered she had read and remembered that particular interview. "That's exactly where we'll discuss it," he admitted.

"It's been a pleasure, Mr. Ventura. I hope we meet again."

He took her slim hand and held it just a fraction of a second longer than he should have. "I hope so, too, Miss Foster."

* * *

"Interesting bird," said Nigel as he and Brent volleyed the ball back and forth across the net. They were on the beach, just a short walk from their office.

"Marla Foster?" Brent jumped up and spiked the ball. Nigel dived for it and missed.

"Not bad. Of course, I'm just warming up," said Nigel, facedown in the sand.

"Of course."

Brent looked up as more than a dozen members of his staff came down the street and trotted across the sand to join them in a game. It was lunchtime at Ventura. Two women and one of the men held a number of small children by the hand. Brent financed a day-care center for employees' children, which was attached to the central lunchroom, and parents who worked for him usually brought their children outside during their breaks and lunch hours.

"Hah! Nigel!" cried the company accountant, wearing denim cutoffs and a tank top.

"G'day," said Nigel.

"Prepare to eat sand."

Brent grinned. "These games have been getting so vicious lately."

"That's because your accountant cheats," Nigel confided loudly. "Can't trust the blighter."

More than a dozen staff members engaged in a rousing game of volleyball while others cheered from the sidelines or played in the surf. After two humiliating defeats, Brent and Nigel sat out a game to discuss business.

"Freemont, Fox and Linsford are the biggest agency. They have the longest reach and the most contacts," Nigel said.

"But...?" Brent prodded.

"One, they're extremely conservative. I don't know if they're right for us or we're right for them. I don't know if they'll understand us."

"And two?"

"Two, we're a desirable client to Freemont, but they've got a number of bigger fish in their stable—excuse the mixed metaphor. You saw how their faces fell when we said we didn't plan to budget for television and radio."

"You like the agency we saw on Monday."

"They're more our style," Nigel admitted. "More adventurous, unconventional. And we'd be one of their most important clients. On the other hand, they're also more limited."

"Your recommendation?"

Nigel shrugged. "You've always liked giving business to the underdog. I recommend we go with the smaller agency."

"Mmm." Brent frowned and stared out at the vast expanse of ocean before them, blue and a little gray. The color of a woman's eyes.

"You're thinking of the woman," Nigel said suddenly, surprise evident in his voice.

Brent squinted into the sun. Age, maturity, experience and grief—none of it had trained his features into impassivity. It was sometimes embarrassing that at the age of thirty-eight his face was an open book to his friends.

"Well, I'll be," said Nigel with annoying enthusiasm. "She caught your eye, didn't she?"

"She had a lot of dignity, which has been missing in everyone else we've talked to. Sincerity, I guess," he said carefully.

"Sure," said Nigel coyly.

"What's that supposed to mean?"

"Just that I'm glad to see you may be taking an interest in someone at last."

"I'm not 'taking an interest' in her," Brent said impatiently. Of course he wasn't. He just wanted to find the right person for Ventura. "She seemed to have the sort of attitude and character we're looking for. She seemed to have an instinctive grasp of what we need."

"You're going to base an expensive decision like this on her? On one person?" Nigel asked. He seemed more amused than incredulous. He'd been with Ventura too long to be surprised at the way his boss ran things.

"No, of course not." Brent caught the volleyball as it flew his way and tossed it back into the game. "If we're going to keep growing at the rate we have been for the past few years, before long we could outgrow the agency you're leaning toward. Why not start out as we mean to continue, to coin one of your own phrases. Someday we may be interested in national television advertising."

"You've always said that our products aren't for people who are sitting in front of the telly on Saturday."

"The point still holds. Why sign with an agency we may outgrow again?"

They always discussed everything, so Brent couldn't understand why he felt so uncomfortable having to explain his reasoning on this occasion. He'd hired good-looking women in the past without feeling defensive about it.

Hoping to end the discussion, he turned to Nigel with an accusing look. "You've dragged me around meeting these greaseballs for two solid weeks, we've wasted plenty of good surfing hours discussing the problem, and my ears are ringing from all the presentations I've had to listen to. I want to choose an agency *now*, and I want to choose one we won't outgrow, so I won't have to go through this again."

Nigel stared at him for a long moment. His assessing look irritated Brent.

"Well?" Brent prodded.

Nigel smiled beatifically, lay back in the sand, turned his face to the sun and closed his eyes.

"Nigel," Brent said with barely concealed impatience.

"I think you sound like a man who's made his decision, despite all my good advice," said Nigel whimsically.

Brent nodded. "I guess I have."

"Want me to call Freemont, Fox and Linsford? After my nap, I mean."

"Sure." Brent momentarily thought of Warren Tallman and the other grasping businessmen present at today's meeting. Despite Marla Foster, he hated giving such quick satisfaction to the rest of them. His lips curved into a slight smile as he said, "On second thought, no. It can wait till morning. Let them sweat for a while."

"Whatever you say." Nigel settled into the sand with the obvious intention of dozing off.

Brent continued to sit, staring out to sea. He suddenly wished Katie were there with him, just as he had wished for her so many times in the past three years. The intensity of his longing caught him off guard.

The first year without Katie had been sheer hell, and he had ached for her every single moment. The pain had finally eased somewhat during the second year, and he had learned to be grateful at least for the years they had had together. By now, nearly three years after her death, Brent thought he had at last learned to accept her absence and his own loneliness. Usually when he found himself missing her these days, it was a soft feeling of regret mingled with remembered fondness.

He couldn't understand the sudden restlessness and yearning that assailed him as he watched a couple of lovers walk hand in hand along the beach. What had gotten into him?

Two days later, Marla knocked on Vernon McConnell's office door. He had been at the meeting with Ventura. He would understand, she thought disconsolately.

"Marla, come in!" Vernon greeted her enthusiastically. "Do you know how to work this thing? It's from that new electronics client, and for the life of me, I can't..." He shrugged helplessly and fumbled with an ungainly piece of abstract art that he held in his hands.

"What's it supposed to be?" Marla asked.

"A radio. It's supposed to double as a tabletop sculpture. I ask you, would you put anything like this on top of your table?" He grimaced.

"No...." She smiled in spite of herself.

"Of course not. You've got impeccable taste."

"Let me have a try." She took the multicolored plastic blob from him and started trying to find the On switch.

"Did you venture down here for any special reason?" Vernon asked. The offices of the creative people were emphatically separated from the offices of the "suits"—the accounts services people. The creatives insisted that the suits acted as if they were going on safari in darkest Africa when they stalked into this part of the building.

"'Venture'? Funny you should use that word," Marla said.

"You heard Ventura is signing with us?"

"I heard it in passing."

Vernon frowned. "That stinks. Anyone could see that you were instrumental in winning his favor. You should have been specifically informed."

"I also heard," she said, trying to keep her voice calm, concentrating hard on the bizarre radio in her hands, "that someone else has been assigned as account executive."

She didn't know what she touched, but suddenly Madonna's voice started blaring out from the hideous little piece of pop sculpture.

"Yikes! What did you do?" Vernon leaped out of his chair, bumping his head on a blow-up rubber crocodile that hung over his desk.

"I'm not sure."

"Can you turn it down?"

"I'm not sure," Marla repeated.

They spent a few fruitless minutes trying to turn the radio off, or at least down. It remained a mystery. Vernon finally opened the door and handed it to his secretary. "Deal with this, will you?"

Vernon quickly closed the door and put a hand on the blow-up crocodile to stop its swinging motion. He picked up the yo-yo he often relied on in moments of intense cogitation and sat down again.

His eyes were full of commiseration when he said, "I guess you also heard that Warren Tallman has been assigned as account supervisor."

"I see."

"Between you and me, he wound up with someone less qualified than you as the account executive." He flung the yo-yo out and expertly reeled it back in.

"You mean he absolutely rejected working with me and absolutely insisted on working with a man," Marla muttered.

Vernon nodded. "I'm sorry. I was gunning for you. I thought we could do a great job together on this account. However, it cannot have escaped your notice that Warren's father-in-law is still chairman of the board."

"I remember it every time Warren opens his mouth," Marla said wearily.

"And after that mess with the Diablo Boots account . . . I realize Warren was the one who handled a simple situation badly, Marla. But in the eyes of management, you're the one who wound up with egg on your face."

Marla nodded. She lowered her eyes, determined not to get emotional. "I'm going to be let go, aren't I?"

If anyone knew for sure, it would be Vernon. He had an uncanny ability for finding things out before anyone else.

"Now stop that. There was no talk of—"

"Oh, come on, Vernon," she said impatiently. "Since I was *booted* off the Diablo Boots account, and since the textbook company decided we were too expensive and dropped us, all I've got of my own is the pocketknife account. One *small* account. It's been over a month, and they haven't assigned me to anything else. I've offered to help on other accounts, I've requested new assignments, and now, even after yesterday's presentation, they're still not going to put me on Ventura's account." She sighed heavily. "People are laid off for far less reason in this business. I'm on my way out."

"Marla, I don't want to see you go—and I happen to know that a number of senior people feel the same way."

If Vernon said so, she believed him. But it didn't lift her sinking spirits. "Unfortunately, I've got the chairman of the board and his son-in-law pitching against me, and I've just struck out a third time. I'm out of the game, Vernon. I'm not kidding myself."

There was a long silence between them. And what really, Marla thought, was there left to say?

"If I can think of some way to help you, Marla—"

"I appreciate it, Vernon, but I'm a big girl. Those are the breaks. I knew it was a tough business when I got into it."

"If you weren't so determined to do everything yourself, you might find this business a little softer. If, for instance, you had let me help you when the troubles with Warren and Diablo Boots had started—"

"Hindsight is a wonderful thing," she said wryly. "Thanks for your time, and your concern." She shrugged. She was ready to burst into tears, but she didn't want him to know that. Instead, she said lightly, "I guess I'll go revise my résumé."

Outside Vernon's office, she found his secretary banging the noisy pop art radio against her desk.

"What do you think I should do with it, Marla?"

"Give it to someone else to deal with. That's what *he* did."

Marla went back to her office. No one had said anything official yet, but she and Vernon both knew she was right. She was finished at Freemont. Ventura had been her only hope of redemption in the eyes of the board. She figured she should probably get a head start and begin packing up her things.

She loved her office. It was bright and airy, decorated with her successful campaigns for the California State Park System, Plethora Textbooks and Rawlins Pocketknives. She had removed all evidence of the Diablo Boots campaign.

She never wanted anything in her office to remind her of that terrible experience.

She had been warned by her colleagues about the frustrations of working with Warren Tallman, but she was ambitious and she had wanted that Diablo account badly enough to risk trouble.

In the end she had wound up with more trouble than she knew how to handle, both from the client and from Warren Tallman. She had learned two important lessons the hard way. One disastrous mistake several years earlier had taught her never to get too close to a client. This more recent mistake had taught her never to let a client get hostile.

They were the only two real mistakes she had made in her carefully plotted, diligently pursued career, but they had both been costly and humiliating. It hadn't helped to be reassured by her colleagues that it could have happened to anyone. Marla expected more of herself.

Now she had been denied the Ventura account, the one hope she had of saving her career at Freemont. She tried to rally her self-confidence. People got hired and fired in advertising with monotonous regularity. At thirty-one, Marla made good money, had good credentials and knew she had a reputation for professionalism and reliability. She would eventually find another job.

But her shattered self-esteem wouldn't let her mind rest, and she couldn't stop the tiny internal voice that scolded her for the way she had mismanaged her career. She was going to lose her job, and she was bitterly ashamed.

She was also scared to death. The whole reason she had struggled to get her M.B.A., the reason she had worked so hard in advertising for the past three years, was because she had come from such a financially insecure and unstable background. She had sworn to herself that she would never go through that kind of worry and turmoil again.

She groaned as she remembered that she had promised her mother she would send her some money. Why did her mother have to be getting divorced again right now? Marla couldn't help pay for another divorce if she was out of work.

"It never rains but it pours," she muttered.

The phone rang. She wondered who it was. Her mother again? Her summons to be fired? She picked up the receiver.

"Hello?"

"Marla? Vernon. You have a guardian angel, my dear. Guess who just telephoned the director of new business in high temper."

"I don't feel like guessing," she said morosely.

"Brent Ventura."

There was a dramatic pause. "Well?" Marla prodded.

"Ventura's new account executive phoned him a little while ago. Ventura himself phoned back to find out what the hell is going on. He's made it absolutely clear, my dear, that if we want his account, you must be the one to work on it."

"What?" Marla sat bolt upright in her chair.

"Yes. I gather he also gave Warren Tallman quite an ear bending." Vernon chuckled with glee. Like Marla, he had also had bad experiences working with Warren. "You know, I suspect Ventura doesn't actually trust us," he added in a puzzled voice.

"Who else knows about this?"

"No one, yet."

"Oh, Vernon." Marla's voice was full of relief, happiness and anticipation. Then she frowned. "How on earth do you find these things out?"

Vernon chuckled evilly. "I never reveal my sources, my dear." Then he sighed. "Oh, I wish I could have seen Warren's face when Ventura called."

"So do I," said Marla wistfully.

"Congratulations, Marla. Glad we'll be working together, after all," Vernon said before hanging up.

Marla stared thoughtfully out her window. She not only wished she could have seen Warren Tallman eat crow, she also wished she could have seen Brent Ventura standing up for her. He had probably been pacing back and forth like a caged lion, snarling into the telephone as he championed her, running his big, tanned hands through his crisp, dark hair. . . .

Marla blinked and then laughed at herself. She was fantasizing like some silly teenager about a man she had only met briefly. Admittedly, no healthy woman could have ignored his graceful, muscular body or his boyishly candid eyes, but he undoubtedly had very practical reasons for demanding her as his account executive.

Her phone rang again. It was Warren Tallman asking to see her in his office immediately. Marla smiled with pure pleasure as she grabbed a few things to take into the meeting. She suspected Warren would omit telling her that Ventura had demanded her services; just assigning her to the account would gall him enough without admitting his error.

She knew Warren and his father-in-law would be watching her closely for the slightest mistake, the faintest hint of inefficiency or unprofessionalism. Well, they would be disappointed, she thought with determination. She would do her best work ever on this account. She fully expected to earn the promotion that had been hinted at before the Diablo Boots fiasco had halted her steady advancement in the agency hierarchy.

"I owe you one, Ventura," she whispered as she left her office, making a silent promise to the man who had given her this sought-after opportunity to redeem herself.

Chapter Two

At Brent's suggestion, Marla visited his company a few mornings later. By that time, they had already spoken together several times on the telephone. She enjoyed their brief conversations. After the Diablo Boots disaster, Marla was glad that she and Brent Ventura were apparently going to get along well.

If she was a little too aware of how deep and sexy his voice sounded on the phone, if she remembered a little too well the feel of his hard, strong hand pressing against her own in the conference room... Well, he was too attractive to ignore, but she could certainly control any unprofessional impulses she might have. She was certain of that.

Ventura's headquarters were a series of connected solar buildings close to the beach at the edge of La Jolla, about fifteen miles north of downtown San Diego. As Marla parked her beige Toyota in Ventura's tree-lined parking lot, she reflected on how inspiring it must be to work in such a lovely location.

When she entered the first building, a woman wearing ruggedly casual Ventura clothing approached her with a friendly smile. "Can I help you?"

"I'm Marla Foster, here to see—"

"Oh, yes. I'll show you where to go."

Marla had tried to dress to suit the occasion. Having guessed that Brent didn't favor formality, she wore a simple cotton outfit of blue and aqua shades. She noticed, however, as she followed her companion through several airy offices and courtyards, that she was still overdressed. Everyone she saw was wearing either Ventura sports clothing or blue jeans and T-shirts.

She followed the woman into a large building that seemed to be at the center of the complex. Inside, there were no rooms or corridors. It was one open area, filled with desks, telephones, sporting equipment, paperwork and men and women who were all noisily pursuing their business.

"This is the Bull Pen," said the woman. "I don't see Brent, but he's probably—"

"Miss Foster!"

Marla recognized the blond Australian, Nigel McBain, as he approached her. He was dressed in jeans like everyone else.

"Hello, Mr. McBain."

"G'day. Call me Nigel. And you're Marla, right?"

She nodded. "I'm pleased you and Brent decided to go with our company."

She wondered why her comment seemed to amuse him. His eyes fairly twinkled when he said, "To be honest, it was mostly Brent's idea."

Rising to the challenge, Marla said smoothly, "I intend to prove to both of you that he made the best choice."

Nigel smiled enigmatically and said, "This should be exciting. Well, why don't you come over here and have a seat?" He drew her away from the woman who had escorted her. "Can I get you anything? Cuppa tea? Coffee? Tonic water?"

"No, thank you."

"Brent's around here somewhere. As soon as he realizes what time it is he'll pop up." Nigel showed her to one section of the room where two enormous desks stood. A couple of comfortable chairs sat between them, and a big couch was aligned against the wall. "This is it," Nigel said dramatically. "Nerve center of Ventura Incorporated. I sit here, and Brent sits there."

Marla was intrigued. "The president and vice president of the company sit right out here, in the open, working in a pool with all these other employees?"

"This is kind of a special section, all of the senior people, more or less."

"Still, it's unusual not to have a private office with a secretary outside the door turning away everyone who doesn't have an appointment."

"Brent spoke to M.B.A. students at Stanford a few months ago, and he told them that the office is arranged in this way to make him accessible to his employees and to promote brainstorming and combined energy."

"That's very progressive thinking," Marla said thoughtfully. She wondered if Brent had business qualifications she hadn't yet learned about.

"But I know the real reason," said Nigel with a leprechaun grin.

"What's that?"

"With all these people and all this chaos, it's hard to tell when he's missing."

"Missing?"

"Out surfing or swimming. Back in the workshops playing with new gadgets. Or even playing hooky and wandering around in the mountains somewhere."

"Management By Absence," Marla said with a smile, remembering the article she had read. "How does he run such a successful company, in that case?"

"Oh, he's got a lot of theories about that, too. I'll let *him* expound on that."

Marla looked around. They had constructed a tiny ski lift that ran continuously across the vast room. She looked questioningly at Nigel.

"That's for messages." Then, as an afterthought, he added, "And pranks."

One entire wall was covered with photographs. Brent was in most of them, Nigel in about half. They always seemed to be in remote locations, clinging to rocks or sheer cliffs, balancing on surfboards, sitting in kayaks surrounded by rushing water and big rocks, hiking with backpacks or cross-country skiing.

"What are these?" she asked in awe. The word *sportsman* hadn't conjured up these death-defying pictures in her mind.

"This is Brent rummaging around the Karakorams in Pakistan. This is the two of us and Jackson Thomas climbing the Vinson Massif in Antarctica—never been so bloody cold in my whole life."

Nigel obligingly explained photo after photo to Marla. There were pictures of Brent traversing an ice field on Mount Edith Cavell, dangling from a ledge in the Shawangunks, meeting the challenge of Changabang, Trango Tower and Bugaboo Spire.

"Where was this one taken?" Marla asked, looking at a particularly breathtaking photograph.

"That's the southwest ridge of Cerro Fitzroy in Patagonia. About six years ago."

"Did you go?"

"No." Nigel sighed. "That was the year Brent and I agreed the company had grown too big for us to climb with each other anymore. We couldn't both be away for an extended period at the same time. And, not to sound gloomy, we couldn't die together and leave the company in chaos."

Marla stared at him, starting to realize how much more there must be to Brent Ventura than met the eye. Of course, he was obviously no ordinary businessman. Now she was starting to suspect that he was also more than a clever entrepreneur with fresh ideas.

"Who's the woman in this photo?" she asked, indicating a riverside scene.

"Brent's wife, Katie."

"He's married?" She couldn't understand the sudden plunge her stomach took, as if it mattered to her whether or not a client was married. She became aware of danger signals in her head as she waited for Nigel's response.

When he finally answered her, she thought she could guess the reason for his hesitation. "Brent's widowed. She died in a boating accident almost three years ago."

Marla looked back at the woman's broad smile, her dirt-smeared face and her long, frizzy black ponytail. Her vivacity shone through, even in an old photograph.

"How terrible," Marla said softly. She felt a soft wave of sorrow as she thought of Brent losing his wife.

"It was," Nigel agreed quietly.

Marla didn't say anything more. She didn't want to pry or to mouth trite phrases. Both would have been inappropriate.

"Well, here you are at last!" said Nigel when Brent joined them. "Not that you were missed. He's never around when you need him," Nigel confided to Marla.

"I founded a whole company just so I could be gone whenever I felt like it," Brent said unrepentantly. "Good to see you again, Marla."

She returned the greeting and offered him her hand. His grip was strong and firm, and his palm was like warm, smooth leather, callused from his active life.

He looked wonderful, dressed as he was in sturdy, pale gray Ventura clothing. His trousers fit his narrow hips like a plastic wrap, moving easily as he moved, and the width of his shoulders made him look indestructible. His dark brown hair waved crisply around his tan face, shiny and healthy and thick. He grinned at Marla, and his eyes were sparkling and friendly, green and glowing and hypnotic. She almost had the impression that he had been looking forward to her arrival.

After a moment, she realized she was staring at him like an adoring teenager. Something made her glance at Nigel, and the smirk on his face brought a rush of blood to her cheeks. She cast around for something professional and intelligent to say and found to her astonishment that her mind had gone blank.

Nigel gave an elaborate sigh and said chidingly, "Brent, why don't you offer to show Marla around?"

Brent looked startled. "Oh. Yeah. Why don't I show you around?" he said like a slow child.

"That would be great," Marla said in a rush, glad to have things getting back on track. Where was her reassuring, well-controlled, professional cool?

"Can I come too?" Nigel's Australian accent seemed to be getting thicker, as if he were trying not to laugh—or strangle.

Brent frowned at him. "No. You stay here and do some work or something."

Nigel grumbled theatrically and went back to his desk.

"This is the center of the operation—all the managing officers work in here," Brent explained to Marla. "Felice and Nigel are in charge of our marketing. They should be able to provide you with most of the information you were asking me about the other day on the phone. Felice's desk is over there—I don't know where she is right now. She's an exhausting person, let me warn you."

Brent smiled again, and Marla felt the full impact of his charm. He looked like a man who had smiled a lot. When he grinned at her, deep grooves marked his cheeks and laugh lines crinkled around his eyes. She could see the tiny telltale signs of grief in his face, too, in the slight furrow between his brows and the hollows under his cheeks. She wondered if those were put there by the death of his wife.

He must have been a very handsome youth. His natural good looks, Marla thought, had only increased through the years with maturity and experience. He had a wonderful face. And his dark, sun-burnished hair didn't yet show even a touch of gray.

She forced herself to focus on professional questions. "With your company growing so fast, I'm surprised you don't have a full-time marketing director."

Brent inclined his head. "Nigel has said the work load is getting too big for him and Felice to handle along with their other responsibilities. Maybe if this ad campaign brings in more business, I'll finally hire a marketing director."

He showed her through the six buildings and three court-yards that made up the Ventura complex, explaining the extent of the operation as they went along. She saw the sportswear design and sewing rooms where prototypes were tried out, workshops for camping and sports gear, head-quarters for the six retail stores run directly by Ventura, headquarters for the catalog and mail-order business, the financial office and the wildlife, nature and outdoor sports research library.

"It looks like you're doing some rearranging," said Marla when Brent proudly showed off their research library.

"Since I founded the company, we've annually given ten percent of our pretax profits to organizations that help pre-serve and restore the natural environment. I've decided, in addition to that, to found our own institute for nature and wildlife protection."

"That's wonderful," said Marla enthusiastically. "The company's level of social consciousness can be a big help in our ad campaign."

She was sorry she had said it a moment later. The shining pride on his face was replaced by a look of cynical resigna-tion. The warmth stopped flowing from him. Biting back an inexplicable desire to apologize for her comment, Marla felt slightly annoyed. She hadn't said anything crass or inap-propriate. Ventura's commitment to wilderness preserva-tion, properly handled, would undoubtedly be one of the qualities that attracted their particular target market and made the consumer choose them before their competitors.

Brent would have to acknowledge and accept that. But Marla sensed that this wasn't the right time to insist.

She tried to reestablish the friendliness that had existed between them prior to her comment. When she began asking him about surfing, he finally warmed up again. Within minutes he was waxing eloquent about his passion for the sport.

"I could never be one of those guys who follow the waves around the world and think of nothing but the surf. I'd miss other sports too much—climbing, skiing, kayaking. But the thrill of riding a good wave is better than success, better than fame, better than scaling Everest, better than sex." He paused for a moment. "Well, maybe not better than sex."

He grinned at her again, and Marla could have sworn he was flirting with her. She smiled uncontrollably in response and felt her pulse accelerate just a bit. She looked away and took a breath.

He was the client, she reminded herself. Even if he did flirt with her, he was absolutely off limits. You didn't date the client. No exceptions.

Except one, she thought bleakly, and what a mistake that had been.

"Is your love of surfing the reason you built the company here by the ocean?" she asked in her best professional tone of voice.

"Partly. Originally we were up in the Sierra Nevada, but that was an inconvenient location for a lot of people who wanted to work for us, and it was awfully far from the water. We decided to move down to the sea about ten years ago. The surfing off of La Jolla is great, maybe the best in the country. We started small, since real estate is so expensive here, and we expanded at a rate we could afford. Lately, I feel like my real estate is worth more than my company."

"Well, you're the first client I've ever worked with who picked his company's location because the surfing was good," Marla said wryly.

"Oh, it's even better at my house," he said with enthusiasm.

"Where's that?"

"I live right by Windansea Beach. The best surfing this side of Hawaii." He cocked a brow at her. "Do you surf?"

"Are you kidding?"

"You're fit, trim, graceful—it's a reasonable question." He laughed. "You should see the look on your face."

"Just the thought of sliding around on a little board in the middle of a churning sea is enough to make me want to pass out."

"You don't like the water?"

"Oh, I love the water. Calm, placid, clear water. And I like less death-defying relaxation. You know, a little swimming, a little snorkeling—something I don't have to confess to life insurance companies."

"Still, you should give surfing a try. This way," he said, leading her through another courtyard.

"Where are we going?"

"The tank."

"What?"

He smiled slyly, his green eyes sparkling as they narrowed. Marla caught her breath. He wasn't flirting. He just had a natural sensuality that emanated from him in hot waves.

"Come on," he said. "You did bring a swimsuit, didn't you?"

"In my handbag," she said, lifting it to indicate. When they had arranged this meeting, he had insisted she bring one. She hung back as he opened the door to a windowless building.

"There's a changing room inside."

"What?" she repeated.

"I'll change, too, so you won't feel self-conscious," he assured her.

They walked into the building. There were two employees, one male, one female, both wearing swimsuits, working on the equipment inside.

"Oh, no! The boss is back again!"

The two employees flopped down onto the tile floor. One slid into the deep, still pool of water that dominated the room.

"Brent, we can't get anything done if you keep dragging people back here to try out—"

"Just one more person. That's all. I promise. No one else for the rest of the week," Brent assured his bedraggled employees. He sounded like a naughty kid trying to assuage his parents.

"What are we trying out?" Marla asked suspiciously.

"It's a surprise. You can change in there." Brent pointed to a cubicle with a curtain drawn across it.

Marla decided to do as requested. She entered the tiny cubicle, took off her clothes and put on her copper-colored, one-piece bathing suit. She had played tennis, eaten raw fish, attended conferences, flown across the country and test-driven cars for her clients, but this was the first time she had ever been asked to go swimming with one.

"If he wants me to climb Mount Everest, the account's in real trouble," she muttered. She stepped out from the cubicle and saw Brent, splendid in practical Ventura swim trunks and a tank top, talking with his employees.

They all became aware of her presence at the same moment. Brent turned toward her, and she suddenly felt her face go warm. She was glad her suntanned skin didn't easily show her blushing.

He behaved with perfect propriety, however, and said they'd be ready in just a minute. She was both relieved and surprisingly disappointed that he hadn't noticed her a little more. She was certainly noticing him.

He had a beautiful body—long and lean, hard and muscular, tan and rugged. It was obvious he spent far more time challenging himself in the outdoors than sitting behind his desk.

She approached the group. Brent's employees smiled at her. It occurred to Marla that everyone she had seen so far at Ventura seemed to be having more fun at work than most people had on vacation.

"Get it started up, kids," Brent said.

"What exactly are we doing?" Marla asked as his employees scrambled out of the way.

"Our newest toy. Surf simulation."

He led her to what appeared to be a diving board. As they got closer, she could see it was actually a surfboard supported by three mechanical pillars. The floor all around it was cushioned with thick, water-resistant pads.

"Give it a try," Brent said. "It's as close to real surfing as you can get without risking injury. A great way to get started."

"I don't think I want to get started," Marla said doubtfully.

"The Japanese businessmen who were here *loved* it," he said enticingly. "Couldn't tear them away from here. Felice said they had to eliminate the rest of their scheduled day, they spent so much time with it."

"It's great!" added the strapping blond man who was setting everything up. "You'll love it."

"Well . . . I always try to be a good sport," Marla said at last. She didn't want the client to think she was an old fussbudget the very first day of business. And she didn't want to disappoint Brent, who looked eager for her to enjoy his new toy.

"Now there's nothing to be afraid of," Brent said. "It's absolutely safe, and even if you fall, it'll be like falling on a mattress." He helped her climb up onto the surfboard, which was about four feet off the ground. "The beauty of this thing is that you don't have to wait for the perfect wave. We can create it for you."

He explained how it worked. One person controlled the shifting motion of the board and the other controlled the water, which would roar around Marla and splash her from all directions.

"What do I do?" Marla asked.

"Hang on," said Brent.

He gave her some pointers on how to stand, balance and follow the motion of the "waves." Then he went to stand on the other side of the tank.

"Why are you going all the way over there?" she called.

He grinned. "It gets pretty wet by you."

"Okay, Marla, here we go. Brent says it's your first time, so we'll start you out slow," said the woman.

Marla gasped and crouched slightly as the surfboard slowly shifted under her feet. Water started spraying at her from six directions very gently. She could see that most of it rolled toward the deep pool and figured the whole room must be designed that way to keep it from flooding.

After a few minutes she started to get the hang of the shifting, sliding motion and stopped worrying about falling off in an ungainly heap.

"This is fun!" she called out.

"Crank it up a little," Brent told his employees.

"Hang on, Marla!" said the woman.

"Yikes!" Marla crouched lower and threw her arms out for balance as the board tilted sharply to the side and water splashed against her. Under Brent's instructions, the staff slowly increased the level of difficulty during the next few minutes until water was drenching Marla from head to foot and she was laughing and gasping as she tried to stay on the wildly tilting surfboard. Except for the people standing nearby and the comfort of knowing there was safe padding beneath her, she felt as if she really were daring the waves. The exhilaration was unlike anything she had ever known. Her adrenaline pumped so furiously that she didn't even feel the discomfort when she tumbled off the board at last and bounced on several delicate parts of her anatomy.

She was laughing and drawing in deep gulps of air when they turned off the machine and Brent came over to join her.

"What do you think?" he asked.

"I'm glad you convinced me to try it," Marla admitted. "I've never done anything like that before. Now I can understand why you're so passionate about surfing."

He nodded. "I've invited my parents to come down and use it so they'll understand. They think surfing is about the craziest thing they've ever heard of."

"Do they live around here?" Marla asked as Brent helped her to her feet.

"Nope. Montana, where I grew up. They visit about once a year, but they're happier when I go home. They hate traveling." He handed her a snorkeling mask.

"Now what?" she asked.

"You said you like snorkeling. Have you ever tried our gear?"

"No," she admitted.

"Come on, choose a pair of flippers and let's get in the pool," he urged.

"Mind if we go back to work?" asked the blond young man, who had finished cleaning up the surfing simulator.

"We won't get in your way," Brent assured him.

"Sure," said the woman, and rolled her eyes at him. He smiled sheepishly.

Brent and Marla paddled around the pool as he showed off Ventura equipment and innovations. "You should be wearing one of our swimsuits, too," he said.

"Why?" she asked.

"They're designed to last longer and dry off quicker. They also stand up to tough punishment. I'll have Felice give you one before you go."

All in all, the time spent in the tank was a wonderful icebreaker. Marla felt easier with Brent than she had ever felt before with a client at their first meeting. They talked comfortably and laughed a lot. It usually took weeks to build that kind of rapport with the client. Sometimes it never happened.

When they were done playing, Brent showed her where she could clean up and get dressed. Then he took her back to the Bull Pen.

"Is that the time?" he said, glancing at the clock on the wall above his desk. "No wonder I'm so hungry."

"What time is it?" Marla asked.

"Almost one o'clock. I get up early and have breakfast before seven, so I'm usually ready to eat half the lunchroom by this time of day. Hungry?"

"Well, perhaps I should speak to Felice and start getting some of the information I'll need—"

"You can do that after lunch. Coming, Nigel?"

"No." Nigel winked. "Meeting a woman for lunch. She digs surfers."

Brent propelled Marla into the Ventura lunchroom, where the staff could eat, take breaks and gather to talk to each other or to clients. "We don't have a cook or anything, but different vendors come by every day to sell their food at lunchtime."

They got a couple of submarine sandwiches and sat down at one of the big tables in the lunchroom, which was decorated to resemble a wilderness lodge.

"How did you get started in this business, Brent?" Marla asked. "Were you raised to be a devoted sportsman?"

"Not really. When I was a boy, one day my dad decided we should do some father-son activities. We tried fishing and hunting, but those expeditions were failures since we couldn't bring ourselves to kill anything and we hated guns and knives. Finally we settled on camping, and we used to go a few times a year.

"As a teenager I started getting into canoeing and white-water rafting. I was seventeen when I started climbing, and that changed my whole life. All I wanted to do was save enough money to go back up."

"How did you get interested in surfing?"

"A friend convinced me to spend a season on the coast and try it. I was twenty years old at the time. I was completely hooked after that. Over the next few years I got into kayaking and cross-country skiing. I took up archery when I broke my leg and couldn't move around for a while."

"Isn't it unusual to do so many different sports?"

"Not among my staff, it isn't. I don't believe in specializing in one sport. It makes a person boring and obsessive. I think you're physically and socially much healthier if you diversify. Of course, people who concentrate on one sport would say I'm a dilettante."

"I don't see how they could," Marla said, "considering some of the feats you've accomplished. Dilettantes don't wander around the mountains of Nepal—"

"Oh, yes, they do," he assured her. "There are actually very few places left that haven't been turned into tourist heaven." He looked a little bleak as he considered this.

"How did you make a living before you founded the company?" Marla asked, changing the subject.

"I was a blacksmith."

"What?" Marla couldn't hide her surprise.

"My father was a blacksmith, and he trained me. For my nineteenth birthday, he gave me enough tools and equipment to start my own independent business—quite an expensive gift, by the way. For years I traveled around, working out of the back of a pickup truck, just interested in making enough money for climbing, surfing and kayaking."

"I'm such a city girl," Marla said with a soft smile. "I guess I thought of blacksmiths as something that only existed in Colonial Williamsburg."

"Oh, no, there are still blacksmiths, especially anywhere that people use working horses."

"So how did you get from being a blacksmith to being a company president?" Marla persisted.

"When I was in my early twenties, I started feeling like I couldn't find climbing gear that suited my needs. I felt that everything I used had design problems or simply wasn't durable enough. I figured there had to be better possibilities. Being a blacksmith, I knew how to make things, so I tried making a few pieces of my own equipment. On my next climb, my equipment was so noticeably superior that a friend asked if I would make something for him. By the end of that year, so many people were requesting my designs that I finally couldn't afford to make them as a favor anymore."

"So that was the beginning of the business?"

"Yes. It was very casual at first. I made everything at cost, just charged for the materials and my time. Then I met Nigel. He had just finished his M.B.A. We became climbing buddies, and he started nagging me, saying I should be making a profit, expanding, promoting, patenting— Damn, did he nag! Still does."

"Was he the one who convinced you to found the company?"

"No, that was my idea. I did it alone, thirteen years ago. After a year I decided I could afford to hire one person. So I hired Nigel away from the big coffee company he worked for. They thought he was crazy for leaving, since I only offered about a quarter of what they paid him. But he came."

"And now you're both successful businessmen," Marla murmured.

He shifted restlessly. "I don't think of myself that way. I never liked businessmen. I still don't. Bunch of dishonest slimes. I was just a hardworking blacksmith. Now I'm just a guy who enjoys his hobbies and makes a living helping other people enjoy theirs."

Marla looked down at her half-finished sandwich. "I'm full."

There was a short silence.

"Maybe you'd like to talk to Felice now?"

"Yes." She rose from her seat and smiled politely as their eyes met. She wondered if Brent Ventura would decide she was just another dishonest, untrustworthy vulture.

She would do everything in her power to make his advertising successful. He had expressed faith in her by specifically requesting her at the agency, but she was, after all, one of that dread species—a businesswoman. She would have to do a very good job to prove to him he could believe in her.

He had a curiously naive approach to business. The jokes about his continual absence made him sound almost as irresponsible as one of her mother's husbands, and yet she couldn't believe he could run such a successful business with so little sophistication.

There was definitely a lot to be learned at Ventura Incorporated. There were pitfalls, too, she acknowledged. She hadn't counted on finding Brent Ventura quite so appealing. The memory of his enthusiasm as they paddled around the pool together stirred feelings that were different but just as strong as the sensations aroused by his physical prowess and candid friendliness.

She would have to tread a careful path between client compatibility and her own inappropriate desires.

Chapter Three

Brent was sorry he had told her how he felt about businessmen. As soon as he saw the subtle change in her face, he had wanted to make amends. He had been enjoying her company so much that he had temporarily forgotten the nature of their relationship. While talking freely, he had put his foot right in his big mouth.

Well, it was his true opinion, and it was too late to take back the words. He glanced up from his work and looked out the window. It was late afternoon. Marla had been locked up with Felice since lunchtime. They were going over the mail-order business and Felice's marketing concepts.

He, too, had been working solidly since lunch, despite his pretense of owning the company just so he wouldn't have to work. His biggest priority truly was to have plenty of free time, but that meant he had to effectively utilize the time he spent at work.

Anyhow, he loved his company and his work. And that had been an important source of purpose and comfort to him after Katie's death.

In fact, that first year of being alone after seven years of marriage had been so hard that free time was usually the *last* thing he had wanted. He had thrown himself into expanding the company as he had never done before, as he had never planned to do. That period of uncharacteristic obsession with work was largely responsible for the enormous increase in business Ventura had experienced during the past three years.

Ironically, he hadn't done it to become richer. He had never cared about money as long as he had enough to pursue his hobbies and put a roof over his head. He had done it to hold himself together after losing the most important person in his life. And now graduate schools and business companies sought his advice, hoping to emulate his methods.

No one could possibly want to emulate the grief he had gone through. And he didn't appreciate the envy or admiration of strangers who considered him a clever businessman.

He did, however, appreciate the support of his family and friends during that terrible period of his life, and he was grateful to have the opportunity to spend his life doing things he loved.

"Brent?" said a voice behind him.

He already recognized the smooth, slightly husky tone of Marla's voice. He stood and turned toward her. She, Felice and a young man from the mail-order department were loaded down with files, catalogs and papers.

"I'm going now," Marla said. "I'll spend the next few days looking over all this material, then I'll be back to discuss strategy with you, Felice and Nigel."

"Have fun," Brent said wryly, eyeing the bundles of material she would have to plow through.

"In the meantime, if there's anything else you want to discuss, don't hesitate to call me."

"I won't."

They stood staring at each other. He felt oddly reluctant to see her leave.

"Well, I'll be seeing you," she said at last.

"Right," he said, and watched her go.

Although it wasn't his habit, he had already looked for evidence of a wedding or engagement ring on her left hand. There was nothing. No husband or fiancé. A lover, perhaps? She was a very good-looking, intelligent, personable woman, with an underlying air of sexuality that was becoming more and more noticeable. A lot of men before him must have been attracted to her, and most of them must have been free.

Then, as the thought struck him, he was astonished to realize he *was* attracted to her. He had noticed her from the first moment he saw her, had looked forward to seeing her today and had enjoyed her company. He liked the way she looked in that pretty cotton thing she was wearing, and he loved the way she looked in her modest swimsuit.

She was slim and feminine and soft. Not athletic and strong like a lot of his female friends—like Katie—but still fit and sleek and graceful.

He felt suddenly guilty, even disloyal. Had he been seriously attracted to a woman since Katie's death? If he had, he couldn't remember her. There had been no time for women. For so long he had simply worked himself to exhaustion, pursued his hobbies vigorously and tried to accept his loss. He had finally started to recover and had learned to live again, taking an interest in his friends and family. He smiled and laughed and challenged himself. He felt whole again, with one exception. There was no woman in his life.

Nigel nagged him, naturally. In this case, so did Felice and his parents; he needed to put his tragedy behind him and find someone to share his life with. He, too, believed in sharing life, but you didn't simply forget a woman like Katie. After being married to the woman who was both his best friend and his lover, he wasn't prepared for the dreary ritual of scoping out women, chatting through auditionlike dates, going through ridiculous mating dances while deciding whether or not to become lovers, and listening to speeches on the nature of commitment and one's own room to grow.

He and Katie had simply fallen in love, gotten married and been happy together. She had just happened along in his life. He didn't think he could go out shopping for a woman.

He didn't idealize Katie's memory. More than once he had even felt a rush of anger at her for the way she had died. Her own carelessness and recklessness, often a subject of discord between them, had caused her death. But he had known the satisfying joy of a truly happy relationship, and he wouldn't settle for something less just for the sake of not spending his nights alone.

He bicycled home that evening, as was his habit. His parents telephoned for a chat, and they commented on how distracted he sounded. His mother fretted that he wasn't getting enough rest.

He went for a late swim in the surf, hoping to clear the jumbled thoughts and irrational panic in his mind.

It was strange and unsettling, after nearly three years, to suddenly feel attracted to someone again. And if he could have described the woman he imagined would wake him out of his grief-induced sleep of the senses, he wouldn't have guessed it would be someone like Marla. A city girl, a businesswoman, sleek, refined and smooth talking, with chic clothes and an expensive haircut.

That long, dark golden hair, he thought as he toweled himself dry on the beach. He had wanted to touch it. It had looked soft and smooth, and it gleamed like silk. In his mind he saw the rise and fall of her breasts in her swimsuit, her nipples hard from the cold water and sharply defined against the wet material. He saw the soft valley of her cleavage, her lashes spiky and pointed against those clear hazel eyes, her smooth thighs tensing as he helped her to her feet....

He drew in a sharp, surprised breath as he felt his body harden with arousal. He closed his eyes and ran a hand over his face as a mixture of chaotic feelings washed through him: desire, guilt, sadness, and above all, a curious feeling of relief. He knew in that moment that he really would go on to live fully in all ways. He was healing.

He felt grateful to Marla. She might not be his kind of woman, but she had helped him take an important step toward believing he would find another woman for himself. He didn't have to bury his heart—or his sexuality—with Katie.

But as he walked back up the beach toward his house, he wished he could stop thinking about Marla. Otherwise it was going to be very difficult to get any sleep that night.

Marla met with Vernon on the Ventura account later that week. They examined a number of catalogs, articles, interviews, photographs and marketing statistics that Marla had garnered from Felice—the small, energetic, exhausting, redheaded workaholic who managed Brent's mail-order business.

"Can you believe this?" Vernon exclaimed as he studied a photo of Brent dangling over a gorge in the Himalayas. "Why would someone do this for fun? Isn't life hard enough for him?"

Marla smiled. "That's not even the scariest-looking one. Have a look at this." She handed him another photo.

Vernon's eyes bulged. "He must be insane!" He peered at her. "I don't envy you having to go out to his place and be macho with him."

"He's not like that, actually. Macho, I mean. He's friendly and relaxed and—get this—over sixty percent of his employees, including management, are women."

"Ah. I imagine you'll find a way to include that in every report you write for our esteemed account supervisor."

"It has crossed my mind, but that might be too subtle for him."

Vernon had made it clear that he wasn't any happier than Marla about being saddled with Warren Tallman on this account. However, Vernon's job wasn't hanging by a thread. He knew, though, how important this account was to Marla's career, and he had already expressed his complete support for her.

Marla frowned. Since entering the room, she had been aware of a peculiar buzzing sound. It seemed more pronounced now. In fact, it was coming from inside a file cabinet in Vernon's riotously colorful office.

"Is something in your file cabinet?" she asked.

Vernon gave a heavy sigh. "Yes." He opened the bottom drawer and pulled out a bundle of rags. As he unwrapped it slowly, the buzzing sound mutated into something Marla recognized as a Bon Jovi song. She had already guessed what she would see when Vernon finished unwrapping his bundle to reveal the pop art radio that she had last seen in his secretary's hands.

"My secretary gave it to a copywriter, who gave it to a layout artist, who gave it to the director of new business, who gave it back to me."

"Why on earth did you accept it?"

"I'm starting to think this thing is part of my destiny, irreversibly wound up in my karmic cycle."

"Well, then maybe you should keep it."

"Are you kidding?" he snapped. "It's been driving me nuts ever since I got it back!"

"I can see why," she said as an announcement for a wrestling match pierced her eardrums.

"What am I going to do with this thing?" he asked morosely.

"Give it to Warren," Marla said with a touch of malice.

"Hey, that's an idea!"

"You keep looking over this stuff." She rose to leave and handed him several of her file folders. "I'm going out to Ventura again tomorrow."

"Poor girl."

"Actually it's a lot of fun." She told him about her first visit and all the fun she had had in the tank. "We're going to start our strategy discussions tomorrow. I'll have my written plans on your desk as soon as possible. By the way, I'd like Nathan to write the copy for this campaign."

"Yes," Vernon agreed. "He's my first choice, too."

Since she would be spending all day at Ventura, Marla dressed to blend in the next morning. She wore formfitting jeans, a casual cotton blouse and sandals. She had been looking forward to seeing Brent again; there was no denying it. However, she knew her boundaries; theirs would have to be a friendly but strictly professional relationship. There was too much at stake for her to break the rules.

He looked wonderful in olive-colored clothes, a ready grin splitting his face when she appeared at his desk in the Bull Pen. He swept her heart away with that flashing white smile in his darkened face, those shining green eyes, that easy, masculine grace. She felt light and buoyant as they discussed the material she had been looking through for several days.

She, Brent, Nigel and Felice all went to the lunchroom to spread out at one of the big tables and discuss their plans.

"All right, there are three main things we must agree on for our strategy plan," Marla began. "Who do you want to reach, why should they buy your product, and what proof will you offer to support that reason?"

"Got that, mate?" said Nigel to Brent.

Brent looked distressed. Felice laughed outright. "Brent doesn't like business talk, Marla," she said. "It makes him feel cheap."

"It does," he said defensively. "Maybe you should all just do this without me."

Nigel and Felice both looked exasperated. "We've been over this before," Nigel said. "It's *your* bloody company."

"Look, maybe if I give you a simple example, it will help, Brent," said Marla.

"That would be thoughtful," said Brent, casting a baleful glare at Nigel.

"Take an ad for a fast-food restaurant, for example," said Marla. "Obviously everyone eats at them now and then. But your ad can't be effectively aimed at everyone. So let's say we aim the ad at a target audience of middle-income families with a minimum of two children. Why should they eat at our place? Our ad tells them that their kids will like it better. Polls show that parents make the decision to eat out, but kids make the decision about *where* the family will eat. Now the support—why will their kids like our place better? We can say we give them balloons and such with their food, or we can show them that the food is more appealing to kids or that the service is more child oriented.

"Now, that's just *one* way of advertising a fast-food restaurant. You could offer different reasons and proofs, or you could choose an entirely different target market and a very different message."

"That's clear enough," said Brent.

"So, we need to discuss these points," Marla continued. "Do we want to aim at only one target market, or do we want successive campaigns aimed at different targets?"

"I'm in favor of at least three campaigns on one target so we can gauge results before we start shifting our emphasis," said Nigel.

Felice and Brent agreed.

"Now the question is, who will our target be?" Marla said. "Thanks to your mail-order business, and to Felice's excellent records, we know who already buys your equipment. You are in the lead as the supplier to serious, dedicated sportsmen, people for whom the outdoors is a way of life as opposed to something they do twice a year.

"The next part of the market you probably need to dominate are those people who go camping once a year, or surf a little, cross-country ski a few times a winter, or are going on their first climbing expedition soon. Your equipment is expensive, but it is economical in the sense that it seems to last forever."

"That's the idea," said Brent.

"Therefore," Marla continued, "we're not going to appeal to bargain hunters or discount shoppers, but we don't have to aim strictly at higher income levels. This target market is not decided necessarily by income so much as by pursuit of quality. The 'you pay more because you get more' strategy."

They continued to discuss their strategy in depth, defining their market, their goals and their guarantees. Brent clearly had no patience for business. His eyes glazed over and he was squirming in his chair like a teenager by the time they were done talking. Marla agreed to return when she had finished writing the first draft of the strategy plan.

Marla worked hard on the strategy documents all of the following week, making several calls to Ventura every day, requesting more information from Freemont's research department and meeting with Vernon. She was a firm believer in a complete, detailed and well-researched strategy. Everything rested on that. Writers, artists, photographers, clients, executives and production people could all waste an awful lot of time and money if the strategy wasn't clearly, crisply and correctly defined right from the start.

She was extremely pleased with her completed first draft. She felt it might even be her best work ever. Ventura was an inspiring company, after all. Before taking the document back to the client, she presented it to Warren Tallman for approval, since he was her supervisor.

Vernon was in her office with her, expressing his own approval of the strategy, when her phone rang.

"Hi, Mom," said Marla in surprise when she heard her mother's voice on the line. "What? Mom, calm down, I can't understand you."

It took several more minutes of urging her mother to calm down before she could understand what had driven her to distraction.

"I'm sorry the reconciliation isn't going to work, Mom." Marla had said it before, about her mother's other husbands. "No, I don't know why men are like that. Yes, I thought he seemed very nice when you met him, too," she said patiently. She glanced over at Vernon, who was discreetly making notes in the margin of her report and pretending not to hear a word she said.

"Look, Mom, can we talk tonight? I'm in the middle of a meeting. I'll call you, okay?"

She hung up and ran a hand across her face. She had thought that moving to the West Coast and distancing herself from her family would help ease the trauma of these ephemeral marriages, but she found herself tense and upset by her mother's call. Shades of her childhood and youth in an unstable home haunted her for a few moments. Men came and went, and her mother depended on one after another rather than learning to take care of herself. Four failed marriages had taught her nothing. When this one was officially over, her mother would wait around helplessly, hoping for a new husband to look after her.

"Trouble at home?" Vernon asked at last.

"The usual," Marla said bleakly. It was the truth.

"Marla?" Her secretary, Yvonne, stuck her head in the door. "We're having lunch together today, remember? Hello, Vernon. I suppose you're going to impose your company on us."

"Well, if you insist," said Vernon.

Marla was able to forget her troubles over an enjoyable lunch with her colleagues. However, more trouble arose as soon as she got back to the office.

Warren Tallman had numerous objections to her strategy document, and she spent the rest of the afternoon closeted in his office with him, defending her document and explaining Ventura's requirements. It wasn't until late the next day that her secretary was finally able to type up the revised version.

The only pleasure Marla derived from the meeting with Warren was when she asked him about the faint buzzing sound coming from inside his desk. Rather than show her Vernon's karmic pop art radio, he turned red and denied hearing anything. Marla supposed he felt his virility was threatened because he couldn't turn off a plastic radio without help.

Once Warren had approved and initialed the written strategy, it was time to take it back to Ventura for their reaction. She called Brent, excited about showing it to him and even more excited about seeing him face-to-face. It had been nearly ten days—not that she was counting.

At Brent's suggestion she drove out to Ventura late that afternoon, after work. She had handed him a copy of the strategy as soon as she arrived.

"I've also brought copies for Nigel and Felice," she said.

"They're not here today. Nigel had to leave right at five o'clock, and Felice is at the warehouse."

"Well, you'll all need a chance to read it and discuss it anyhow before you get back to me with suggestions."

She couldn't keep her eyes from straying over him. He looked rugged and healthy and relaxed, as usual. He had an air of confidence and candor that was rare in Marla's experience. She couldn't help smiling however, at the look of dismay that crossed his face when he glanced through the papers she handed him.

"I'm sure Nigel will explain it to you," she said, surprised to hear herself teasing him.

He tossed the papers onto his desk. "I should have stayed a blacksmith. No target markets, no strategies, no per capita income. Just me, my tools and my job."

"Now that's not true," she countered. "You had to make your services known. Even knocking on doors or passing the word is a form of advertising. And you must have said something to make people want to use your services—told them you were the most reasonably priced or the best trained or the most reliable."

He shook a finger at her. "Businesspeople have a way of interpreting everything to suit their values."

"Ah, but—"

"Look, instead of arguing, why don't I take you for a walk on the beach and show you where we play volleyball? The water looks beautiful this time of day, when the sun starts going down."

His warm, deep voice made it sound too enticing to refuse. The light in his eyes was friendly and innocent, nothing more, but it tugged at something inside her. It couldn't hurt to enjoy just a little more time alone with him, now could it? After all, building a rapport with him was an important part of her job.

"Okay. Let's go."

He led her down the street and across the sand to the water's edge.

"I love the ocean," he said pensively, looking out as they walked side by side along the shore. "You know, the first time I ever saw the sea I was twenty years old."

"That's funny, so was I," Marla said.

He looked surprised. "Really? You're not a native Californian?"

"Is anyone?" she asked dryly. "No, I grew up in Chicago."

"And you never went to Fort Lauderdale on spring break? I thought that was a rite of passage for midwesterners."

"Only for some. We didn't have a lot of money, and I worked all holidays as a teenager, trying to save up for college. I was very ambitious, serious, full of purpose." She smiled wistfully. "I guess Fort Lauderdale would have been wasted on me."

"I take it you got to college?"

"Yes. And when I was twenty I worked as a camp counselor in a plush summer camp for wealthy kids in Massachusetts. One of the other counselors invited me to spend the last week of the summer at her family's home on Cape Cod. I decided I wanted to live by the ocean someday."

"Yeah, after the first time I saw it, I could never stay away for long," he agreed. "Did your parents mind you moving so far away from them?"

She hesitated before replying, "My mother did."

"And your father?" he pressed.

Marla shrugged noncommittally.

Brent sensed that she didn't like talking about her family. He wondered why but felt that this was hardly the time to ask probing personal questions.

The wind blew her long blond hair away from her face and lifted her simple linen skirt to give him a teasing glance of thigh. There was a quality about her that made him think of the old saying, Still waters run deep. On the surface she possessed a calmness and confidence that he respected and appreciated. He found her enjoyable, even comforting in an unfamiliar way. But there were moments, like this one, when he was aware that she had many other qualities—mystery, sadness, sensuality and strength—that she kept hidden during business hours.

He wondered if she revealed them after the sun went down. He was tempted to keep her on the beach long enough to find out.

And why shouldn't he? he thought suddenly. He had thought she wasn't his type of woman, but what the hell did that mean, anyhow? Wasn't he underestimating her to suppose that he knew everything important about her just because she dressed elegantly and worked in the business world? He liked her, he enjoyed her company, he had professional confidence in her, and she was the first woman who had been able to arouse his interest since the death of his wife.

Wouldn't he be a fool not to pursue this further and find out exactly what it was about her that excited instincts he had begun to fear were dead and buried?

He opened his mouth to speak and then snapped it shut again. He hadn't asked a woman for a date in nearly ten years. How did he begin? He tried to remember.

"There are a lot of great seafood restaurants around here," he said, giving her her cue.

"Yes, I suppose so."

A beautiful beach, a beautiful man, she thought. It seemed she had always been busy working her way through high school or college or graduate school, and that had left little time for idle moments with no beginning or end. She envied Brent his dedication to pleasurable pursuits. Such a frivolous, carefree existence seemed foreign and exotic to a woman like her, who had always been so stoic and hard-working.

"Do you like seafood?" he said.

"Some of it."

She thought of Warren Tallman and his father-in-law, the chairman of the board. She thought of how hard she had worked to get this job at Freemont, Fox and Linsford, how much youth she had sacrificed to it.

"Do you like shrimp?"

"Yes," she said absently.

Brent frowned. She wasn't helping. He must be going about this all wrong, he thought, but he pressed on. "There's a place about a mile up the beach that makes great scampi."

"Really?"

He took the plunge. "Do you have plans tonight?"

"I . . ." She had planned to call her little sister—not so little now at twenty-six—to see if she could provide a clearer perspective about her mother's situation. Knowing her sister, it was doubtful.

"I mean, are you hungry?" Why had he even started this conversation? He hadn't felt this awkward since he was a gangly fifteen-year-old.

"Huh?" Marla stopped walking and turned to stare at him.

He looked into her wide hazel eyes. "Will you have dinner with me tonight?" His voice was low and much more serious than he had intended.

Marla looked away and then looked back at Brent. The setting sun touched dark, burnished highlights in his hair, and his silhouette was overwhelmingly big and masculine against the western sky. She had never seen anyone so beautiful.

"I don't know...." she stammered stupidly.

"I want to spend time with you," he said slowly.

Her heart started pounding at the intimate tone of his voice. He wasn't talking about an agency dinner where they would chat about the account, she realized. He wanted a date. He'd expect them to sit in the candlelight somewhere, telling each other personal things.

"Brent, I'm your account executive." Her voice was husky.

"I know that," he said blankly.

She realized he didn't understand the implications. She wanted to explain, but at the same time she was afraid of making a fool of herself. What if he didn't realize he put out heat waves like a hot stove? What if he merely wanted to be friendly?

"Marla, this was hard for me to ask. Do you think you could at least give me an answer?"

There was a vulnerability in the question that tore through her. His shirt was open at the neck. His skin looked warm and smooth, lightly dusted with dark hairs. Would the hair be thicker on his chest? Would it descend in a thin line down his belly to his groin?

This is playing with fire, she thought desperately. She was undressing the man in her mind, and all he had actually done was ask her to eat with him.

Alarm bells went off in her head. She must be the model of professionalism, the epitome of proper conduct, if she didn't want Warren Tallman to boot her out of the agency. She, of all people knew better than to put her career in even the slightest jeopardy for a man.

"No, I'm sorry, I can't, Brent."

"Oh. Well... Walk you back to your car?" he said as lightly as he could.

"No, thanks," Marla said quickly, dying to end the scene. "You finish your walk. I'll call you in a few days to get your reaction to the strategy, and we'll all have lunch or something, okay?"

"Yeah, sure. See you, Marla."

Brent watched her walk away. He felt a rush of humiliation. This was rejection, and it wasn't pretty. He was at a complete loss. He had known when he asked her to go to dinner with him that there were a dozen reasons she might say no. It hadn't occurred to him until he saw the look of dismay in her eyes that she just might not want to spend her free time with him.

He sighed deeply, wishing he had left well enough alone. Maybe he had been wrong. Maybe he wasn't ready to meet another woman yet. Or maybe he had been right when he had assumed that Marla just wasn't someone he should be interested in.

Well, he could have bungled it even worse. He could have grabbed her roughly and smothered her with kisses. If he had, he probably would have had to start looking for a new ad agency first thing in the morning, he thought wryly. Marla didn't look like someone who appreciated brute force.

Unable to sleep that night, he did something very unusual for him—he turned on the TV and watched an old movie. Clark Gable, a rough and rugged guy, was falling for a cool-as-cucumber dame wouldn't tumble. Gable grabbed the woman roughly and smothered her with kisses. She fell madly in love with him on the spot.

"Well, I guess it works for some guys," Brent muttered.

Chapter Four

Nigel sat cross-legged atop his desk in the Bull Pen and read through the documents Marla had left for him. Brent lay on the couch nearby, ostensibly doing the same thing but actually replaying yesterday's scene over and over in his mind. Maybe he was punishing himself for having wanted to be with another woman, even after all this time. Or maybe the things Katie had found endearing about him didn't appeal to other women.

Or maybe Marla just didn't like him very much.

"She's got good sense," said Nigel.

"What?" The word came out of Brent's mouth like a gunshot.

Nigel looked at him sharply. "Your advertising woman. She knows what she's doing," he said succinctly.

"Oh." Brent relaxed again and stared at the ceiling.

"What's got into you, mate?"

"Nothing."

"You look like a kicked puppy."

Brent glared at him. "I am too old for that description."

"Nevertheless, it fits." Nigel peered at him slyly. "Or is *lovesick* the word I'm searching for?"

"Lay off." Brent tried to sound ominous.

Nigel ignored him. "The two of you could hardly stop staring at each other the last time she was here."

"That's an exaggeration."

"Felice noticed it, too."

"Have you two been talking behind my back?" Brent snapped.

"For the past three years."

There was a heavy silence. Brent frowned and studied his hands. Nigel and Felice had been sympathetic, supportive and patient by turns since Katie's death. They both believed it was in his best interest to get involved with a new woman. Naturally they would pounce on whomever they perceived to be the first likely candidate.

Nigel heaved a sigh. He put down his file folder and contemplated Brent seriously. Since it was lunchtime, there was no one within hearing distance. He said gently, "You're not feeling guilty, are you?"

Brent shrugged uncomfortably.

"More than anyone, she would have wanted you to find someone new. Wherever she is, she'd be happy for you if you and Marla...uh..."

"Subtle as ever," Brent said dryly.

"Don't tell me you haven't thought about it," Nigel said in a lighter tone.

"Forget it. She's not interested," Brent said tersely.

"Of course she is. She looks at you like—"

"She said no."

"Aha! So you've been making progress!"

"Nigel," Brent said in exasperation, "I asked her to have dinner with me. That's *all* I asked for," he added as he saw Nigel smirk, "and she refused. She wants to keep it strictly business. End of discussion. She wasn't being coy."

"No," Nigel said thoughtfully, "she's not the coy type. But she's got hidden agenda—you can see that."

"*I* can't."

"That's because you're smitten."

"I am not 'smitten.' I just . . . I mean, I thought . . . She's very . . . Oh, forget it. I'm going for a swim."

"Sure, mate. I'll finish going over this report, and we can talk about it later. Then we'll invite Marla around."

Brent glowered at the exaggerated innocence of Nigel's tone and stalked out the door. Why hadn't he just kept his mouth shut? Men were supposed to tell their buddies about their conquests, not their rejections.

When he reached the beach, he pulled off his tank top and dived into the surf wearing only his shorts. The sea was choppy, and striving against it gave him satisfaction. This was something real and physical he could concentrate on, and the exertion brought him pleasure. The awakening of long-dormant needs and feelings that had no outlet had so far brought him only frustration.

When he came out of the water a half hour later, he felt calmer. It had been naive to suppose that the first woman he had been interested in since Katie's death would simply tumble into his arms. And he certainly wasn't going to embarrass either of them by opening the subject again. Her refusal had been clear. That was that.

It was at least an hour before he was aware of the persistent yearning pulsing inside of him again, stronger than ever.

She tortured herself all day. Had she been too rude, too slow to answer, too arbitrary in her refusal? Had she offended him, or even worse, hurt his feelings?

Had she jeopardized the account?

"This is the fourth time you've wandered into my office. Are you *sure* there's not something you want to talk about?" Vernon said in exasperation that afternoon.

Marla once more considered asking Vernon's advice. No, no, it was her problem. Maybe it wasn't even a problem. Maybe she had been so boggled by Brent's sheer magnetism that she had mistaken his signals. Maybe he just didn't like to eat alone.

"Marla? Are you listening to me?"

"Hmm? Oh, sorry. What were you saying?"

"I said, 'Gee, Marla, how's the Ventura account coming along?'"

"Oh," she said blankly. "Fine. Nigel McBain called about an hour ago. I'm going out there again tomorrow."

She made a few halfhearted attempts to shoot Vernon's basketball into the basket over his doorway.

"I gave the radio to Warren," Vernon said.

"I know. It's still making a racket in his desk drawer. I wonder what he's going to do with it?"

"*I* wonder what kind of batteries that thing's got."

Marla sighed. "I guess I should get back to work."

She spent half the afternoon staring out her office window and wondering how she should deal with Brent the next time they met. Should she pretend nothing had happened? Should she make a polite and mature attempt to explain her reasoning behind last night's refusal?

She scribbled idly on page after page of scrap paper, aware that her biggest stumbling block was not how to handle a potentially embarrassing client situation. She had done that many times before with success. No, her real problem was that despite all her common sense, she had wanted that intimate dinner with Brent last night so much she could have drummed her heels in frustration when she returned to her empty apartment in Pacific Beach.

"Dumb," she muttered. "Very dumb."

An unproductive day and a restless night were the only result of her fretting. When she drove out to Ventura the next day, she still had no idea what she would do.

By the time she found Nigel, and then they, in turn, found Brent in Ventura's uniquely unstructured environment, she was so fascinated by Brent's appearance that she forgot her unease about seeing him again.

He was in one of the workshops, and Marla felt she was being given a glimpse into his past. He was employing the skills he had learned as a blacksmith, working hot iron with heavy tools, delicately beating it into submission.

She guessed he had been at the task for quite a while. His sweat-soaked cotton shirt clung to his back and muscular arms, defining every ripple and bulge, every sinuous, powerful movement. His dark face glistened with healthy sweat, and his dark hair shone like damp silk.

He saw Nigel signal to him and indicated with a nod that he wanted to finish this piece of work. Marla watched in fascination as Brent skillfully practiced his ancient craft with ease and obvious satisfaction. She was hypnotized by his strength, his control, his steady rhythm and the atonal sound of metal hitting metal.

When he finally straightened and looked at his work with satisfaction, Marla came forward quite unself-consciously and asked him about it.

"This is amazing!" she exclaimed when he showed her the piece of climbing equipment he was designing. "I've never seen a blacksmith at work. It's really skilled work, isn't it?"

Brent looked boyishly pleased with her enthusiasm for the trade his father had taught him. He used a bandanna to wipe his face and the strong, tan column of his throat, then insisted she look at some of the other prototypes he was working on.

"The idea behind most of these designs," he explained, "is to encourage alternatives to chipping and chiseling away at rocks and cliff face as if they were just so much aluminum siding you could replace tomorrow."

She asked him to teach her something about working iron. By this time, Nigel had left the workshop to answer a phone call, and she and Brent were alone. He showed her some of his tools, explained the principles of heating, cooling and working the metal, and then he tried to help her make a small, decorative horseshoe.

"The hard part of this is actually trying not to get stepped on or kicked in the face while you're fitting the shoe," he said wryly.

Marla found the tools unfamiliar and ungainly in her grasp. Brent's arms came around her naturally as he held her own arms firmly and tried to guide her movements.

"Hit it hard. Go on, it won't hit back," he urged.

She felt sheer pleasure—nothing else. No warnings, no worries. He felt good to her, his big hands steadying her arms, his chest pressed against her back, his encouraging, laughing voice near her ear, his breath brushing her hair. It felt too right to be wrong, and they were having too much fun for it to be a mistake.

It seemed to take ages, but at last she held up a little horseshoe.

"Your first project," Brent said. "Well-done."

"Yeah, but you did most of the work. I just made most of the mistakes." Even the most charitable observer would have to admit that her horseshoe was lopsided and dented.

"It's still better than my first horseshoe," he assured her.

"Can I keep it?"

"I insist." He squinted critically at it. "I can't have something that badly designed sitting around the shop. People would get the wrong idea."

She smiled up at him. He was still standing very close to her, and he was so tall she had to tilt her head back to meet his eyes. There was a pleasant glow in their green depths, relaxed and excited at the same time. He smelled warm and musky. Her next comment got stuck in her throat, and she felt some essential organ in her chest tighten perceptibly. How could you not adore this man? she thought suddenly.

His own expression changed subtly. There was a slight hesitation in his manner when he lifted one hand to her face. He swallowed and shifted his eyes away from hers.

"Marla..." His voice was low and raspy. He brushed her cheek with a feather-light touch, then pushed her long hair off her forehead and behind her shoulder. His gentleness made her feel cherished and special.

"Do you think . . . ?" He hesitated again.

"What?" she whispered, moved by the vulnerability in his face, the uncertainty in his voice. This man had scaled mountains, run rapids, conquered the surf. What on earth could make him feel unsure of himself?

He lowered his eyes to her mouth, and though his thick, dark lashes hid their expression from her, she could feel excitement start to rush through her body. He touched his fingertips to her moist lips for a moment, and she felt as if every nerve ending in her body was aware of that delicate, slight caress.

Slowly, with slim, callused fingers, he traced the shape of her trembling lips. Marla's eyes closed of their own volition, and she knew he must feel the quickened pace of her breath against his skin.

"Mmm." It was a small sound, thin and weak, not even strong enough to be called a sigh, but they both heard it as it escaped her throat.

He stilled, and she became aware of an awesome tension building inside him. When he spoke, his voice was unusually deep and strained.

"I haven't kissed a woman for . . . a long time."

It was more of a question than a statement. Marla's gaze flew up to capture his. He looked confused and shy, but more than that, he looked like a man who still knew how to kiss a woman very thoroughly, despite his disclaimer. She was too mature not to recognize pure desire when she saw it in a man's eyes. For just a moment, she allowed herself to bask in the thrill of being desired by this remarkable man.

He lowered his head just a fraction, still uncertain himself. She felt his warm breath across her cheekbones. The physical sensation brought her back to reality with a jolt.

"Wait," she gasped. She backed away in three quick, awkward steps, clutching her absurd little horseshoe.

Brent straightened just as suddenly and stared at her with wide eyes.

"This is a big mistake, Brent." Panic started to seep into her numb brain. She felt her chest rise and fall, heard her breath rush in and out like gusts of wind.

She was prepared for almost any reaction except the one she actually got. He lowered his head and turned away for a moment.

"I'm sorry, Marla. I didn't consider..." His voice trailed off. After another moment of agonized silence, he straightened his shoulders and said, "Let's go tell Nigel and Felice we're ready for that meeting. It's why you came, after all, isn't it?"

She nodded dumbly and preceded him out the doorway. They walked back to the Bull Pen in uneasy, thought-filled silence. She had behaved stupidly, and he was taking it better than she had any right to expect. She would have to make sure she wasn't alone with him again at any time for any reason. It was the only way she could trust herself not to make an even worse mistake.

The meeting went badly. Brent was distracted and restless. Marla felt embarrassed and depressed. Nigel kept being called to the telephone because of a problem in one of Ventura's regional stores, and Felice had a head cold. After one unproductive hour, they all agreed to call it a day and meet again the following week.

Brent watched with painful confusion while Marla high-tailed it out of Ventura as if the building were on fire. His resolve not to force her to recognize his attraction had lasted less than twenty-four hours. He wouldn't be at all surprised if she asked her boss, Warren Tallman, to assign someone else to the Ventura account.

There had been a moment, just a brief moment, when he had thought she wanted him to touch her, when he had thought she returned his fascination. A flicker of longing in those hazel eyes, a softening of that strong-featured face. And then she had jumped like a scalded cat.

He ran his hands through his hair and drained his coffee cup. And his friends and family kept insisting it would be a *good* thing if he got interested in a woman?

"How'd it go at Ventura yesterday?" Vernon asked as he played with one of the Rawlins Pocketknives in Marla's office.

"I don't want to talk about it." The terse words were out of her mouth before she could stop them.

Vernon looked at her curiously. "Problems?"

"No. Yes. Oh, you know how it goes. Bad meeting," she finished vaguely.

"Oh." There was a long pause before Vernon said, "Warren had a little chat with me. He doesn't want Nathan to write the copy on this account. He wants David."

"David!" Marla slammed her coffee cup down on her desk, annoyed with Warren but almost pleased to have a subject upon which to vent her pent-up frustration. "Of all the ridiculous ideas! David is the last thing we need on this account! Not only is he coy and slick, but he never delivers on time, and he always blatantly ignores the agreed-upon strategy."

"I know, but—"

"Anyhow, you're the creative director, so where does Warren get off telling *you* who to assign to the account?"

"Well, he—"

"Besides, if he has objections, why doesn't he come to *me*? I *am* the account exec. I *am* the one who's meant to determine the client's needs. He should talk to me about this before he approaches you. He's never even spent ten minutes alone with Brent!"

"Feeling better?" Vernon asked conversationally.

She took a deep breath and found to her surprise that she did indeed feel better. It was marvelous to be annoyed at someone besides herself. "Self-righteous indignation is good for the soul," she said wryly.

"I do so agree."

"I'll get back to you on the Ventura account as soon as I meet with them again, okay?"

Since Brent was taking a personal interest in the company's advertising, Marla couldn't follow the most sensible course of action, which would be to avoid any contact with him whatsoever. However, she was determined to avoid seeing or speaking to him alone. Nothing but trouble could come out of placing herself in another tempting situation.

There was no mistaking his intention in the workshop yesterday. It made things even worse. It was hard enough to ignore her own attraction to him. Now that she realized he felt a similar pull, she didn't want to risk long-winded explanations and embarrassing apologies. She almost hoped that Nigel had noticed the tension between them and would explain to Brent how inappropriate any involvement between them would be. Nigel behaved as rebelliously as Brent, but he at least seemed to have some understanding of the usual conventions.

During her next few trips to Ventura the following week, Marla was almost convinced that Brent had changed his mind about her. At first, when he didn't join her meetings with Nigel and Felice, she quelled her feeling of disappointment and reminded herself that this was really for the best. Apparently he had realized what a mistake it would be to become too interested in her.

However, despite all her hard work and common sense, she felt positively resentful by the end of that week. She had been to Ventura headquarters three times in four days, and Brent hadn't even said hello to her. She hadn't glimpsed him at all. She even found, to her mortification, that she had lost track of Nigel's words several times because she was strenuously—though surreptitiously—searching for Brent with her eyes.

This is absurd, she thought. I can at least ask about him, for goodness' sake. So she did.

Nigel and Felice exchanged a glance. "He's gone climbing, Marla," Nigel said with attempted casualness.

"What?" The sharp question startled her as much as it did them. She tried to amend her mistake. "He didn't mention he was planning to leave town."

Felice shrugged. "He wasn't. He just called to say he was heading into the Sierra Nevada for a couple of weeks and would see us when he got back." She paused. "He does that sometimes."

"Alone?" Marla asked shakily, appalled at the thought of him dangling over gorges with no one to go for help if he should fall and hurt himself.

"I didn't ask," Felice admitted, "but I doubt if he'll go up alone. He has plenty of climbing buddies."

"I see...."

Marla was grateful that business concerns took Nigel away for a few moments and that Felice excused herself to go take another dose of her cold medication.

Whatever reaction she had been counting on from Brent, she hadn't expected anything like this. She didn't know what to make of it. Was he so disturbed about their last encounter that he couldn't bear to be in the same city, let alone the same building, with her for two weeks? Or had he shrugged off the incident within minutes and decided to go away for two weeks simply because he was restless?

She remembered the jokes everyone at Ventura made about Brent's frequent absence. He was never around when you needed him, Nigel had said. Brent himself had admitted to founding the company just so he could have plenty of free time.

Based on that, she wasn't vain enough to assume he had gone to the mountains to lick his wounds simply because she wouldn't kiss him. Anger at him started to replace her worry. How typically selfish, irresponsible and immature! Didn't he realize they had work to do here? She was about to make the final corrections on the strategy, but the account couldn't go any further until they had Brent's official approval on it. How could he be so frivolous? she fumed silently.

She had already noticed his inability to concentrate on serious business matters. It didn't matter how boyish or endearing or gorgeous he was, Marla knew better than to let even a spark of interest continue to glow inside of her for such an irresponsible man. She knew the consequences of such folly from long experience.

Brent curled up inside his thermal sleeping bag. Although he had wanted to get away from it all for a couple of weeks, he wasn't a solitary man by nature, so he had tracked down a couple of friends he had known were currently camping and climbing near the California-Nevada border.

Someone threw another log on the camp fire and called good-night to him. Although April in San Diego was warm—like all months in San Diego—it was still mighty cold this high up. He allowed himself a moment of smug pride as he recalled how durable and warm the new Ventura clothing designs had proved to be on this trip.

He knew that when he returned home tomorrow, Nigel and Felice would plague him with questions. He sighed and rolled over. Being cared about could be a pain in the neck sometimes, but he knew he wouldn't change it for anything.

He hadn't suddenly disappeared without prior warning for almost two years. It had been a frequent occurrence after Katie's death, and everyone had accepted his need to find peace in hard physical activities, to cherish his memories in the silence of nature, to absorb himself in the things he loved. It had also been his only respite from the way he had thrown himself into company business at that time.

He had stabilized since then, and if he now spent more time playing than working, he at least gave plenty of advance warning. So Nigel and Felice would want to know why he had disappeared like this.

Marla's face appeared before his eyes without warning, and he cursed himself silently. He had thought that two weeks of climbing and camping and camaraderie, two weeks in an environment where a woman like her had no place, had finally banished her image from his mind. And now it rose up before him as if he had only seen her, wanted her, moments ago.

How many times did a woman have to say no before you accepted that she wasn't interested? What kind of man was he that he had let it rock him that much?

It was the closest he had come to a woman, sexually, in almost three years. After the years of numbness, his needs were thundering through him now. He wanted to hold and touch and kiss; he wanted warmth and affection, comfort and intimacy, passion and satisfaction. He wanted flesh against flesh, a woman writhing against him, breath burning in his lungs, strength draining from his quivering muscles.

There had been days in the past three years when he had sadly feared he'd never want another woman again and would therefore miss so much of life. Now he wanted a woman, this particular woman, so much it hurt. And she didn't want him.

Why couldn't it be simple, he fumed, like last time? Katie had met him, claimed it was love at first sight, and by the third date she was dragging him off to the nearest bed, as impetuous as always. Not that he had needed any urging. He smiled reminiscently. She had never given him room for self-doubt. They were married within six weeks of meeting, and the only reason they had waited that long was because he wanted his parents to come down from Montana for the ceremony.

He thought back to his life before Katie. There had been women, and he had been rejected once in a while, and he had always bounced back. But, he acknowledged, he wasn't the same man he had been in his twenties. In those days, he had thought nothing was more important than a great wave or a challenging cliff. His marriage had taught him otherwise. Now, in his late thirties and coming out of mourning, he knew that the most important things in life were at stake when he became seriously attracted to a woman.

Realizing he wouldn't get any sleep with his mind working so furiously, Brent crawled out of his sleeping bag and fed some kindling to the camp fire.

Maybe his real problem was that he was taking this all too seriously. Wanting to have sex with a woman wasn't the same thing as falling in love with a woman and wanting to share your whole life with her. Maybe he should view Marla's response as a sexual rejection, rather than as a rejection of his emotional offering, his character and his life-style.

He smiled wryly, finally able to laugh at himself. Yes, he had definitely taken it too seriously, let it hurt too much. He had come to these mountains for a clearer perspective, and finally, on his last night, he had found it. It wounded his masculine ego to be rejected the first time he had chosen to make a pass at a woman since becoming widowed, but at least he could handle that kind of hurt equably.

He curled into his sleeping bag again, satisfied that he could behave reasonably toward Marla when he got back to San Diego. So she didn't want him to touch her. So what? He could deal with that.

The moment Marla saw him, she realized she had missed him. He looked better than she had ever seen him—darker, stronger, healthier, more relaxed. Whatever he did high up in the mountains, it obviously agreed with him.

He greeted her cheerfully. Her fingers disappeared in his brown, callused hand. His presence overwhelmed her, his broad shoulders dwarfed her, his glowing green eyes made her feel self-conscious.

"You sure look pretty," he said ingenuously.

"Thank you." She didn't even try to stop the pleased smile that lighted her face. After all, she had tried to look pretty today.

He offered her a seat near his big, overflowing desk. "Nigel tells me you guys got a lot of work done while I was away," he said.

"Yes. We just need your final approval on these documents before we can continue."

He looked contrite. "Nigel told me that my absence has held things up. I'm really sorry. I just didn't think."

No, you didn't, did you? But it was hard to be annoyed at this powerful, muscular man who looked at her as though he were afraid she would scold him. Instead, she said, "Where is Nigel?"

"He caught Felice's cold, so he's home in bed."

"Oh."

"But I'll just read this through, and if everything's all right..." He trailed off, already frowning in perplexity as he skimmed over page one.

He propped both elbows on his desk and studied the documents. He looked like a football player studying for an exam, and Marla had the feeling he wasn't absorbing much. After a few more minutes, she caught him peering at her from under his brows. She stifled the urge to laugh.

"Problems?" she asked innocently.

"Nah. Piece of cake."

"You're frowning."

"It's a defense mechanism."

She gave in and laughed. "Is there anything you'd like me to explain to you?"

"Oh, just ten or twelve things." He grinned. "I'm starved. Let's do it over lunch."

It was an innocent enough invitation. He looked naughty and happy rather than intent and serious. He looked too good to refuse. Besides, she reasoned, another refusal might send him back into the Sierra Nevada for two more weeks. "Sure."

They got some sandwiches and sat in Ventura's lunch-room with a copy of the strategy spread out before them. Marla went over it point by point with him, her long, fine-boned hand moving from page to page as she explained everything. She discovered quickly that he understood it all as long as it was couched in layman's terms.

Brent's eyes moved over her face assessingly. He couldn't have omitted telling her she was pretty today. Everything about her looked perfect, from the soft sheen of her thick blond hair to the subtle femininity of her clothes. Best of all was the way her somber face lighted up when she smiled. There was no harm in admiring, after all. She had said no twice, and he knew where he stood with her. There was no danger in being friendly.

"This all seems perfectly in order to me," he said. She accepted his statement professionally, but some sixth sense alerted him that she was disappointed at the blandness of his words. Nigel said she had done awfully good work. So Brent wanted to explain his feelings. Just to clear the air, that was all.

"I'm sorry I'm not more enthusiastic, Marla. It's like Felice said, business talk makes me feel cheap. I design the equipment, I decide what we'll spend and how much we'll charge, and I decide how the company will operate. But this—" he gestured toward the strategy "—isn't my bag. I know you'll think it sounds naive, but I feel like this means we're going to try to *trick* people into buying our stuff."

Her slanted hazel eyes were very serious as she considered his words. "I can assure you we won't say anything about your products that isn't true."

"You don't need to. They're the best."

His response made her smile again. "Then why keep it a secret? Why not tell everyone? And why not start with a specific target market?"

He sighed theatrically. "You reason like the devil himself. No wonder all the ads we see make us feel we should buy things we don't want and don't need."

"Well, admittedly advertising often has an unsavory reputation. There's that old joke, you know. Please don't tell my mother I'm in advertising—she thinks I play piano in a whorehouse."

Brent laughed. "What drew you to advertising, then?" he asked curiously.

"Oh, I like a lot of things about it. I like working with people, getting to know all my clients, learning about different businesses. I like the creativity involved and the camaraderie with my colleagues. There's always a new challenge, a new surprise, an exciting change. And, to be honest, the pay is good, especially when you're working your way up the ladder at a big agency like Freemont."

"And is that what you're doing? Working your way up the ladder?"

"Well, that's certainly my ambition," she said evasively.

He studied her speculatively. Yes, ambition would account for the efficiency and dedication with which she had pursued this account. "Do you really think Freemont is the best place for an ambitious woman?"

She hesitated before responding, aware that his question was perceptive but reluctant to hint to a client that her employer wasn't perfect. "It's a conservative agency," she admitted, "and I might rise to the top faster in a less conservative agency. But when I finished my M.B.A. and started looking for the right kind of job, it seemed sensible to start out in the biggest, most powerful agency in the city. There's greater potential for me there."

"If you say so. But wouldn't you rather work someplace where you felt more at home?"

She frowned. "I do feel at home there."

"Really?" he said skeptically. He couldn't picture Marla at home among the men he had met that day at Freemont. She was too honest, forthright and friendly. She saw him as more than figures in an account book, and he doubted if the others did.

Marla felt unsettled by his question. Of course she felt at home at Freemont. Maybe she had to watch her step, maybe she couldn't always say what she thought to the brass, but that was business. That was real life. Not everybody could create their own ideal working environment just because Brent had, and she was annoyed with him for not realizing that.

"You say business makes you feel cheap, and yet you're a very canny businessman. You implement the most progressive and modern management policies, you use ideal tax shelters and you have a flair for publicity. You must have at least studied the enemy." She raised her brows inquisitively.

The slow grin that spread across his face stole her breath away. Even at work he always seemed to be playing.

"This is going to kill you, Marla, but I really don't know anything about business. That's why I've got Nigel. All those things you just mentioned to me are, in fact, my ideas, but they don't come out of an M.B.A. program or an in-depth study of successfully operated private companies."

"Then what is the secret of your success?" she asked, enjoying the sparkle in his eyes.

"Four words my mother told me when I left home—do the right thing. It's really that simple."

" 'Do the right thing'?" she repeated blankly.

"Exactly. Mom said if you do the right thing, you'll get back double what you put in."

"Well, that's very uplifting Brent, but it hardly explains a company that does nearly thirty million dollars of business a year."

"But it does. I make the very best equipment, I don't skimp on design or materials, and I don't let anything leave my factory that isn't perfect. I charge a fair price, even though Nigel tells me I *could* charge more and not lose customers. I pay all my employees well—more than they would get elsewhere—and I respect them as adults, so I don't make a lot of silly rules or check on their whereabouts.

"Consequently, I sell everything I make and am bombarded with demands for more. All my customers are satisfied, because even if someone writes or phones with a complaint, we bend over backward to help them out. I fire any employees who don't work out, and all the others are loyal, hardworking, long-term employees, who probably do more work for me voluntarily than I actually pay them for." He shrugged. "So Mom was right."

Marla leaned forward and propped both elbows on the table. "It sounds too much like a fairy tale to me."

"But if I know you, you've seen our sales figures, our public relations files and have talked to the staff, and you know it's all true."

"Well..."

"Aha! You just don't want to admit I'm right, because you're not sure it fits into the business world that you know."

Marla smiled at his enthusiasm. "And your pretax donations to conservationist organizations? Is that also the right thing?"

"That's just about the *most* right thing. Where are we going to climb and camp if it's all cut down, mined or covered with factories? Where will I swim, surf and sail if all the water is polluted with toxic chemicals and all the fish have cancer?" He shook his head sadly. "When I was twenty and saw the Pacific Ocean for the first time, I thought it was something so vast that no one could hurt it. I was wrong."

Marla leaned back, moved by his tone, and voiced a sudden idea. "Maybe your campaign could include the right thing, Brent."

"How?"

She shrugged. "I don't know yet. Luckily we have some very good people working on this account. I'm sure, given the nature of your products, that we can find a way to subliminally interest the target market in conservation in relation to Ventura."

"If you could do that, Marla, I might even take back some of the nasty things I've said about advertising."

"Now how can I resist a challenge like that?" she teased.

He grunted. "I have my doubts. It seems like all advertising is based on the promise that if you buy a certain product, someone will give you money, sex or power. We don't offer those things to anyone."

"Then what do you offer?" she asked, curious to hear his answer.

"Freedom." He looked sheepish a moment later and said, "I know that sounds corny, but I believe it."

"It doesn't sound corny. Idealistic, but not corny." She caught his gaze and let him see that she respected his beliefs.

A sudden glow, a tender light, entered his eyes. He placed his hand over hers and squeezed it. "You're too nice to be my account executive."

"Thanks. I think."

She looked so lovely, her strong features softened by some inner warmth, her thick-lashed eyes looking wider than ever. Her skin smelled subtly of woman and expensive perfume, stirring his senses anew. He felt his belly tighten as he looked at her soft pink lips. His mouth went dry.

"So what happens now?" he said huskily. "I mean, with our business."

"Now the creative people enter the scene and start planning concepts and proposals, with me acting as their control." Her voice was unusually low, he thought. Could she possibly feel it, too, this hot cord wrapping around them, squeezing air from their lungs, pulling them closer to each other?

"So we won't see you again for a while?" He didn't even try to mask his disappointment.

"Actually, I'd like to bring a few of my people out to meet you and have a look around Ventura. It's bound to inspire them."

"Good. I'll see you then," he said.

He escorted her to the front of the complex but didn't walk her to her car. As long as they were around other people, he knew what he would and wouldn't do, but there were no other people in the parking lot.

Because after today there was no point kidding himself that she was just a sexually attractive woman to him. He liked her too much to just want her body. He was fascinated by the contradictions in her, by the things he didn't yet know or understand about her. Her eyes made him feel tender, her smile made him feel happy, and her very presence made him feel hungry and wanting. So he had a feeling that if she said no again, he wouldn't accept it equably. He'd want to know why.

He was confused. There were moments when he was sure she liked him. Sometimes her smile was full of fondness. He was positive he'd caught her looking at his body, and although he wasn't vain, he knew he had what modern advertising told everyone was a good, rugged build.

He wished he knew more about her. Maybe she thought she was in love with someone else, maybe she preferred the sensitive, intellectual type, or maybe she was recovering from a broken heart. Whatever it was, she was playing her cards close to her chest.

He worked late that night, trying to exhaust himself, trying to occupy his mind. He didn't *want* to be interested in a complicated woman. He didn't think he would know how to cope with her. So why, he chided himself, had he spent so much time today trying to find out how she felt, trying to explain some of his own philosophies?

"Urrgh," he said when he tried without success to stop analyzing and interpreting her comments and gestures.

He peddled home in the dark and started making dinner in his kitchen. He had moved to the small house near Windansea Beach two years ago, wanting to live someplace that wasn't full of memories of his marriage, recognizing that it would be healthier to live without daily reminders of Katie.

Tonight, for the first time in quite a while, the house seemed unbearably lonely and silent.

He resented the way his whole life was being affected by a woman he didn't understand, a woman who pretended she had no interest in him. He did something he hadn't done for a very long time. He opened an old photo album and started trying to actively call up memories—good times with Katie, sweet moments from their life together.

He put down the photo album a half hour later, stunned and disturbed. The photos and the memories didn't have the same effect on him anymore. They were just memories now. He was grateful for them—those years had shaped and changed him and enriched his life—but they were over.

The door to the past had swung shut forever in his heart tonight, and he was being pulled forward into the future, lured by a pair of mysterious hazel eyes.

Chapter Five

Marla returned to Ventura a few days later with four members of the creative department who would be working on the account, including Nathan the copywriter and Vernon. She had quite intentionally not brought along Warren Tallman's choice for copywriter.

She knew Warren would eventually confront her about her resistance to the other copywriter, but she cared too much about this account to let it be mangled by Warren and his favorite lackeys. Brent was right, Freemont was a conservative agency. But there were still quite a few outlandish free spirits in the creative department, and she was determined to see that Ventura benefited from their talents.

Brent greeted the team with his customary ease and hospitality. She was pleased to see that Vernon and Brent hit it off, now that they were in a more relaxed atmosphere than that of their first meeting. Brent and Nigel showed them all around the Ventura complex and answered their questions. The tour took quite a long time since Vernon couldn't resist playing with all the toys that staff members either worked on or kept at Ventura to use for recreation. Marla thought dryly that they must be what Vernon and Brent recognized in each other. They were two grown men whose primary interest was playing.

Nathan and Nigel hit it off, too, since they both had a peculiar turn of phrase and obviously liked to think they were undiscovered philosophers. All in all, as they gathered around one of the tables in Ventura's lunchroom, Marla allowed herself the luxury of believing this would be the account that boosted her career at Freemont. Everything seemed to be falling into place.

She felt eyes on her and looked up to lock gazes with Brent. He was the serpent in near paradise. If she was going to blunder anywhere, it would be with him. Somehow knowing that didn't make her any surer she could avoid all the pitfalls in her path. If he was this gorgeous but not so endearing, or if he was gorgeous and endearing but didn't radiate such sexuality, or if he was all of those things but didn't look at her as if he wanted to devour her...

She caught her breath as she realized that that was *exactly* how he was looking at her, and it was the first time. Even in those rare moments when she had seen a flicker of desire in his eyes, it had been mingled with hesitation and uncertainty. Something had changed, she realized, and this powerful, devastating man no longer looked confused. In fact, he looked positively predatory. Marla swallowed. Her hands fell clumsily to her lap as all her muscles seemed to go liquid and limp. She felt her lips part involuntarily and saw his burning green gaze shift to her mouth.

She could hear the cacophony of voices around them, but she had no idea what they were saying, since their actual words were drowned out by the thud of her heart. Brent's eyelids flickered, and she could feel his lowered gaze moving over her body like warm honey, flowing and smooth and tangible.

She became aware of the rise and fall of her breasts as she drew in rapid breaths, of the friction of the lacy cups of her bra against her skin. Her linen slacks caressed her belly and gripped her thighs. The chair she was sitting on pressed firmly against her back and her bottom. Every sensation was heightened where his eyes touched her. She was trembling inside and wondered if he could tell.

She knew she should break the spell, show him how forbidden and impossible this was. But drawn by a force stronger than common sense and aware that she was at least safe from herself since they were surrounded by her colleagues, Marla basked in his glowing eyes and let herself admire him.

When he relaxed and stretched out in his chair, he didn't collapse like most men of her acquaintance. He looked like a panther—supple and firm, coiled and ready to spring into action if need be. His shoulders were broad and square, and she had a tingling awareness of how easily he could sweep a woman off her feet.

After so many days and nights of forbidding it to herself, she finally let herself imagine how he would make love. Her eyes slid down to his taut, narrow hips. He would ease them gracefully between her thighs, lifting her hips with his big hands. He would probably be gentle, but he was so strong there would still be an enormous sense of vigor and power when he thrust inside her. She pictured him in the moonlight, his back arched, his muscular arms steady beneath his weight, his dark, burnished head thrown back, his legs tensed and a fine sheen of sweat glistening on his bronze skin as he moved again and again in nature's steady pulsing rhythm, probing deeper with each thrust, demanding more with each caress, breathing harshly, murmuring to her, murmuring her name....

Desire pierced through her, as strong and sharp as her fantasy, and she drew in a quick breath, her eyes flashing up to his face. His eyes narrowed and his lips parted. She realized, with a sinking feeling of desperation, that he knew.

Her face must have mirrored her dismay, because the faintest of smiles, soft and reassuring, touched his firm lips. He looked at her with obvious satisfaction now, as if she had somehow pleased him. She lowered her eyes in confusion, too embarrassed to look around the table and see if anyone had noticed their silent byplay.

She nearly jumped out of her skin a moment later when she heard his voice near her ear, low and unusually gravelly. "More coffee?"

He had stood up and was leaning over her. His warm breath brushed her hair. She could smell him, that faintly warm, musky, fresh-air scent that clung to his skin. He rested a hand on the back of her chair as he leaned closer, and heat radiated out from him to engulf her.

"Coffee?" she croaked in a voice quite unlike her usually smooth, round tones.

"Yeah, I think another cup of coffee is called for all around. Whaddaya say, everyone?" Nigel asked.

The insufferable innocence of Nigel's tone made Marla look at him sharply. His nose was still red from his cold and his eyes were all puffy, but she had the uneasy feeling he was suppressing a smirk. Much to her relief, everyone else at the table was either absorbed in conversation or poring over file folders. A general group grunt indicated that another cup of coffee would suit them all.

"I'll get it," Felice said. Now that she had recovered from her cold, she was once again a bundle of dynamic energy and apparently found it hard to sit still for more than five minutes. Nigel glared at her resentfully.

Brent sat back down and grinned at Marla. She had the distinct impression he was enjoying himself now. The slow-burning sensuality of a moment ago was gone, and he seemed to be playing again. She wasn't sure what this new sport was, and she was even less sure of her skill at it.

"Hey, Brent!" A muscular young woman came up to their table and handed him a manila mailing envelope.

"This just came in the mail. It's from your buddy, Carmichael Hall. I thought you'd want it right away."

"Thanks!" Brent eagerly took the envelope from her hand and ripped it open. He pulled out a letter and what appeared to be an eight-by-ten-inch photograph. "Well, I'll be damned. Hey, Nigel, Carmichael's on the Marsyandi River."

"No kidding?" Nigel leaned across the table and reached for the photograph. "It's about time that blighter wrote to us. How's he doing?"

"You can read his letter when I'm through." Brent apologized for his preoccupation, explaining to the others that this was an old friend he hadn't heard from in more than a year. Then he continued reading the letter, grinning and occasionally chuckling at his friend's account of his life during that time.

"Where's the Marsyandi River?" Nathan asked Nigel as the group passed the photograph around.

"Nepal," Nigel answered. "Carmichael's a world-class kayaker."

Marla's eyes widened as she leaned toward Vernon to see the photograph. It depicted a sinewy red-haired man about Brent's age in a kayak on a rushing river. The little boat looked too frail and slim to afford him any kind of protection in such fierce waters, but the exultant grin on his face assured her he was enjoying himself.

"People do this for fun?" Vernon said incredulously.

"It's not as great as surfing, but it does have a certain charm," Nigel said airily.

Vernon frowned and studied the picture more closely. "Wait a minute, wait a minute. Nigel, that's Ventura clothing he's wearing, isn't it?"

"Of course it is," Nigel said, as if that should be obvious.

"Marla, take another look at this," Vernon said excitedly.

She did, and this time she also noticed the distinctive Ventura river shorts, short-sleeved shirt and waterproof vest.

"Do a lot of your friends send you photos like this?" Vernon asked Nigel. "I mean, pictures of themselves engaged in sports while wearing Ventura clothing?"

Nigel shrugged. "Yeah, I suppose we've got plenty of these."

Vernon handed the photo back to Nigel and leaned back in his chair with a thoughtful frown. Within moments he was bouncing around a small rubber ball and ignoring everyone else. Marla knew he had just had an idea for the account and was now going to spend time mulling it over.

It seemed the right time to break up the meeting, since Brent and Nigel were interested in reading their friend's letter, and Marla's colleagues clearly wanted to go back to the office and brainstorm. She rose to her feet, relieved to find that her legs weren't trembling, and suggested she and her colleagues get back to work.

"It's all right, I know the way out of here by now," Marla said when she saw Felice and Nigel hop out of their chairs to escort her and her crew to the door.

Brent put down Carmichael Hall's letter and looked at her. His expression, for once, was unfathomable. Seeing her opportunity, Marla beat a hasty retreat before anything else unexpected could pass between them.

She was already out the front door and walking across the parking lot when she heard his voice behind her.

"Marla, could you come here for just a minute?" he called.

She turned around to see him standing on the front step. She didn't want to leave him behind; she didn't want to go back in and deal with him. She froze.

"There's something I forgot," he said.

She recognized that she couldn't neglect a professional duty just because she was afraid he might say something about the way they'd been undressing each other with their eyes. And if he did bring it up, it was her job to apologize and explain why that mustn't happen again. Perhaps she should explain it anyhow, since things could definitely get out of hand if she didn't put a stop to it now. She had already put it off too long, for one reason or another. Thus fortified, she told Vernon she would be out in just a moment. Nathan and the others had already gone ahead in a separate car.

Brent pushed the front door open and stepped aside to let Marla reenter the building. His body heat reached out to her as she brushed by him, and she practically skittered inside. Get hold of yourself, she chided, and stop acting like a teenager.

As soon as she entered the front office, she realized it was empty. When she had walked through just a minute earlier, there had been two employees there. She knew instantly that Brent must have told them to leave. She whirled nervously to face him.

He closed the front door and leaned back against it. He looked at her steadily without saying anything. The speculative, assessing look in his eyes made her feel absurdly guilty.

She wet her lips and took a deep breath. She'd be damned if she'd just stand here like a schoolgirl until he felt like speaking. She was a businesswoman, and a busy one at that. She cleared her throat and tried to sound pleasantly cool.

"You said you'd forgotten something?" Much to her annoyance, her voice sounded slightly choked.

He nodded. "Something important."

He made no move but just kept staring at her. She shrugged, feeling helpless beneath his piercing regard. "What?"

It was as if her question catalyzed him into movement. He pushed himself away from the door with one smooth ripple of muscle and stalked forward like a jungle cat. She took a step backward without thinking, only aware that she felt scared and excited at the same time.

He stopped directly in front of her. Then, in a movement so sudden it made her gasp, he grabbed her shoulders and pulled her against him.

"Uh," she said. Where had that sound come from? She meant to say something like "don't" or "stop it." Instead, she stared at him helplessly, unbearably conscious of the smooth strength of his arms as they practically lifted her off the floor, the hard wall of his chest pressing against her breasts, his muscular thighs tensed against the cradle of her hips.

Any objection she might have made fled from her mind the moment his expression softened. His eyes grew lambent and tender, sending her senses reeling, and his lips parted and lowered toward her own.

"Silly me. I forgot this," he murmured, his breath entering her mouth an instant before his lips touched hers.

Her eyes closed and her mouth opened to him as easily as if he had willed it—which he may have, for all she knew. Whatever she had imagined or let herself fantasize, it hadn't equaled the exquisite, tortuous pleasure of his lips on hers.

His mouth was warm and moist and seeking. She could feel his fierce concentration as he probed her lips gently— rubbing, teasing, exploring. It was only his intense focus that let her believe he hadn't kissed a woman for a long time, because in every other way he seemed to have practiced until he was perfect.

He was insistent, but not brutal or forceful. His big hands still gripped her shoulders, holding her near enough for his kisses but keeping her farther away than she wanted to be. Unable to move in his iron grasp, she finally let her purse drop to the floor with a thud and put her hands on his hips.

A small sound escaped him, a tiny moan swallowed by his sudden intake of breath when she touched him, and it thrilled her to excite him with a mere touch. She tilted her head, drowning in his sweet, warm kisses, melting under the smooth, moist feel of his mouth against hers. She wished he would use his tongue, but she tried to be patient, sensing that he wanted to take it slowly, to explore each sensation to its fullest, to relearn all the pleasures he had denied himself since... Since the death of his wife?

The thought made her heart flood with tenderness and wonder, and she slid her hands up his sides, reveling in the supple hardness of his waist.

Oh, Brent, Brent, she moaned silently, letting herself experience what she had tried so hard not to imagine.

With obvious reluctance, he pulled his mouth away and ended their kisses. He rested his forehead against hers.

After a moment, his husky voice cut across the sound of their breathing roaring in Marla's ears. "That's what I forgot." He kissed her forehead softly. "Don't let me forget it again."

Marla went rigid, realizing that she had just done exactly what she had known she mustn't do. What's more, she had enjoyed it, encouraged it, participated in it too enthusiastically to pretend she had merely tolerated it.

She pushed her hands against his waist, but he still held her firmly by the shoulders. She tilted her head back and looked into his face. He looked so affectionate it threw her into a panic. It would have been easy to shake him off if he'd had the gall to look smug or lecherous.

"We have to talk about this," she said in a rush. She had to make him understand that this was absolutely taboo.

He smiled easily. "We will. Next time I see you. Try to make it soon, okay?" He brushed his lips across hers with devastating tenderness and gently pushed her away. "You'd better go before Vernon comes in here looking for you." He looked sheepish. "Or before the secretaries realize I sent them off on a wild-goose chase."

Marla gaped at him speechlessly as he scooped her purse off the floor, folded her hand around its strap and guided her out the front door. He gave her an encouraging little push and then waved at Vernon, who was leaning against the side of her car and flinging his yo-yo around.

Marla walked to her car, as stiff and mechanical as a windup toy. She could feel Brent's eyes burning into her back. She didn't dare turn around to look at him one last time. She was too afraid she'd do something dumb—like run back to him for more.

She got into the car, started the engine, waited for Vernon to put on his seat belt and then peeled out of the parking lot.

She blamed herself. How could she have behaved so unprofessionally? She was a grown woman; she had seen trouble on the horizon. Yet instead of heading it off in a mature and forthright fashion, she had deluded herself into thinking she was being tactful by not speaking openly to Brent about her reservations. And what a lie that was. She hadn't said anything to him because she enjoyed him too much.

She wanted him to desire her, and some deeply buried and extremely stupid part of her had wanted to keep alive the tiny, ridiculous and dangerous fantasy that they could share something personal together. She had kidded herself that they could be professional friends and sensibly control the exciting sexual tension that vibrated between them.

She had told herself she was learning to like and respect him too much, to admire his integrity and idealism too thoroughly, so she couldn't put him off with rules and regulations about their personal interaction and limitations. And so, naturally, after their silent sparring in the lunchroom today, Brent had assumed their relationship should take what he considered to be the next logical step forward.

It didn't matter that she had put him off before. She had sent out silent signals today that no man could ignore or misinterpret. She must have been out of her mind!

She should have stopped it before it began. Now it would be messy and awkward. She regretted having let things come this far. She regretted even more the necessity of cutting off a man like Brent Ventura.

But this account would make or break her at Freemont, and there was absolutely no way she was going to jeopardize her career over her attraction to a man. Particularly one who played more than he worked, and who, by all accounts, was never around when you needed him.

"Something wrong?" Vernon asked, bracing himself as Marla screeched to a halt before a red light. "You don't usually drive like Mario Andretti."

"Some days," Marla said between clenched teeth, "I could just kick myself."

Her mood didn't improve when they got back to the agency. Warren Tallman had left a message that she was to see him as soon as she returned.

"Do not pass go, do not collect two hundred dollars," Yvonne said dryly upon giving her the message.

Marla walked down the hallway to Warren's office, talking to herself, reminding herself to be calm and cool, forcing herself to put her personal problems out of her mind for the moment.

As she had expected, Warren lividly demanded to know why she hadn't taken David along to Ventura.

"David who?" she asked politely.

"David what's-his-face! The copywriter I told Vernon I wanted to see working on this account!"

"Ah, David Moran, you mean. Vernon did mention to me that you had said something about David, but since you didn't approach me about it—" she raised her brows significantly but kept her voice smooth and pleasant "—I assumed you had realized he wouldn't be suitable for this account and had changed your mind about him."

Warren reddened and looked speechless. And what could he say? Marla thought wearily. She was right. When he rose and went to close his office door so they wouldn't be overheard, she remembered that being right was very little protection against a man like Warren.

Instead of sitting down again, he stood towering over her and looking down his nose at her. Bless his heart, she thought wryly, he's been reading some of those modern power-play manuals. She assumed a relaxed pose, remembering that royalty sat while others stood. Two could play at Warren's silly games.

"You were not my first choice to handle this account, Marla," Warren said ominously, "and after the Diablo Boots scandal, I must frankly admit that I'm not sure you can handle it."

"I have handled a number of accounts quite successfully," Marla replied, working hard to keep all trace of resentment out of her voice.

"*This* is an *important* account," he said, dismissing her previous three years of commendable work at the agency. "The senior executives agree that Ventura is an unpredictable client." Marla thought back to the day Brent had phoned in anger and demanded they assign her to the account. Yes, he could be considered unpredictable.

"Therefore, we can't afford a single mistake or misstep," Warren continued. Marla resisted the urge to remind him that *he* had already made the mistake of not assigning her to the account in the first place. "Until I can feel sure that your handling of the account is adequate to the purpose, I must insist all my recommendations be followed—" he raised a spindly forefinger to forestall her objection "—without debate. The board is watching this one very closely, Marla. One slipup, and you could quickly become expendable."

And since Warren's father-in-law was chairman of the board, it would take only a hint from Warren to get her fired. It would do no good to remind this pompous ass that the whole reason her job was in jeopardy was because of his incompetent handling of the Diablo Boots affair. How ironic that now she must either follow his absurd advice to the letter or else lose her job. And if she followed his advice, she felt almost certain they would lose Ventura. Warren had all the skill and sensitivity of a tree stump, and this was a special and challenging account.

"Therefore," Warren continued, "I expect to see David..."

"Moran," she supplied tersely. He could at least learn the names of his own colleagues.

"Yes, I expect to see David Moran included in all activities involving the Ventura account. Understood?"

Holding herself together by force of will, Marla said calmly, "Understood. If you'll excuse me now, I have a lot to do." Like explaining to Vernon that you're pulling rank and stepping on his toes, she added silently.

"Of course." He smiled pleasantly, and the effect made him look somewhat reptilian. He was obviously pleased to have won this argument. He even tried to be placating. "You just conduct yourself like a good girl, and I'm sure we can find something else for you to work on when things settle down with Ventura."

If he patted her arm, she would bite him, she thought savagely. She left Warren's office with all the dignity she possessed, refusing to let him see how angry and humiliated she felt.

She found herself unconsciously walking toward Vernon's office a few minutes later, having paced off some of her initial anger. She knew she would have to tell Vernon about Warren's ultimatum. But even more than that, she wanted to be with colleagues she liked and respected. She wanted to be in an atmosphere that would remind her of why she even cared about this damned job.

She found Nathan sitting with Vernon in his office. The two of them were fussing over a brightly colored plastic piece of pop art from which George Michael's voice was trumpeting forth.

"Marla, Marla, come have a look at this," Vernon said. "This thing is amazing! We should send it to NASA. Do you realize how long it's been playing nonstop?"

"You sound pleased," Marla said, pulling up a chair and watching Nathan try to figure out how to turn it off.

"I am! I've *finally* figured out how we're going to market this hideous thing. It plays forever! We won't even be lying when we say it."

"Yeah, in the meantime, what am I going to do with it?" Nathan said morosely.

Marla looked at the long-haired young man. "How did it wind up with you?" she asked.

"Warren Tallman gave it to me two days ago. He said he had heard that you and Vernon had taken me out for my birthday without telling him, so he wanted to give me a little something."

"That stinking cheapskate!" Marla had never imagined that even someone as self-centered as Warren would stoop to passing off unwanted junk as a thoughtful birthday gift.

"That's what Vernon said," said Nathan. He frowned. "I'm trying to figure out who I can sucker into taking it."

"Hey, Nathan!" said Yvonne, sticking her head into Vernon's office. She was holding a lunch bag from a local carryout deli. "Your car just passed me by in the street."

Marla frowned. "Don't you mean you just passed by his car?"

"No. It's being towed. Illegal parking."

Nathan sprang out of his seat. "Holy cow!"

Vernon groaned. "Not again? Nathan, how many times have we talked about this propensity of yours to park wherever the spirit moves you?"

"I'm a taxpayer!" Nathan howled. "It's a sign of fascist inegalitarianism to tell me I can't park my car on a public street!"

Marla rolled her eyes. Vernon put his head in his hands. Yvonne sneered at Nathan and said, "And is paying parking tickets another sign of fascism?"

Marla suspected Yvonne's irritation was the result of concern. She knew Yvonne had been mooning over Nathan for a couple of months. Unfortunately for Yvonne, Nathan was peculiarly obtuse about everything except his work.

"You don't pay your parking tickets?" Vernon gasped. "Oh, Nathan, Nathan..." He sighed. "Go find your car. And take *this* with you," he added tersely, handing him the blaring radio.

Yvonne looked pleadingly at Marla. "It's all right," Marla said. "You can go with him. I won't be needing you the rest of the day."

Yvonne dashed after Nathan, leaving her carryout food on Vernon's desk. "My, my, it's been an exciting day so far," he said dryly, digging into the lunch bag. "Care for half a chicken sandwich?"

"Thanks, but I've lost my appetite."

"Problems?"

Marla told Vernon about her conversation with Warren. They both acknowledged how this could handicap their work on the account.

"David Moran has his talents, but he's arrogant and unreliable," Vernon agreed. "Above all, his specialty is slick and coy catchphrases, which you've already said Ventura doesn't want."

"We'll just have to exercise strict control on him and make sure he stays close to the strategy," Marla said.

"Listen, I think I've had a brilliant idea, Marla. I got it while we were looking at that picture of Brent's kayaking buddy on the Marsyandi River."

"Oh?"

"I want the two of us to get out to Ventura again this week to go through every single photo they've got of employees, friends, sports fiends and Ventura himself. Nigel said there were plenty. Can you arrange it?"

"Sure."

Make it soon, Brent had said. A shiver shook her. All her physical instincts longed to reach out to Brent, but her sense of self-protection, especially after her chat with Warren, told her she must tactfully but firmly resolve the mess she had gotten herself into this morning.

Though she felt battered and weary and certainly in no need of further reminders of what folly it had been to melt into Brent's arms, another reminder came to her loud and clear that evening in the form of a telephone call from her mother.

"John is still adamant about not giving you any alimony?" Marla asked in concern.

She sat wrapped in her bathrobe, toweling her hair dry from her shower, as her mother brought her up-to-date on her divorce proceedings. Marla agreed with her mother's previous estimation that she couldn't live on the meager wages she earned at her unpensioned job as a beauty salon receptionist. Three previous divorces had left her in similar straits.

"What does your lawyer say about John's resistance to paying alimony?"

"That's why I'm calling," he mother answered hesitantly. "I hate to ask you for money again so soon, but legal fees are outrageous, and..." She trailed off.

Marla rubbed her fingers across her tired eyes, trying to work out how much she could afford to send. "It's okay, Mom. How much do you think you need?" Her face crumpled with dismay when her mother estimated how much more she would have to have in the next few months to cover the legal costs of fighting for an alimony she might not even get.

Marla responded evenly, promising to send a check in the mail that week. As she said goodbye, she fought back her anger and resentment. Why, after four failed marriages, did her mother still refuse to understand that the only way to survive was to learn to take care of yourself? In between her husbands, she looked to Marla not only for financial support, but also to sort out the mundane, bureaucratic problems of life in the adult world.

Marla was tired of being emotionally and morally tied to a grown woman who refused to act like one. She was resentful of having to continually give her mother considerable sums of money that she had worked her tail off to earn. She was sick of being the family member the others counted on to be stoic and reliable. Above all, she was fed up with hearing from her mother and sister about how "lucky" she was.

Her life was going well because she had taken firm control of it, dammit. Everything she had done since she was eight years old had been geared toward making sure she would never have to rely on someone else for her security.

This bout of resentment ended, as it always did, in a rush of guilt. Despite all her mother's faults, she had never chosen a man in a mercenary fashion. She had believed herself to be in love with each new husband, and she was devastated by each new divorce.

Giving in to her misery at last, Marla opened a bag of chocolate chip cookies and started munching with determination. And what, she wondered with mingled longing and sadness, was Brent doing on this lonely evening?

If she were a mountain, he would study her carefully before his climb to the summit. He would explore her base, investigate her height and breadth, learn about her strong and weak spots and find out all about her seasonal patterns. He would study her until he knew which side would yield to his efforts in the most satisfactory and exciting way.

Could he do less with a woman? Especially this particular woman? He had jumped the gun this morning, grabbing her and smothering her with kisses like that, but he couldn't help remembering that it had worked for Clark Gable fifty years earlier. Besides, after the way her eyes had burned through him in the lunchroom, he finally knew without a doubt what she had tried so hard to conceal from him.

She wanted him, too.

He didn't know why she hadn't wanted him to know, or why she was fighting their mutual fascination. Sometimes it was fun to take a trial run up the base of the mountain without preparing, just to get a taste of what he would enjoy later on. It had been that way today.

It had been so good to touch a woman again after so long. No, not just *a* woman. *This* woman. He didn't yet know why she was the one he had waited for all those lonely nights, but having discovered her, he acknowledged that after Katie, he hadn't been prepared to settle for anything less than this relentless fascination and excitement.

He shook his head with a wry smile as he walked along Windansea Beach that evening. Marla Foster was as different from Katie as silk was from leather. But it didn't matter. She was the woman he had chosen to start over with, even though he had resisted the idea at first. Even though *she* was still resisting it.

So now he would have to do his preliminary work. She had said they needed to talk, and she was right. He knew almost nothing about her—only what his heart sensed, only what his body felt. He had a wealth of information to fill in about who she was and how she lived and what she wanted.

Most of all, he had to find out why she denied her own instincts, why she tried to keep herself from wanting him. There could be a thousand reasons, and if he was a better man, he might move more slowly, be more patient with her.

Instead, he had jumped her today, not only because he couldn't stand to go another moment without tasting those full lips, but also because he wanted her to know that he knew she felt it, too, and that he wouldn't let her hide any longer.

He sat down in the sand at the shore's edge and watched the dark sea heave and swell under the starlit sky. He wished Marla was there with him, even if only in companionable silence. Now that he was lonely for a woman who was actually alive and breathing, he found the solitude intolerable. He wanted to start sharing again, now, right away, before another precious moment of life ticked by.

Yes, they would talk. Soon and seriously. Then they would both know what she was afraid of.

Chapter Six

As soon as Marla saw Brent, she realized that he didn't intend to pretend for anyone's benefit that their last meeting hadn't altered their relationship. Oh, he was tactful, even subtle, but he let Marla know that things had changed and he intended them to go on changing.

Handle it, she ordered herself. But it was so hard to be stern in the face of his boyish grin, so difficult to resist his friendly questions, so impossible to pull her hand out of his warm, strong grip as he led her over to a mountain of photographs piled up on Nigel's desk.

"You weren't kidding when you said you had plenty of these, Nigel," Vernon said, looking at the pile in awe.

Nigel sneezed. "G'day," he said morosely.

"Still got that nasty cold?" Marla said sympathetically.

He nodded and sniffled. "They say it's going around. But I know who gave it to me." He cast a baleful glare at Felice's empty desk.

Tactfully changing the subject, Marla said, "I want to thank you for responding so thoroughly to our request for old photographs." She surveyed the pile ruefully. "I hardly know where to begin."

"I'm glad you asked," Brent said. "Until we started rummaging around and putting these in one pile, I didn't realize how many photos we had. We should put them in some kind of order."

He was standing close to her. He had relinquished his hold on her hand, but his body heat engulfed her. Every time her eyes met his, his expression became warm and intimate. She was starting to shake inside, wanting to respond, trying not to. She had to find time to talk with him today, no matter how obvious her efforts to get him alone. She couldn't let this thing between them grow any more powerful.

"How shall we organize this?" she said in a rush, gesturing to the pile of photos.

"Well, first of all let's figure out what sort of thing you and Vernon are looking for," Nigel said.

Marla nodded to Vernon, letting him explain his idea. He said, "I think the best way to illustrate your products and their uses in magazine layouts is to use photos that show real sportsmen—and women—engaged in real activities. It will give your ads the veracity Brent has expressed concern about."

"The best photos," Marla continued, "would be those in which Ventura clothing and equipment are plainly visible."

"Standing up to punishment," Vernon added.

"Famous events, daring feats, well-known adventurers," Marla said.

"The kicker is," Vernon concluded, "we also need good photography. That photo of your pal on the Marsyandi River gave me the idea, but it was actually a lousy photograph."

"What do you think, mate?" Nigel asked Brent.

"I like it. I like it a lot."

"Then let's get started," Nigel said.

"This will probably go faster if we divide the photos into two piles," Vernon said.

Brent divided the pile down the middle and pushed half of it toward Nigel. "You go over those with Vernon. I'll show these to Marla."

Within a few minutes, the four of them were spread out across Brent and Nigel's area of the Bull Pen. Brent and Marla sat on the floor in front of his desk, their heads close together as they leafed through both black-and-white and color photographs of different sizes. Nigel and Vernon were just a few feet away, their conversation clearly audible, and other employees were milling around the area. Since this was hardly the opportunity she sought to talk alone with Brent, Marla forced herself to concentrate on the photos in his hands.

"Hey, Brent!" Nigel called. "Remember this?" He tossed a photo across to them.

"Good Lord!" Brent studied the photo and smiled slowly. "Boy, I was young then."

Marla leaned closer to him curiously. "What is it?"

He showed her a photo of Nigel and himself, dripping wet, holding their surfboards and posing in front of the ocean. Brent was waving a trophy over his head. Brent's face was smoother and fuller in the picture, his hair longer.

"This was a surfing competition in Hawaii, fourteen years ago," Brent explained to Marla. He added in a stage whisper, "Nigel's never forgiven me for beating him in front of all those beautiful women that day."

"Modesty wasn't one of his strong points, even then," Nigel told Vernon.

A moment later Brent let out a muffled exclamation as he pulled a photo out of his own pile. "Here's one I would like to forget." He grinned and showed the picture to Marla. He and five other men sat around in about eight inches of mud, looking thoroughly disgusted and demoralized.

"What happened?"

"What didn't happen?" he countered wryly. He spent the next ten minutes recounting a climbing expedition on which everything that could go wrong *had* gone wrong. Bad weather, faulty equipment, insufficient supplies and group disharmony.

The two of them continued on that way for some time, occasionally finding the kind of photos Marla was looking for but mostly laughing over memories and wild stories. Brent and his friends were an adventurous group. She could tell by the whoops of laughter coming from Nigel and Vernon that they were progressing as slowly as she and Brent.

She enjoyed Brent's company and sharing his memories to the fullest, but she felt sad because she knew that she must, absolutely must, put a damper on the glowing light in his eyes and the swelling joy in her heart. For the moment, under the auspices of work, she could safely enjoy just a little more of this special time before she had to face reality.

After leafing through some fairly dull and fuzzy shots of more surfers, Brent suddenly picked up another eight-by-ten photo and studied it closely. A soft, reminiscent smile curved his firm lips, and a tender expression flooded his whole face.

He glanced up at Marla, and then, without any hesitation, he handed the photo to her like an offering. "Look," he said simply.

She knew who it was the second she glanced at the photo of a woman in a kayak. She had seen this woman's picture once before. She looked at Brent.

"My wife," he said. His eyes held hers. "You know I was married?"

She nodded solemnly. "Nigel said she died in a boating accident almost three years ago."

Brent nodded. "She was a water lover. Swimming, kayaking, rafting, sailing." He grinned. "She *hated* mountaineering, though. I took her climbing just once. It was the closest she ever came to walking out on me."

Marla was curious to know what kind of woman he had obviously loved so much. "How did you meet her?"

He leaned back. "I met Katie about two months after we moved the company headquarters here. She wrote for an outdoor adventure magazine and was supposed to do an article about us. She came out here to interview me, and I asked her out before the interview had even begun." He grinned again. "After we were married, we used to argue about who had swept who off their feet."

"Whirlwind courtship?" Marla said, pleased for him that the memories seemed comfortable for him now, full of reminiscence, devoid of pain.

"You could say that. I was afraid she'd get away if I didn't marry her right away. And she was just plain impetuous. Reckless, actually."

Marla smiled slightly, hearing echoes of other old arguments in his tone. "Did marriage calm her down?"

"Are you kidding? You would think that in my marriage, my wife would worry about me—dangling over gorges, scaling cliffs, skimming along on surfboards. But instead, I was always wondering what my wife was doing—running rapids without a life jacket, kayaking without her helmet, swimming in strong currents." He shook his head.

"She probably *did* worry about you," said Marla, worrying a little herself at the thought of his adventures.

"There's no need to, actually. I'm very thorough. I check and double-check all my equipment, I watch every step I take, I never give up a foothold till I know I've got a firm handhold.... That's why I'm still alive and kicking."

His face clouded briefly. Marla went silent, too, watching him closely. A slow, dawning awareness was growing inside her. She realized he wanted her to know these things. He wanted to tell her the rest. Nigel and Vernon were shouting with laughter again, and Marla knew that she and Brent had enough privacy for her next question, the question she knew he wanted her to ask.

"How did she die?" Her voice sounded low and full to her own ears.

He lowered his eyes and studied his hands. "She went up to Oregon to visit her family and do some sailing. I stayed down here because things were so busy. I talked to her on the phone the night before.... Just the usual things two people talk about. She said she was going to take her old dinghy out the next day for old times' sake. I told her to check the hull and rigging, to wear a life jacket, to check the weather report." He shrugged. "All the same stuff I always told her. She said, as usual, that I was such a killjoy and I shouldn't nag her so much, and that she knew what she was doing. I told her I loved her. She said she'd call again in a day or two."

He took a deep breath. "The next night her mother called me in a panic. There'd been a storm that day, and no one had seen Katie since she sailed out of the bay." His face crumpled and he suddenly looked older. "I flew up on the first available flight. We found her body the next morning." His voice grew softer. "No life jacket. They found what was left of the boat later that day...."

Marla could picture the awful, painful scene in her mind. Brent, usually concerned about his wife's recklessness in an exasperated and affectionate way, suddenly thrown into sickening terror and dread when she didn't come back from the sea after a storm. The phone call from Katie's mother delivering the blow; the flight north, during which he must have prayed and hoped and panicked; the hope-filled, fear-racked search for his wife all night long; and then the discovery of her lifeless body, confirming death and finality. He must have imagined her death a thousand times in his mind: her struggle to live, her terror, her helplessness, her last moment of consciousness before drowning....

"How terrible," she whispered.

In a perfectly natural human gesture, she put her hand over his. He turned his hand over and clasped hers, entwining his fingers with her own, then rubbing his other palm over their joined hands.

He looked up and let his eyes meet hers. His expression was more serious than she had ever seen it. "It was the worst thing that ever happened in my life," he whispered. "It's something I wanted you to know about me."

She nodded slowly, holding his gaze, too aware of him needing her to think about anything else at that moment.

They gradually became conscious of the life and noise going on around them, of Nigel's voice cheerfully piercing the air. Brent loosened his grip and Marla slowly pulled her hand away from his.

After a moment of stillness, he made a vague pretense of leafing through more photographs. It didn't matter that their hands were no longer joined, she realized dimly. He had bound her to him by telling her his story. Their hands might as well still be clasped for all the success she was having at trying to separate herself from him.

They silently passed a few photos back and forth. Marla saw nothing that interested her, and she was still wrestling with the implications of Brent's tale and the emotional upheaval it caused. After a few more minutes, Nigel finally called out to them.

"You two are awfully quiet over there. What's going on?"

"Marla, Marla," Vernon said, chuckling, "you've got to look at this." He walked over to where she sat and showed her a huge color photo of a kayaker who, in an improbable midair twist over a rushing river, was taking off his helmet to wave it at the camera. He was also sticking out his tongue. "I love this!"

Marla smiled and passed the photo to Brent. He smiled, too, and said, "Good old Carmichael. Always a ham."

"What have you found so far?" Vernon asked.

Marla handed him the three photos she thought were good prospects, explaining what Brent had told her about each one. Her voice sounded normal to her, but everything else about the scene seemed unreal, pale and insignificant compared to the silent communication still going on between her and Brent.

"Any luck?" Nigel called absently from his post.

Brent looked at Marla again, and whatever he saw in her eyes apparently decided him. "I'm tired of staring at photos. I'm going for a walk on the beach to clear my head." He rolled gracefully to his feet, then looked down and held out his hand. "Marla?"

She knew he was providing her with the opportunity she sought to talk alone with him. She took his hand and let him haul her to her feet. "Sure, I'll go with you."

"Hey, Vernon, have a look at this!" Nigel said, relieving Marla of the necessity of discouraging Vernon from joining them.

Marla followed Brent out the back door and into the California sunshine. They reached the street and started to walk toward the beach. They remained silent. Marla didn't know how to begin the necessary conversation, and Brent seemed content to just walk in silence for a while.

They arrived at the beach and walked across the sand to the shoreline. Brent stared out across the water for a few moments, then suddenly turned to her.

"I wanted to tell you about my wife because I think it concerns you."

She frowned in confusion, not sure what he meant.

He scuffed the sand with his foot, then touched her arm to steer her to the left with him. They started walking along the shoreline.

"It was a good marriage, and I loved her very much," he said bluntly. "It took me a long time to get over her death—maybe until just recently. That's why I haven't been involved with another woman since then. That's why I've been slow to decide...I mean, slow to realize..." He took a deep breath and tried again. "I don't want to wait for another business appointment to see you again."

Her heart swelled with fondness, despite her sensation of panic. He wasn't like any of the smooth talkers she had known in her life. He was as honest and forthright as a child. But he spoke with a man's need and a man's emotion. She wished she could have given him anything and everything he desired. But she couldn't.

"Brent, we have to talk." She stopped walking and put her hand on his arm to stop him, too.

"I know." He squinted against the sunlight as he turned to look at her again. He reached out and lightly caressed her cheek. "I hardly know anything about you." He shrugged. "But it doesn't matter much. Just like it didn't matter then."

"It matters," she insisted. She twisted her hands nervously while he waited for her to explain. "Can we sit down somewhere?"

"Sure."

He led her to an open-air café near the beach, where they sat in the shade under an awning. Brent ordered coffee for both of them. Once their coffee arrived, Marla wrapped her hands around her mug and tried to find a way to begin. His first question startled her.

"Is there someone else?"

Her eyes shot up to meet his. He looked as vulnerable as a puppy as he waited for her answer.

"No, no one. I mean . . . I go out now and then, but not with anyone I—" She stopped herself. Her *personal* life had nothing to do with her reasons for not wanting to get involved with Brent.

"Someone in the past?"

She nearly said no, then she remembered. "Sort of."

"Did he hurt you?"

"Yes, but not in the way you think."

He looked puzzled.

"Brent . . ." She sighed and looked away for a moment. This was going to be even harder than she had feared. "I didn't intend for things to go this far between us," she said honestly.

"Neither did I."

She looked at him in surprise. Maybe he already knew what she needed to explain to him.

"I'm not a kid anymore, Marla, and I felt...maimed when I lost Katie. I didn't think I could bear to go through meeting and, uh, courting someone again. And I have to admit, I didn't think at first that you and I could possibly have much in common." He reached across the table to touch her hand. "But I can't stop thinking about you, and I couldn't be so drawn to someone who's wrong for me."

She had smiled involuntarily at the word "courting," but his intense expression and soft touch filled her with longing. She felt an almost physical pain when she said, "Brent, we can't possibly get involved with each other."

"Why not?" He didn't seem at all perturbed by her words. She realized with a jolt that he had been expecting her to say something like that.

"Because I'm your account executive," she blurted out.

"And?" He still looked perfectly at ease.

"It's absolutely forbidden for the account executive to get personally involved with the client."

"Oh, come on. Account execs call their clients on the phone, take them to lunch, play tennis with them, buy them drinks. Even I know that, Marla."

"I mean sexually involved."

He frowned. "I'll have to reread my agency agreement. I don't recall it saying that I couldn't touch you."

"It's an unwritten rule."

"Then we don't have to worry about it."

"*I* do. It's *my* job that's at stake."

"Wait a minute. You're saying that you could lose your job for spending your free time with me?" He saw her hesitate, so he said more bluntly, "For sleeping with me?"

"Yes."

He pulled his hand away from hers and leaned back. He looked puzzled. At last he said, "I don't understand. Why?"

"Because a client's account is worth thousands, even hundreds of thousands of dollars to the agency. If, hypothetically speaking, I had an affair with you, when we quarreled or broke up, you could choose to leave the agency when you left me. Therefore, my personal life would cost the agency a lot of money. If it was a big enough account, one that had a dozen specialized people working on it, they could all lose their jobs when you took your business away. Do you see how catastrophic that could be for the agency and its employees?"

"Well, sure."

"Good." She was both relieved and perversely hurt that he was taking it so well.

"But what if things, hypothetically speaking, worked out between you and me? What if, for example, the account executive and the client she was sleeping with got married? Then it would be all right, wouldn't it?"

"I don't know. I guess that would be all right, but the account executive would probably have been removed from her post before things got that serious. I think she would be reassigned after the marriage in any case, to avoid personal and professional conflicts. But that's not the point, Brent."

"No, I guess not," he agreed. "Well, don't worry about it. If we fight or break up, I promise not to take my business elsewhere. Okay?"

She almost choked on her coffee. She had thought he was getting the idea. She would have laughed at the simplicity of his argument under other circumstances. "It's not quite that simple, I'm afraid. I may trust you—"

"Good."

"But my superiors wouldn't and couldn't condone my behaving unprofessionally just because I trusted a good-looking man to keep his word."

"So we won't tell them."

"Oh, Brent." She smiled in spite of herself. He was so naive about some things.

"I don't get it. You've been staying out of reach all this time just because of some unwritten code that you're not supposed to get involved with me? Doesn't that smack a little bit of authoritarianism? It's not enough that you have to account to Freemont for your working life, now you're going to let them dictate your personal life, too?"

"In this case, I have to. My career depends on it."

"I've already told you that I won't—"

"I know. But what they believe is what counts. And if they learned—as they would be bound to, sooner or later—that I was sleeping with one of my clients, your personal guarantees couldn't save my job."

"They'd really fire you for that?" he asked in amazement.

"They'd fire *me*," she admitted.

He caught the emphasis. "Why do you say it like that?"

"I'm sort of on probation at the moment."

"Don't tell me you slept with another client?"

"No!" She saw the gleam in his eyes and realized he was teasing her. "My last account blew up in my face, Brent. If anything goes wrong with your account—*anything*—I'll be let go."

He leaned closer now, interested in her statement. "Will you at least tell me what happened?"

She frowned for a moment, aware that it was also a violation of ethics to tell a client about internal agency trouble. But this, she reasoned, was an entirely personal conversation. He knew she was attracted to him, and he had a right to a full explanation of why she wouldn't give in to her desires.

"Well, my first two years at the agency were very successful," she began.

"I can believe that. I don't understand half the stuff you shove in front of me, but Nigel says you're very good at your job."

She felt pleased for a moment that her new clients had recognized that. She continued, "Then almost a year ago, Freemont got the Diablo Boots account."

"Yeah, I've heard of them. I've got a pair of Diablos myself."

"Well, Warren Tallman, my account supervisor on this account, also supervised that account. He didn't want me on the Diablo account, but I wasn't going to let that...stinking chauvinist," she said finally, enjoying the feel of the words on her tongue, "stop me. It was a huge account, the president and the marketing director of Diablo liked me, and several senior Freemont people who liked my work agreed that I should handle it."

"So you got the account?" He could see the determination and ambition in her face that he had sensed before.

"Yes, much to Warren's dismay. I had been warned against working with him, but... Anyhow, things went pretty smoothly for the first six months. Then my contact at Diablo left them for another job. She was replaced by an older man. He detested me at first sight."

"Why?" Brent asked, startled. He couldn't imagine anyone not being taken with her, as he had been.

She shrugged. "He was older and was embittered about not having risen higher in the company at his age. He hated seeing women in business just as much as Warren does. He said I was hard to talk to, that I was a bad listener, that I dressed provocatively—"

"He was a fool. You're about the easiest person to talk to I've ever met, and that's because you're such a great listener. Although, I have to admit, I find you pretty provocative, too."

She smiled in spite of herself. She wished he wouldn't flirt with her; it made him impossibly appealing.

"Anyhow, I made a very bad decision then. I should have realized that the conflict was destructive to the account, but I wanted that account too much." She took another sip of her coffee. "So the client complained about me to Warren one day."

"And Warren called you into his office, chewed you out and took you off the account?"

"Now that's what you would expect to happen, isn't it?"

"It didn't happen that way?" he asked curiously. He claimed to know little about business, but he certainly knew how to handle staff and clients.

"No."

"What did he do?"

She nearly ground her teeth as she remembered her humiliation. "He called a special meeting of the board to discuss the problem."

"What?" Brent's eyes widened.

"Yes. I was called upon to attend. Warren explained to them my severe mishandling of the account and client. Of course, the entire company knew about this meeting, so conversation ceased in every room I entered for the next two weeks."

"Why did the board let him—"

"His father-in-law is chairman of the board," she said flatly.

"Good Lord," Brent said softly. "So instead of simply handling an awkward but fairly ordinary problem at his level, he brought the entire company down on your head."

Marla nodded. "But I have to admit, Brent, that the initial mistake was mine. I should have given up the account the first day I realized the new client didn't like me. That's professional behavior."

"So you were a pariah after that?" he asked quietly, thinking how hard the humiliation must have been for her.

"Yes. The only reason they didn't fire me on the spot was because they managed to keep the account with the agency. But it got worse for me. About a month before you came to Freemont, my other big client, Plethora Textbooks, left the agency."

"Why?"

"They said we had become too big and costly for their needs. They were very nice to me. They insisted they had always been happy with my services. They even gave me a bunch of textbooks at our last meeting." She shrugged. "So when you came to the agency, all I was handling was one small pocketknife account."

"You must have wanted my account very badly," he murmured thoughtfully.

"I did," she admitted. Her gaze held his. "It meant more to me than you can imagine when you called the agency and demanded my services."

"Even though you knew it meant you'd be working with Warren again?" he asked shrewdly.

"Maybe I can handle him this time," she said faintly.

Brent didn't like the thought of that man as Marla's superior. "And he's watching you very closely, is that it?"

She nodded. "I'm sorry, Brent. If there were a single client in the world I'd break the rules for, it would be you."

He smiled and tried to take her hand again, but she pulled it slowly away from him.

"Warren's already told me that my behavior and results must be exemplary on this account. One slipup, and I'm gone." Her eyes pleaded with him to understand.

He looked away. "I have to admit that of all the reasons you might not want to be with me, this one never entered my mind." He shook his head. The hypocrisy and rigidity of the business world never failed to amaze him.

"Then you understand why our relationship has to be strictly professional?"

He looked at her long and hard. She thought he was scrutinizing her the way he must scrutinize a difficult cliff.

"I understand why you're concerned about your position at the company," he said carefully. "We'll find a way to work it out."

Shock rippled through her at the determined look on his face. He had listened so calmly and sympathetically, she had thought she was getting through to him. She realized now that he only regarded this as a difficulty to be overcome, rather than as the ultimatum she had intended it to be.

"Brent, we can't—"

"I admit there's a lot I have to think about now that you've told me this. But don't you think you have a lot to think about, too?"

"Like what?" she said blankly.

She saw temper flare in his green eyes for the first time since she'd met him. "Like the things I've said to you. That I understand your difficulties at work, and I don't want my personal feelings for you to compromise your career any more than you do. That I've already tried resisting my feelings, and it doesn't work. And," he added, his voice getting low and gravelly, "there's also what I told you about losing my wife. Do you think I talk about Katie to just anybody?"

"No, of course not," she said quickly. She realized he thought she had disregarded the private grief he had shared with her, and he was hurt by it. It amazed her time and time again how much vulnerability this bold adventurer could express when he was with her. "Please don't think that. I'm proud you felt you could tell me about her."

He relaxed a little and his expression softened. "I know you're ambitious, Marla. But I can't believe it's not possible for us to find a way to spend time together." He hesitated before adding, "Unless what I'm feeling is one-sided."

He didn't plead or cajole or demand. He simply waited for her response. "You know it isn't," she said softly. "You knew it the other day before you kissed me—and you certainly knew it after the way I responded."

"Just checking." He wriggled his dark brows. Marla smiled involuntarily, wondering if she would ever be able to stay on an even keel around him. He kept kicking her legs out from under her; he was tender and serious one moment, teasing and flirtatious the next, powerful and daring, yet honest and vulnerable.

He grinned at her. "We'd better be getting back." He tossed some money on the table to pay for their coffee. When she protested, he said, "I really don't think I can let you put this one on the agency expense account, Marla."

"No, I guess you're right," she agreed wryly.

"I don't suppose I can talk you into holding my hand on the way back?" he said hopefully.

Her heart flipped over, but she said, "It's not a good idea Brent."

He shrugged. "Next time."

She took a breath and tried again. "I don't feel like we've exactly settled things."

"We haven't," he agreed cheerfully. "But then, our business has already taken us weeks and it's still not settled. Would you expect our feelings to be easier?"

"I would expect we could both recognize, as mature adults, that our feelings aren't important in this case."

He looked shocked. "Don't say that, Marla. Our feelings and our personal lives are a hell of a lot more important than how clever your ad campaigns are or how many pitons and carabiners I sell as a result of them."

She shook her head. "That's naive, Brent."

"You really think so?"

She thought of her mother and sister, two women who always let their feelings dictate their lives and had never used common sense or forethought. Look where it had got them.

"Let's go back," she said bleakly. What could Brent understand about her determination to run her life sensibly and successfully? He, after all, had made a fortune out of playing.

He looked at her peculiarly, aware that she had suddenly shifted gears. He decided not to press for an explanation, realizing in that instant that although she had been honest with him today, she hadn't laid all her cards on the table. He had already learned she was a complicated woman. But their mutual honesty today had only deepened his need to know more, to share more, to be with her.

Her dark blond hair gleamed in the sunlight as they walked back to the Ventura buildings. Her head was bowed as she wrestled with personal thoughts he knew she didn't want to discuss. Some lingering sadness softened the beautiful angles of her face.

He wanted to hold her and comfort her, to be comforted in return. He wanted the warmth of her skin pressed against him, the softness of her breasts in his hands, the sweetness of her mouth exploring his. He wanted her to whisper her darkest secrets and most secret desires to him.

Soon, he promised himself, soon. Because he wouldn't have climbed all those mountains and surfed all those waves if he was the kind of man who gave up the first time an obstacle got in his way. If Marla didn't know that yet, she would learn it before long.

Chapter Seven

Well?'' Vernon asked Marla apprehensively as she stalked into his office several days later. "What did Warren want to see you about?''

"He thinks we're exercising too tight a control on David Moran. He wants him to have more freedom in his copywriting. He hates our concept about using real people in real situations for the Ventura ads. And he loathes my promotional ideas. Have I left anything out?''

She slumped into a chair and aimed Vernon's basketball at the basket with vicious force. Her aim was so far off the mark that she hit Vernon's blow-up crocodile and nearly hit Vernon, too.

"Yikes!'' Vernon threw himself to the floor. A moment later he peered theatrically over the top of his desk at her. Marla smiled reluctantly. "Feeling better now?''

"I guess so.''

He stood up. "It's not so bad, Marla. Everyone else on the creative team is doing great work. We'll make three conceptual proposals to Ventura. Let David work on the copy of one proposal all by himself. That'll give us the other two unhindered, and two out of three ain't bad.''

"You're right, of course," Marla agreed. It was the obvious solution. She ran her hands through her normally tidy hair, mussing it even further. She hadn't been the same since her conversation with Brent in the beach café.

She couldn't sleep well, wasn't hungry and kept forgetting things. She kept wanting to talk to him again, wishing she could change the situation but knowing she couldn't, plagued by the conviction that their conversation had brought them closer together rather than driven them further apart, as she had intended. She already cared too much about him, and she suspected she hadn't convinced him not to care about her.

Marla didn't know what would happen next with that unpredictable man, but she had a feeling things would get harder before they got easier.

Her emotional condition was affecting the usually calm, collected way she dealt with everything else. It had taken every ounce of willpower she possessed not to tell Warren what an unimaginative, unprincipled jerk he was during their conversation this morning. Why, she wondered desperately, couldn't any one of the half dozen senior people she really respected be supervising this account?

What's more, she had neglected to call her mother again, feeling unable to cope with her responsibilities in that woman's chaotic life. Marla had also snapped at her sister the previous evening when she had phoned from Chicago to complain about her own family's financial troubles.

"Go get a job," Marla had told her tersely.

Why couldn't she have just met Brent through friends or by chance? she wondered morosely. Then they wouldn't have had to worry about all the messy complications of subterfuge and professional ethics. She could enjoy the man without feeling their relationship jeopardized her career and her whole way of life.

"Marla, you look shattered," Vernon said as he poured them both a cup of coffee from the percolator on his file cabinet. "Why don't you go home early today?"

"I can't."

"You're pushing yourself too hard." He paused and looked at her shrewdly. "Or is something besides the account bothering you?"

She shrugged and looked at her coffee cup with intense absorption.

"I won't pry, but if you ever feel like talking..."

"Thanks, Vernon." She smiled wanly. Despite Warren and his ilk, despite inconvenient rules and unwritten codes, there were a lot of great people in this business. "How's Nathan's work coming?"

"Good. Everything's kicking into shape. When are you going back to Ventura?"

"I'm not sure. Why?"

"I'd like you to get a bunch of their stuff for us to work with. You know, clothing, equipment, that kind of thing. Something that will give us some more ideas."

And that was how Marla wound up driving out to Ventura the next day. It could have waited, she admitted to herself as she turned into Ventura's parking lot. But *she* couldn't wait any longer. She wanted to see Brent the way she wanted to draw her next breath. Not that she was going to let anything unprofessional happen.

She found him waiting for her in the Bull Pen. Nigel and Felice were nowhere in sight. Brent's expression was intimate, tender and entirely personal when Marla walked up to greet him. Her heart started thudding almost painfully in her chest, excited by his attention, horrified at the implications.

He ignored her proffered hand. Instead, he took her slim shoulders between his brown hands and squeezed them briefly. He stood close to her, studying her face with a lazy half smile and absently caressing her bare arms.

"You look beautiful," he murmured.

She would have bitten her tongue off before admitting that she had changed clothes three times that morning before deciding on this short-sleeved linen blouse and skirt.

She took a shaky breath, trying to get control of the situation. He smiled, his laughing eyes telling her as clearly as any words that he knew she was excited and didn't know what to do about it.

"You said you wanted to collect some clothing and equipment?" he asked, stepping back and capturing one of her hands in his.

Marla nodded dumbly. Everything about him reached out to her, mocking her rational rejection of her growing desire for him.

Finally she pulled her hand abruptly out of his and said, "Yes. Can we get them right away? I'm afraid I don't have much time."

His eyes narrowed at the attempted coolness of her tone. He shrugged after a moment and said, "Sure. Come with me."

He led her to the back of the complex, to the small building they had never entered before. He opened the door, switched on the light, led her inside and closed the door behind them.

"We always keep a few samples of everything on the premises for visitors, journalists and friends," he explained, gesturing to the well-organized shelves and packing cases full of Ventura products.

"What would you recommend?" she asked, not sure where to start.

He was so quiet she turned to face him. He was leaning casually against the door, studying her with narrowed, predatory eyes. "I recommend that you relax. You're wound up like a spring."

She nodded in acknowledgment of his observation. She looked at him accusingly and said, "You shouldn't touch me like that."

"Like what?"

"The way you did when I got here."

He straightened away from the door and started walking slowly toward her. "I can't help it," he said.

She had never heard his voice sound so steely and deliberate. She tripped over something before she realized that she had started backing away from him. "I told you—"

"I remember what you told me. Watch your step," he chided as she bumped into a shelf behind her. "What are you afraid of?"

"Stop it. We're not going to—"

"Careful!" He grabbed her arm to halt her backward progress just before she fell over a packing case. "And to think I thought you were graceful when we met."

"You shouldn't notice things like that about me! We're in business together!" she snapped, trying to control her frantic breathing.

"Now that's a ridiculous thing to say," he murmured, sliding his big, warm hands up her bare arms. She shivered involuntarily, loving the slow seduction of his touch, the rough caress of his low voice, the wave of body heat reaching out to her. "The only reason I trusted you that day was because I noticed how special you were."

He pulled her closer. Her hands trembled when they brushed the denim of his jeans. Her skin tingled as he slid his arms around her and smoothed his palms up the length of her back.

"Brent, please," she begged in a voice choked with longing.

"Mmm." He lowered his head and pressed his lips to hers.

It was nothing like last time. He knew exactly what he wanted and what she wanted, and he was assaulting her with all the determination he would have brought to Mount Everest. Marla felt her muscles quiver and weaken in awe and exultation.

He wrapped his arms so tightly around her she could hardly breathe, but she would willingly give up oxygen for him. His mouth moved hungrily across hers, insisting, tasting, plundering. He kissed her with raw need and blatant sensuality, thrusting his tongue inside her mouth to entangle her own in a hot, silky duel.

Her eyes closed, her head tilted back, and reality was lost in a swirling black sea of delight, hot and erotic, strong and overpowering. Without thought or conscious decision, she slid her arms over his shoulders and wrapped them around his neck, trying to pull him even closer.

He pulled his mouth a fraction of an inch away from hers and slid his hands across her shoulders to cup her face between his palms.

"Look at me," he said in a rough voice.

She opened her eyes, unable to refuse him. She could feel his breath against her lips, warm and sweet, entering her mouth to feed her lungs as she gasped for air.

"Someone might come in," she said weakly.

"I locked the door."

Her heavy-lidded eyes flew wide open at that. "You *planned* this?"

Brent grinned, enjoying her flare of temper.

"That is the most . . . most . . ." She sputtered futilely.

"You can't throw this away, Marla. No matter how ambitious you are, you can't ignore this."

He kissed her again, and she had to agree that there was no way to ignore him. His lips rubbed warmly, moistly, insistently over hers—probing, nibbling, teasing, devouring. His arms enveloped her, making her feel small and feminine and utterly surrounded by his musky warmth.

She smoothed her hands down his back, dying to touch the body she had surreptitiously admired so many times. His shoulders amazed her—as wide as the sky, as solid as granite and as smooth as a pool of honey. She tugged in momentary frustration at the cotton barrier of his shirt, wanting to feel his hot skin under her palms.

His hair was like wild silk, wrapping around her fingers, springing up between them with exuberant luxuriance. She

loved the way his head moved when he kissed her, the way
his muscles bulged every time he caressed her, the way he
growled and murmured in his throat.

His hands moved boldly over her, shaping her soft bottom, measuring her slim waist, massaging her back, pulling
her hair to tilt her head farther back. He smoothed her hair
away from her face and kissed her forehead, her cheekbones, her chin, her neck.

Marla made a tiny sobbing sound, involuntary and revealing. She needed this in the same way that she needed
food and drink. Everything in her had been crying out to be
touched and held and cherished by him. She had ignored it
until it hurt too much to be denied. And he had waited until he could see she was ready to break into a million pieces
for want of his touch. How had he known? she wondered
blissfully.

He slid his hands down to her breasts and touched them
through the fine fabric of her blouse. Marla moaned, feeling pleasure close to pain as her nipples peaked under his
stroking palms.

"Marla, Marla," he murmured hoarsely, pulling her close
with one arm and kissing her so hard her head fell back,
spilling her long hair over his arm. His free hand pulled her
blouse out of her waistband and slipped underneath the
flimsy material.

When she felt his palm against the sensitized skin of her
midriff, stroking up toward her breasts, she clutched his hips
and started nuzzling his neck, wanting him, wanting every
sensation they could give each other.

He pushed aside the lacy fabric of her bra and touched her
breast tentatively. Marla forced her eyes open to look at his
face. She saw the wonder, the tenderness, the intense desire
in his expression as he caressed her with infinite gentleness.
Her breast felt swollen, and the nipple ached beneath his
questing fingers.

"Oh, God, it's been such a long time," he said brokenly.
He pressed his forehead against hers. She hugged him, feel-

ing so tender toward him she thought her heart would force its way out of her chest.

Brent put a hand on her bottom to lift her slightly and pull her against him. He pushed his rigid manhood against the V of her thighs and sighed.

"I want you," he whispered raggedly. "I want to make love to you. I want to touch every part of you, feel your legs wrap around me, feel myself inside you."

He wrapped both arms around her again, holding her tightly, rubbing his hands urgently across her back, under her blouse. Marla moaned and struggled to press herself closer, impossibly closer, as his words stirred up erotic images that couldn't be controlled, that had to be satisfied.

It would be just like that; she knew it. It would be so good, it would fill her and complete her and burn her to ashes. She slid her hand down his flat stomach, intent on touching him, intent on reaching for the fastening of his jeans.

He drew in a sharp breath and grabbed her hand. He pushed her away almost roughly. Their eyes met, their labored breathing harsh in the silence of the storage room.

"I don't want the first time to be in here," he said at last. A small, wry smile touched his mouth. "We'll try it sometime, but not the first time." He held her gaze. "Come home with me."

"Now?" she asked weakly.

He hugged her again. "Of course now. I don't want to walk around in this condition the rest of the day."

She smiled at the teasing in his voice.

He cleared his throat. "Come with me?"

It was the hardest thing she had ever done, but she backed out of his embrace. Unable to bear breaking contact totally, she held his hand as she stepped farther away from him. Now that he had stopped assaulting her senses, she needed to think.

"Marla," he said huskily, watching her closely, "couldn't you just feel for a change?"

Her face crumpled. "No," she whispered. "No."

He realized he was losing his advantage. He almost swept her into his arms again, but he was too honest. If she could still have second thoughts after what had just passed between them, then her misgivings were a bigger hurdle than he had realized.

Marla released his hand, straightened her blouse and sat down gracelessly on top of a packing crate. She lowered her head, feeling deflated and intensely frustrated, but also scared. After a moment she felt him sit beside her and put his hand on her thigh.

"Why not?" he asked softly.

"I didn't get where I am by just feeling, Brent. I always think first."

"And where are you that's so important it matters more than this?"

Her eyes flashed up to his face, and he saw a spark of resentment there. It surprised him.

"I realize that my career doesn't seem very important to you, since you've got close to a thirty-million-dollar company and think playing with your toys is the most important thing in the world, but it matters to me."

"Of course—"

"Don't placate me," she snapped.

He realized they were getting closer to the core of the problem. He had never seen her so impatient or tense before.

"Do you think someone just handed me my job?" she said in exasperation.

"How did you get it?" he asked, not sure what she was driving at.

"The hard way."

"Go on."

She sighed, wondering why she felt it was imperative to explain this to him. "When I got out of college, I had huge loans to pay off. Mostly because . . . well, never mind. Anyhow, I got a job selling radio time to advertisers. It didn't take me long to figure out I'd never get anywhere without an M.B.A., so I worked long enough to pay off all my loans and put away some savings. Then I worked full-time for four years by day and went to graduate school at night.''

''That's a lot of work,'' he admitted, impressed by her determination.

''For four years I didn't take a vacation or read novels or work out or make new friends. All I did was work, study and pay my bills. All so I could get that M.B.A. and start a good career.''

He frowned. ''You did all that so you could work under some skunk like Warren Tallman and refuse to sleep with me because it's against company policy? Sounds like a lot of wasted effort.''

If she hadn't been angry before, she was certainly angry now. ''I've been at the agency for three years, and they were about to promote me to a job just like Warren's when I screwed up on the Diablo Boots account! I already make more money than anyone in my family has ever made, and I don't rely on anybody to pay my way or ensure my security. That alone is worth all the effort.''

''Look, maybe I could talk to your superiors and explain that I really want—''

''To sleep with me? That's all I need!''

He scowled at her. ''Obviously, I would be more tactful than that. But I'm the client, so maybe I—''

''Brent, forget it. It won't work.''

''How do you know?'' he challenged.

She was silent so long he thought she wasn't going to answer him. Then she released her breath in a long sigh of resignation and said, ''All right. I'll tell you how I know. My final year of grad school I was still working for the radio station. One of the clients was . . . a very attractive man. He asked me out, and he made it clear it was a purely personal invitation.''

She shrugged wearily. ''I knew the station wouldn't like it if they knew, but I was already interviewing for a new job, preparing to resign as soon as I finished the M.B.A. program in a few more months. And,'' she added softly, ''I was so lonely. I just wanted to be with a man I liked.''

He wanted to hold her again, but he forced himself to remain still. ''What happened?''

''We went out a few times. I decided that his attractiveness was only skin-deep, and I told him as nicely as possible that I didn't want to see him again.'' She wrapped her arms around herself. ''A few days later he took his business away from the radio station. He told my boss it was because I had led him on and then rejected him.''

''Did they fire you?''

She shook her head. ''Not exactly. They were a smaller, more liberal company than Freemont, and I was the top person in my department. But even so, they were furious, and I wound up resigning a little sooner than I had intended. After all, my personal life cost them a lot of money.''

Brent leaned forward and propped his chin on his hands, thinking over her story and not liking the obvious conclusions.

''Now you know the two biggest mistakes I've ever made,'' Marla said. ''I can't afford to repeat either of them.''

He sat up again and frowned at her. ''Wait a minute. Do you honestly think I'm some kind of macho, self-pitying creep who would go whining to the agency if you dumped me?''

''No, I—''

''Damn right I'm not. And I resent being compared to some immature jerk you were stupid enough to find attractive in another era of your life.''

''And I resent being backed into a corner because you can't keep your libido under control,'' she shot back, stung by his comment.

"I also don't like being told time and time again that I am less important to you than my account. I think it's about time you put *me* first."

Marla jumped to her feet. "You *will* not understand, will you? You must have fallen off one of those mountains and landed on your head! I will not let you jeopardize what I have worked years to build!"

"*What* have you worked years to build? A job selling things you don't make to people who don't want and can't afford them? A life where you let other people dictate who you'll spend your time with? A code of—"

"I think I've heard quite enough," she said furiously. She was shaking. She couldn't remember ever having been so angry in her life.

"No, I think there's a lot more to say," he said, standing up and walking toward her.

"I do *not* need a lecture on how to run my life from someone who spends all his time on a surfboard or dangling over gorges and is never around when you need him!"

"Fine! Why don't you just go back to your per capita income reports and target markets? That's what really counts with you, isn't it?"

"You have no idea what counts with me. We can't all live in an endless volleyball match, Brent. Some of us have to work for a living and act like adults. And that," she said tersely, "means *you* can't have every damn thing you want. Including me."

They stared at each other in shocked silence. Brent looked as if she'd just slapped him. Marla thought her legs would refuse to support her in another moment. Brent stepped back and ran a hand through his hair in agitation. He didn't think he'd been so mad at anyone in years.

If he had forgotten the astonishing glory of a woman's body in the past three years, he now realized he had also forgotten something else. Caring about a woman could hurt like hell at times. And the only person who could comfort you was usually the woman who was busy hurting you.

Suddenly, for the first time since Katie's death, he felt like crying. He clenched his teeth and pressed his lips together. He looked at Marla and felt a violent emotion, something so close to hatred that it rocked him. How could she *do* this to him when he had shown her how hard it was for him to enter the mating dance once again?

"It's a damned shame that the first woman I've wanted since I was widowed is a walking business machine," he said roughly. He pushed his way past her and started to leave the storage room.

"I still need to get samples of your merchandise for—"

"Just go away," he said tiredly. He paused by the doorway and spoke to her without looking back. "Call Nigel. Have someone else come out to get the stuff. This is my company, and I really don't want you here right now."

He walked out the door and disappeared. Marla stared after him, feeling as if she'd been kicked in the stomach. It took her the longest time to be sure she had heard him correctly.

Yes, the client she had started off liking so much, the client she had done everything in her power to deal with on a pleasantly professional basis, had just thrown her out of his company.

Her movements were stiff and jerky as she picked up her purse and made her way out of the storage room, through the Ventura complex and out to her car.

She put her key into the ignition and then just sat there, trying to take it all in. She felt her insides quiver painfully. She buried her face in her hands, and a low, animal sound escaped her throat as she tried not to cry. She never cried. She had always been the stoic one in her family. Marla could always face every situation with calm competence.

She started her car and reversed it out of the Ventura parking lot. She took deep, painful gulps of air as she drove, willing herself not to cry, forbidding herself the soft luxury of tears.

How had she made this mess? What had prompted her to fight with him, to start making love with him, to give him so many reasons to be angry with her? The road swam before her eyes, and she pulled into the first lot she saw. It was a convenience store. She got out of the car and got herself some coffee.

"Are you okay, lady?" the cashier asked in concern when she paid for the carryout coffee.

Marla ignored him and took her coffee out to her car. She took a sip of it without even blowing on it, wanting the scalding feel of it in her mouth to shock her back into reality.

Of course she burned her tongue. She gasped and clapped a hand to her stinging lips and cursed when she felt two big tears slide down her cheeks.

What the hell had she just done?

When she got back to the agency, she called Nigel and told him she would be sending Vernon out to collect the products they needed from him. He sounded a little confused, but she made herself attribute that to his head cold. She could tell by his congested voice that he hadn't yet shaken it off.

Vernon also looked puzzled when she told him she had decided it would be best for him to go out to Ventura alone and collect what he wanted from Nigel. She made sure her expression gave nothing away, but she locked herself inside her office the rest of the day, not sure how long she could keep her mask from cracking and crumbling.

She hardly recognized herself in the angry woman who had fought so frankly and insultingly with Brent today. She couldn't remember ever having spoken to anyone that way.

She also couldn't remember having abandoned herself to pleasure the way she had before their argument. She was a normal, healthy woman, and she didn't think she had any hang-ups, but she had never before experienced anything so powerful, overwhelming and extraordinary as what she had felt in his arms.

She remembered his lips on hers, his intimate whispers, his gentle hands on her breasts, the look of awe and wonder on his face when he touched her. No other man had ever looked as if touching her shook him to the core. No other man had ever made her feel so cherished and desirable and mysterious.

She wished she could laugh at the irony of it all. In effect, she had offended him personally because she was afraid of what he would do if she offended him personally. She had refused his affection for professional reasons, but she had sailed into the fray without a thought when he got angry. It had been bad enough when the chemistry between them had merely been potential. Now they had been through a full-blown eruption together.

What next? she wondered bleakly.

She worked herself into a state of exhaustion the rest of the week. She received several phone calls from Ventura, but always from Nigel or Felice. She asked about Brent, wondering if he had gone away again. She only got vague answers that he was "around somewhere."

Vernon went to Ventura's headquarters at the end of the week. When he returned, he entered Marla's office with an unusually grave and troubled expression. Fear coursed through her the moment she saw him.

"What's wrong?" she said.

"You're not going to like it."

"What?"

"Ventura has stepped up the schedule. They want to see a full presentation of our proposals next week. On Monday."

"What?"

Vernon nodded. "I don't get it. Brent seemed like such a friendly, relaxed guy the couple of times I met him."

"Brent told you he wanted the presentation next Monday?"

"Yeah. And when Nigel said he thought that was short notice, Brent nearly bit his head off."

Marla sank into her chair, feeling sick at heart. If only she could turn back the clock or call back angry words. Surely, even in management's eyes, insulting the client was worse than sleeping with him.

"Can we be ready?" she asked Vernon.

He shrugged. "I'd rather not find out. Can't you talk to Brent? He's always seemed sweet on you."

"What do you mean by that?" she asked sharply.

"You know. He likes you, he flirts with you, and he acts like he respects you. If anyone can change his mind, it's probably you."

Marla had a feeling that her pleas would only make things worse, but she promised to try. After Vernon left her office, she got up her courage, dialed Ventura's number and asked for Brent.

Brent stared at the phone for nearly thirty seconds when Nigel told him Marla was on the line for him. Finally, conscious of his friend's curious gaze, he picked up the receiver and tentatively said, "Hello?"

"Brent, it's me."

He heard the breathlessness in her voice and guessed she was as nervous as he was. He hated telephones. He wanted to see her face, her wide hazel eyes, her thick blond hair. He wanted to hear her slightly husky voice without the mechanical hollowness the telephone gave it.

"Yes?" he said.

"I have to talk to you. Have you got a moment?"

His heart twisted in his chest. They did have to talk. They couldn't let those angry words and harsh insults be the end of what was blossoming between them. He still felt raw, stunned at how angry she had made him, shocked at how much her anger had hurt him.

"Sure, go ahead," he said. She knew—she must know—they couldn't let it go. All she had to do was meet him halfway. If she could just make him believe a little, he'd do anything for her.

"I've just spoken with Vernon. I understand you want to move the presentation up to next Monday."

His blood froze. She had called to talk business?

"Yes, that's what I told him."

There was a long silence. Finally she said, "I . . . I have to apologize for the way I spoke to you the last time I saw you, Brent. After all my talk about professionalism, it was inexcusable. It was unforgivable, but I have to ask your forgiveness, anyhow."

Her apology was hurting him more than her anger.

"Is that what you called to say?" he asked gruffly.

"That and . . . and to ask you not to let your personal feelings influence your decisions about the account. My team is doing wonderful work, but to demand they deliver a prepared proposal in just a few days puts a lot of pressure on them. Perhaps if we set the date for, say, a week from Monday, or two weeks . . ."

He hadn't known he could be even madder than he was already. The force of it scared him. "Me and my messy feelings. We just keep getting in the way of your job, don't we?" he snapped.

"Brent, please—"

"I have my doubts about this whole enterprise, Marla, and I'm beginning to regret hiring an ad agency more than you can imagine. You've got until Monday to convince me that you and your company are worth my time, effort and aggravation, and if you can't, I'm throwing in the towel."

"But you—"

"I never wanted to get involved with you people in the first place," he continued, working himself into a fine rage, "but I let Nigel talk me into it. And nothing, absolutely nothing, about your company has convinced me yet that I wasn't right."

He was furious. How could she taunt him like this? How could she telephone him just to tell him once more that his market potential mattered more to her than the way he felt about her?

"All right. If that's your final decision, then I'll make sure my team is prepared for the presentation by Monday. Please have your secretary call mine to arrange the time. Goodbye."

Brent put down the receiver softly. He suddenly felt a little guilty. Wasn't he doing exactly what he had said he wouldn't do, putting her under professional pressure because he wasn't satisfied with the way things were working out personally?

She had sounded shaken. Even if she was shaken for fear of her job rather than because he was angry at her, he was still responsible for her distress.

"Game of volleyball, mate?" Nigel asked.

Brent looked over at his friend. Nigel was studying his new surfing magazine with intense absorption and swigging orange juice from a half-gallon pitcher. Nigel knew better than to ask a direct question when Brent was this upset. Instead, Brent realized, Nigel would just wear away at him, poking and prodding, nagging and trying to catch him off guard until he found out what was wrong.

"Volleyball?" Brent said. "Nah. Not in the mood."

He was going to keep his guard up this time. This one hurt too much, and it wasn't over yet. That was why he had set that sudden deadline. The sooner he could get this business over with, the less time he'd have to spend avoiding Marla.

If the presentation was all right, maybe he could just turn things over to Nigel or Felice and tell them to keep Marla out of the building when he was there from now on. If the presentation was awful, then he could just drop Freemont and put this whole unpleasant experience behind him.

He crumpled a piece of paper and threw it into the hoop over his wastebasket. On the whole, he thought he preferred the numbness of mourning to the pain of wanting.

Chapter Eight

Marla had heard stories of terrible catastrophes from her colleagues, but until the day of the presentation to Ventura, she hadn't known it was possible for so much to go wrong all at once.

"Nathan's in *jail*?" she demanded.

Yvonne nodded mutely.

"You mean, he's not coming to the meeting with his final draft because he's in *jail*?" Marla seized Yvonne by the shoulders, willing her to deny it.

Yvonne nodded again and started to cry.

Marla took a deep breath and tried to think logically. "All right. Why has he been arrested?"

"For all those parking tickets he didn't pay. He ignored the warnings and final notices and...and...he's in *jail*!" Yvonne started sobbing loudly, overcome by worry for the man she had adored with unrequited affection for the past few months.

"Calm down, calm down. He'll be all right," Marla said soothingly. She guided Yvonne to a chair in her office and called Vernon on the intercom. "You'd better get in here. We've got serious problems."

She was handing a cup of coffee to Yvonne moments later when Vernon showed up. They had all worked together until late Saturday night, planning to finalize their presentation this morning. Brent Ventura and his associates were coming this afternoon for the meeting.

The second Marla saw Vernon, her heart sank. "You look awful," she said bluntly.

"Achoo!" He pulled out a handkerchief, sneezed again and wiped his red nose. His puffy, red-rimmed eyes looked morose. A fine film of perspiration covered his face, and Marla suspected he was running a fever. "I caught Nigel's cold," he said unnecessarily.

"Oh, Vernon. Here, have some hot coffee," Marla said.

Vernon accepted the steaming cup gratefully and plopped into the chair next to Yvonne's. "What's wrong?" he asked. He sneezed again and groaned. "Nigel *said* the first couple of days of this bug were hell."

Marla broke the news while Yvonne took in shaky gulps of air. "Nathan's been arrested for not paying all those parking tickets."

Vernon's eyes bulged. His first words made Yvonne glare at him. "Where's the final draft of his work?"

"I don't know. He was supposed to finish it yesterday so we could insert it in the presentation this morning. Do you suppose it's in his apartment?" Marla said.

"Could be. Has anyone talked to him?" Vernon said.

"*I* have," said Yvonne, "and can't you two think about anything except this account? Nathan could be being brutalized at this very moment!"

"I doubt that," Vernon said. After a moment, he added, "Not as long as he keeps his mouth shut, anyhow."

"Well, one of us has to go see him in jail and find out where his final draft is," Marla said.

"I'll go!" Yvonne said, hopping out of her chair.

"All right," Marla agreed. She and Vernon both had too much to do in the next few hours to run around town searching for Nathan's final draft. "And call me right away. Find out how much his bail is, too. Maybe I can get him out of there in time for the meeting."

Yvonne scooped up her purse and dashed out of the office. Vernon rubbed his sore throat absently and looked at Marla. "Now what?" he said.

"We'll have to get everything else together as planned and hope Nathan finished his final draft before he was arrested. We'll also have to tell Warren about this." She took a deep breath and squared her shoulders.

"Do we have to?" Vernon pleaded.

Marla met his gaze with mutual understanding. It wasn't unusual in this business to work long, frantic hours in an effort to make a deadline, but the past few days had been especially fraught with conflict and frustration. Warren kept interfering much more than was usual for a man in his position, making it clear at every opportunity that he didn't trust Marla's judgment or capabilities and fully intended to have her fired if things didn't go well today.

The strain had been hard on the entire creative team, since there were also divisions within the group. Two of the people had been assigned due to Warren's influence after the others had already enthusiastically planned out their concepts, and the two newcomers didn't share ideas that were even remotely similar with the core group's. Marla had had her hands full trying to keep everything running smoothly and according to the strategy she had worked out, and Vernon had lost his temper several times under the conflicting pressures.

"Look, I'll tell Warren," Marla said. "You go get something for that cold and complete the work we talked about Saturday, okay?"

"You're a noble woman, Marla," he said. "I'd give five years of my life never to speak to Warren again."

By the time she was done talking with Warren, Marla had decided that Vernon had underestimated the value of never speaking to him again.

"I told you from the beginning I didn't want that irresponsible, left-wing hippy on this account!" Warren had raged at her.

Marla had stood her ground, refusing to let Warren intimidate her. It was hardly her fault that the best person for the job had managed to get himself arrested at a crucial moment.

"We'll just have to scrap that entire section of the representation," Warren concluded. "I never liked those concepts, anyhow, and I think your promotional ideas for it are absurd."

"We can't scrap weeks of work!" Marla protested. "What do you suggest I replace it with at the last minute?"

"We'll just have to go with David Moran's work and that of the people I requested—over your objections, I might add." He looked at her accusingly.

Marla felt almost physically sick at the thought. That particular concept was in opposition to the whole character of Ventura. She felt sure Brent would detest it. She cleared her throat and tried to appeal to Warren's business sense, afraid it was a wasted effort.

"The concept you favor in this presentation is off strategy. I have spent enough time with the senior officers of Ventura to know—"

"I will not have you mess up this important presentation with half-completed, badly conceived work!" Warren snarled.

"That's what I was about to say!" The steel thread of her temper finally broke, and she lost all sense of caution. "We worked damn hard on this presentation, and I'm not going to let you ruin it with coy, slick, overblown ideas that this client will detest!"

"How dare you speak to me that way!" Warren raged.

"I know this company inside out, and I will include the concepts most likely to appeal to them in today's presentation. *That* is my professional responsibility, *not* deferring to you."

"That does it," Warren said through gritted teeth. "You'd better enjoy today's presentation, because unless a miracle happens, it's going to be the last one you make at Freemont."

Marla walked out of his office without even responding to his threat. As soon as she collapsed into a chair in her own office, she wondered what had become of the stoic, calm, reserved woman she had always been. She had already alienated the client, and now she had shouted at her immediate superior.

What else could go wrong today?

A few hours later, she found out.

Nathan's final draft had been on his person when he had been arrested, and it was currently being held by the police department, along with his other personal effects. None of them could get their hands on it until they bailed him out.

In addition to her rent, car payment and usual bills, Marla had just sent a huge check off to her mother, so she wouldn't have enough money to bail Nathan out until the next payday. Everyone else on the account was in a similar situation—except Warren, whom no one dared to ask. Nathan forbade them to tell his parents he needed to be bailed out of jail. So he—and his final draft—were stuck there for the time being.

A half hour before Brent and the others were due to arrive, Marla and Vernon met in her office again. She started speaking as soon as Vernon walked in the door, not even glancing up at him.

"We'll have to use Saturday's rough-draft copy in the presentation," she said briskly, going over her notes, "and we'll say something about submitting various final drafts for their approval. With Nathan missing, we need to swing the emphasis to the visual presentation. We'll have to generate a lot of enthusiasm, be very forceful and positive. That's where you come in.''

"Huh?" Vernon said blankly.

Marla glanced up at him with a scowl. "Pay attention, would you? We only have—" She stopped speaking and froze.

Vernon sat before her with a vague, placid smile on his face. His puffy eyes were heavy lidded and half-closed. He looked totally spaced-out.

"Oh, no," she said slowly. She shot out of her chair and rounded the desk to have a closer look at him.

"Sorry, Marla," he said fuzzily. "I took a double dose of that new cold medicine. Extra strength. It's made me a little..."

"Yes, I can tell."

She tried everything she could think of to snap him back to reality: coffee, cold water, a brisk walk. Nothing worked. Just when she needed him most, Vernon was out for the count.

He kept apologizing incoherently, saying he was going to sue the makers of that cold medicine as soon as he felt alert enough to do it. Marla glumly assured him she wasn't angry.

"It's fate," she said bleakly. "Why else would all this be happening?"

The final straw was that Yvonne, frantic with worry over Nathan and exhausted from her hectic morning, had forgotten to type up and photocopy part of Marla's proposal. By the time Brent, Nigel and Felice finally arrived at the agency, it took every ounce of courage and character Marla had to pull herself together and leave her office to begin what would surely be the most disastrous presentation of her career.

In fact, after Warren's repeated warnings, she could count on today's presentation *ending* her career.

Just before she left the safety of her office, she saw the small, crooked horseshoe Brent had helped her make in the

Ventura workshop. Remembering that horseshoes were supposed to be good luck, and far too distraught to scoff at mere superstition, Marla took it in her hand and carried it out the door with her.

She looked so tired, Brent thought when she welcomed him politely in the conference room. Nigel and Felice greeted Marla with easy familiarity, heightening Brent's sense of desolation at the formal, uncomfortable way he and Marla addressed each other.

Once the room had filled with people, several of whom Brent had met before, a secretary made sure everyone had refreshments. After a few more minutes, Marla asked for everyone's attention.

Her opening statements were cool, professional and organized, but he believed he knew her better than that, and he didn't like what he saw. Her wide hazel eyes looked distressed; her mouth was taut; her hands seemed a little stiff and jerky.

Marla apologized for not having some kind of papers to hand out to them. She should have known he didn't want to read that stuff, anyhow. He was aware of Warren Tallman radiating disapproval nearby, and he wanted to slug the man.

Brent swallowed painfully, wishing Marla would look at him just once with something other than that veiled, polite expression he was sure she used for numerous business acquaintances. He wished he could stop wanting to be more than a client to her; he wished she could stop wanting him to be only that. He scowled and tried to concentrate on what was being said around the table.

Marla was launching into an introduction of the first campaign concept when Warren interrupted her. "Why don't we start with our strongest idea first, Marla?"

Marla went still and stared at Warren. It took her only a brief moment to recover her composure, but Brent had noticed the slip. He wondered what was going on.

Two people Brent hadn't met before took over the presentation. What followed was a series of examples of proposed magazine layouts, each more horrible than the last. Wet-lipped, limpid-eyed, long-legged, full-bosomed women lounged around in provocative poses wearing rugged Ventura outfits that, even in these proposed drawings, Brent could see were about three sizes too small.

The body copy of the ads was insipid at best, in Brent's opinion, vaguely promising sex and power to anyone who used Ventura's products. The overall vulgarity of the whole proposal was exemplified by its theme headline.

"'Dare to Wear It'?" Brent said incredulously.

Marla looked helplessly at her colleagues.

"Catchy," said Warren eagerly. "Something people can roll around on the tip of their tongues. The words are memorable, the girls are eye-catching. It gives Ventura that quality of glamour, of excitement—"

"Sex sells," Nigel said blandly. He leaned back in his chair and winked at Felice.

"Well..." Warren gave Nigel a "we're men of the world" look and chuckled.

Brent winced. "Why don't we just move on to the next concept," he said weakly. These ads would make his company the laughingstock of every serious sportsman in the Western Hemisphere.

Marla looked extremely relieved, although Brent's request to jump ahead to the next proposal had everyone scuttling around the room in haste for a moment.

The next concept was her pet project, the one she believed in most of all. She folded her hands nervously in front of her, silently pleading with Brent to like it. She had done it for him.

Vernon rose from his chair and groggily tried to assist her in explaining the layouts and initial ideas for the concept. Her heart started pounding harder when she saw Brent scowl again, as he had done several times since the beginning of the meeting.

Please, she begged silently, I've done everything I could with this mess.

Vernon was so inarticulate she finally maneuvered him back to his chair, trying not to be obvious about it but afraid she hadn't fooled anybody.

"We're calling this the 'Venture Forth' campaign," Marla explained, returning to her post. "Those words will be our headline, and the headline will be exemplified by the feats being dared in each photo layout. Therefore, we'll get the attention not only of sportsmen, but of anyone who even fantasizes about himself as a fearless adventurer or a rugged sportsman."

Brent leaned forward and the interested look on his face gave her courage to continue. Nigel exchanged a glance with Felice, who scribbled something on her notepad.

"Now, we're including more body copy than you'll see in most print advertising, because tone is as important as information here. We want to make the consumer aware that these are the best products for serious sportsmen, but we also want dabblers to feel the company and its products are accessible to them, friendly."

Since Marla had been unable to supply examples of the copy for everyone, she started reading aloud from her copy of Nathan's rough draft, which emulated, as she had hoped, the flavor and character of Brent's company.

Having finished, she continued, "The endorsements of real people are memorable and persuasive. Therefore, for our second launch of the 'Venture Forth' ads, we'd like to collect and edit the comments of well-known and avid users of your equipment."

Marla continued explaining the concepts, filling in details and answering numerous questions from Nigel and Felice. She had expected Brent to be quiet, knowing how he detested business meetings, but she wished he would show some kind of reaction. She still wasn't sure if he liked it or hated it. When they had finished discussing the layout and copy, she took a deep breath and began explaining her promotional idea, aware of Warren's disapproval.

"With the next set of ads, we can announce that Ventura is running a photo contest for the following year. Everyone who uses Ventura equipment or wears the clothing will be encouraged to send in their own photos and their testimonials. That will get the consumers involved, make them look eagerly for the new ads, make them consider how they could participate."

"Now that's an idea," said Nigel thoughtfully. Felice was scribbling furiously.

Brent was keeping his face carefully blank. Marla wanted to drag him out of the room and have it out with him. She wanted to beg him to understand her; she wanted to crawl onto his lap and ask him to hold her. Instead, she finished outlining the promotional campaign.

"We'll charge an entry fee to the contest. Anyone who's willing to go to the trouble of preparing a photograph or essay will probably also be willing to spend between ten and twenty dollars to enter the contest. And that money," she added, looking directly at Brent, "will be donated to an environmental or wildlife charity. In fact, we could even provide space on the entry form to give the contestant his choice of several nonprofit organizations Ventura habitually donates to."

She had bet him she could find a way for him to do the right thing in his ad campaign. She could tell by the glitter in his green eyes that he remembered.

There was an uneasy pause. Then Brent nodded and gave her a slight, rueful smile, acknowledging that she had surprised and pleased him with this. Marla smiled, too, the first real smile that had split her face in a long time. All the tension rushed out of her, and she continued her presentation with a feeling of buoyant confidence she hadn't known for quite a while.

The change in the atmosphere was apparent to everyone, and by the end of the presentation, most of them had forgotten how tense they had all been at the outset. When the meeting finally broke up, everyone lingered a few minutes to chat and congratulate each other.

Marla approached Brent, her eyes soft and vulnerable. He wanted to stroke her hair, kiss her forehead, let her rest her head against his chest. He wanted to beg her forgiveness for the pressure he had unwittingly put her under, even worse, perhaps, than the pressure her superiors had laid on her. He did none of those things, however, too aware of Warren stiffly standing at his side.

Marla smiled tremulously. Finally she said, "Now you'll have to take back all those nasty things you said about advertising."

He smiled and tilted his head as he looked her. "Not really."

She raised her slanted brows, aware of the tender light in his eyes. She had missed him so much. "Why not?"

Brent turned his attention to Warren. He would land a blow for Marla that she couldn't deliver herself. "Because that first presentation, Mr. Tallman, was the single most tasteless, vulgar and juvenile suggestion it has ever been my misfortune to hear. Professionally speaking, I mean."

Warren turned red. He coughed, then sputtered, "Well, that's why we always produce several proposals, Mr. Ventura. To show the client the broad range of...uh..." He glanced at his watch. "Will you excuse me? I'm due at... Glad we were able to find common ground today. That promotion is a smashing idea, isn't it? We'll be seeing you soon, I'm sure."

Brent watched him with a bland expression as Warren backed away from them. He bumped into an artist and snapped at her to watch where she was going.

Marla met Brent's eyes. She tried to suppress a satisfied smile but gave up. Why not enjoy her victory to the fullest? "Thanks," she said softly.

"My pleasure. I try to be gallant around you, even if it doesn't always work out that way."

Her smile faded. "I try to be responsible around you, and I don't seem to have much success, either."

"We need to talk," he said seriously.

"I know." Why try to deny it? She couldn't stop needing him just because she knew she should.

He glanced around the room for a moment before saying, "Meet me tonight? After work?"

She nodded. "Where?" Before he could respond, she added, "Not at the company."

"No," he agreed. This would be entirely personal, without even the pretense of business. "How about that café near the beach we talked at?"

"Okay," she said. "I'll probably have to work late. I'll be there by eight o'clock."

"Okay."

"Hey, Marla," said Nigel behind her. "Tell me, for those 'Dare to Wear It' drawings, did they use real models?"

"Yes."

Nigel grinned. "I don't suppose you've got a few of those ladies' phone numbers handy?"

Brent rolled his eyes. Marla laughed. "You're thinking of using that campaign?" she asked innocently.

"No, of course not. But you can see that a couple of those women need surfing lessons. I feel duty-bound to volunteer."

"That's very noble of you, but I'm afraid I can't give out that information."

Nigel looked so disappointed she had to laugh again. It was such a relief to be able to enjoy life after the past few days.

Then Nigel shrugged good-naturedly and said, "Ah, well, no harm in asking. Nothing ventured, nothing gained."

"Nigel's a walking volume of platitudes," Felice said, joining them. "I'm ready to get back to work, Brent."

"You would be," Nigel said morosely.

"Let's go. This place makes me uncomfortable," Brent said, looking more like his old self.

Just before he and the others left, his eyes met Marla's, reminding her of their date. He refused to think of it as another damned meeting.

She had been right in assuming she would have to work late. Her planned schedule, however, was disrupted by an unexpected summons to the office of one of her superiors. Consequently, she was almost twenty minutes late meeting Brent that evening.

As soon as she saw him waiting for her, as soon as she saw the smooth, graceful way he rose to his feet to greet her, she had an overwhelmingly physical reaction to him. She felt she was being pulled towards him as surely as if they were bound together by a rope. She couldn't stop the smile that lighted her face or ignore the pounding of her heart. She had been a fool all along to think she could handle this with professional ease.

He took her hands in his and held them tightly for a moment. She felt the restraint he was putting on himself, felt his grip tighten as he fought against pulling her into his embrace, and it thrilled her. After a moment he smiled sheepishly, released her and pulled out her chair.

"I'm sorry I'm so late," she said breathlessly.

"I wasn't afraid you had changed your mind," he assured her. He glanced at the waiter who was already hovering over them. "What would you like to drink?"

"Um." She noticed the beer sitting in front of him. "Glass of wine, white and dry," she said to the waiter, just wanting him to go away.

"Did you have a lot to do at the office?" Brent asked.

"Yes, but I got held up because I was summoned to a meeting with one of the senior vice presidents."

Brent frowned. "What now?"

She smiled. "Just the opposite of what you're thinking—of what I thought, too. They're pleased with the way I handled today's disasters and with the way I've handled you." The look they exchanged was ironic. "This senior officer has always encouraged me, and I gather he was just waiting for me to do something right so he could help me out. He's promised me they're going to find me another big client."

Brent's eyes narrowed. "You mean they're taking you off my account?"

"No. We'll work together just the way we have been," she assured him. "They're just showing their faith in me, offering me a big work load. Offering me the kind of work load I *should* have at my salary," she admitted.

"Oh." Brent relaxed again and smiled. "In that case, I'm very happy for you, Marla. But, uh, what 'disasters' was he referring to?"

Marla rolled her eyes. "I hardly know where to begin." She took a sip of her wine when the waiter placed it before her and, against agency ethics, began telling Brent everything that had gone wrong that morning. Now that the worst was over, she was able to laugh about it, and Brent joined her.

"But how did this senior vice president find out about all this?" he asked.

"Vernon, I suspect," she said. "Once he came down from all that cold medicine, I think he met with him to tell him how things had gone, probably on the assumption that Warren's account would be slightly slanted."

Brent grunted. "'Dare to Wear It,'" he repeated incredulously.

"Well, to give him his due, sex does sell. We have dozens of clients who pay us to come up with campaigns just like that. But I knew you'd hate it, and Warren refused to trust my judgment."

"You look smug," he said with a lazy smile.

"I know it's unbecoming, but I can't help it," she admitted. "I feel like celebrating."

"Okay, let's celebrate. What do you want to do?"

She reached across the table impulsively and covered his big brown hand with one of hers. "I'm doing what I want to do," she said softly. "I just want to be with you."

He swallowed. His voice was husky when he said, "Marla, don't . . . I mean, I have to know where I stand."

Her eyes held his candidly. "I'm sorry," she said with feeling, "for the things I said, for the way I acted."

"I'm sorry, too. But I want more than an apology from you."

He watched her carefully, trying not to put physical or emotional pressure on her as he waited for her response. She hesitated only for a moment on the brink, vaguely frightened of the enormous leap she was about to take, sensing for the first time that a lot more than her job would be at stake once she went into his embrace.

"So do I," she said at last.

He made a brief, reflexive movement toward her, then stopped, forcing himself to sit perfectly still. "What about your job?"

She licked her lips. "I'll have to trust you not to jeopardize it." Marla could hardly believe her own ears. That statement alone was evidence of how impossible it was to resist him.

Brent lowered his eyes, feeling ashamed. "That's a lot of trust after the way I've been acting lately. I'm sorry I moved up the deadline and behaved . . . just the way you were afraid I'd behave."

Her throat filled with emotion to hear him apologize so humbly for his anger and actions. "Since you're big enough to snap me in two with your bare hands, I suppose I got off lightly."

His shocked gaze shot up to her face. "I would never hurt you! I've never used violence—"

"I know, I know," she said quickly. His gentleness was one of the things that made him so special. She shrugged. "Since I kept telling you my job was what made me say no, I suppose you just wanted to finish with the whole thing as quickly as possible."

"That's exactly what I wanted," he agreed wearily.

"At least you gave me a chance to redeem myself today."

"And I'm glad I did. You had a lot of great ideas."

"That credit really goes to Vernon and the creative people."

"But the photo contest, with the entry fees going to—"

"Yes, that was my idea," she admitted proudly.

He gave her that familiar boyish grin. "You really are too nice to be in advertising, Marla."

"There are plenty of nice people in advertising. You're just letting your naive prejudices get the better of you because of a few unfortunate examples," she said sternly.

He shrugged. "Anyhow, I'm impressed at how you held together today. Especially thinking I'd bite your head off any minute."

"I had a lucky charm." She pulled her pathetic little horseshoe out of the pocket of her linen blazer and showed it to him.

"Oh, Marla." He smiled, touched.

"Anyhow, I think the wear and tear is starting to show in my face. At the end of my talk with the senior vice president today, he told me to clear my desk and then take a few days off." She grimaced. "He politely indicated that I look like hell."

Brent looked indignant. "You look beautiful. You *always* look beautiful. But—" he leaned over and touched her cheek gently "—you do look tired. I'm responsible for most of that."

"Don't blame yourself."

"But I—"

"I'm used to short deadlines. And . . . if I've tossed and turned a lot at night lately, it's no more your fault than mine."

"I've been tossing and turning, too."

Their eyes locked. She saw the glitter of desire in his expression, felt the intent in the warm palm that cupped her cheek. Something wild and demanding surged between them in the speaking silence of their mingled gazes.

Her breath suddenly seemed to burn her lungs. She felt heat rush straight to her loins, hot and liquid and urgent. Her pulse hammered so loudly in her ears she felt certain he could hear it.

"I live a short drive from here," he said in a low voice.

The restaurant light gleamed on his dark hair and bronze skin. His expression was tender, persuasive. His words stirred up sudden, unbidden images that made her shiver. Afraid her voice would break, Marla nodded in silent response to the question in his eyes.

Brent paid for their drinks, stood and took her arm to guide her out the door. She resisted touching him or looking at him, afraid she'd melt all over him in the middle of this public place if she succumbed even slightly to the desires rushing through her.

"Where's your car?" he murmured.

She led him to it. She slid into the driver's seat, opened the passenger door and started the engine as he got in. "Your car?" she asked briefly, finding it hard to push the words out. She didn't care about details; she just wanted to be alone with him in his house.

"I left my bicycle at work."

She could feel his eyes on her as she drove. After a moment, he leaned over and stroked her thigh. Marla hit the gas pedal so suddenly they nearly ran a stop sign. She shot him a rueful glance.

"Sorry," he said, not sounding sorry at all.

"Better let me concentrate long enough for us to get there," she said dryly.

They were very near, as he had said. A few minutes later, under his direction, she pulled up in front of his house, a small and sturdy structure not far from Windansea Beach. They got out of the car and approached the front door.

"It's beautiful," Marla said. The house had a weathered charm that was apparent even in the dark.

"It's even better inside," he assured her. He opened the door and showed her in.

Brent's house had the best attributes of Southern California architecture without any of the garish flaws or shoddy workmanship Marla had come to deplore. A simple decor with wood and tile floors and white and cedar walls gave it a feeling of spaciousness and masculine elegance. He explained his reasons for selling the house he had lived in with his wife and moving here to start over again. She could see his personality in the friendly coziness of the rooms, with their comfortably rugged furnishings.

There was a breathtaking view of the sea from the terrace at back of the house. Marla walked to the edge of the terrace and leaned against the railing.

"I love it here," she said enthusiastically, tilting her head back to look at the night sky. A billion stars glittered above them in the endless black void. She felt the sea breeze brush past her face and lift her hair away from her neck.

Brent came up beside her and leaned against the railing, too. She smiled brilliantly at him, feeling happy and beautiful.

"I'm glad you like my house. It's special to me," he said simply.

Another gust of warm air blew some of her hair across her face. Brent smoothed it away from her cheek and brushed it behind her ear. Marla stepped closer to him, close enough that their body heat mingled and heightened.

"I feel like I could shatter from wanting you," he said huskily.

She tilted her face up to his, eyes half-closed, lips moist and parted.

"Marla . . ."

"Hmm?" She touched his taut stomach as she had longed to, sliding her palms across the muscles and then up his chest. She heard his sharp intake of breath.

"It's been a long time for me," he said uncertainly.

She opened her eyes fully and looked into his face. He towered over her. The width of his shoulders blocked out the bright moon. The strength of his personality had conquered her resistance, and the force of his sensuality had melted her common sense.

"And now you're nervous?" she said with incredulity.

He nodded mutely, looking like a boy with his first woman.

"Don't tell me you're worried about *your* job?" she said lightly.

He shook his head, refusing to smile at her feeble joke. "I'm worried I . . . um . . ." He looked at her helplessly.

She raised her slanted brows. "You mean you're afraid you've forgotten how to make love?"

He shrugged impatiently. Marla found herself smiling. He scowled. "You won't think it's so funny if we find out I have," he growled.

Marla slid her palms up and down his chest. She could feel his pectoral muscles rise and fall rapidly and knew he wasn't as calm as he was trying to look.

"It's like riding a bike," she murmured confidentially.

"From what I remember, it's *nothing* like riding a bike."

Marla could hear the breathlessness in his hoarse voice, could feel the excited thud of his heart under her palms. She began unbuttoning his shirt, enjoying their reversed positions. Until now, he had done all the convincing.

"Maybe that was a bad analogy," she agreed, working her way down his shirt with trembling fingers. When she started pulling it out of his waistband, his head sagged forward and his knuckles tightened on the railing next to them.

"Do you remember this part?" She slid her arms around his back and pressed a moist kiss against his chest.

He went rigid for a moment, then his breathing accelerated. "I . . ."

"Does this jog your memory?" Marla lightly kissed the hard knot of his nipple, then touched her tongue to it. He tasted warm and salty and so good.

"That's . . ." His hand released its death grip on the railing and came up to cup the back of her head.

Holding him to steady herself, Marla started to slide down. "Is this familiar?" She traced kisses down his chest and across his stomach, darting her tongue into his navel. She knelt and reached for his belt buckle. "Or this?"

"Wait a minute," he croaked. He hauled her to her feet and scooped her up into his arms with one graceful motion. "I remember now, and you're skipping a lot."

Marla laughed at the accusing look he gave her. Their lips met in a warm, reassuring kiss. "Where's the bedroom?" she whispered against his lips.

"Now *that* I know I remember," he murmured.

Marla rested her head on his shoulder and inhaled the musky male fragrance of his skin as he carried her inside the house and down the darkened hall to his moonlit bedroom.

He placed one knee on the bed and they kissed again, a kiss full of promise and hunger. Gently, he deposited her on the bed and then followed her down, pressing her into the mattress with his body.

"You're so big," she murmured.

"You're guessing," he teased, shifting against her.

"I mean tall," she chided. Then she gasped as his hands found their way under her blouse.

He kissed her again and again, hot, sweet kisses, as he explored the smooth skin of her midriff and back. His tongue touched hers teasingly and then flitted away to dart against the corner of her mouth or trace the shape of her lower lip.

Marla groaned and stirred restlessly beneath his questing hands. They were both wearing too many clothes. Her hands tugged at his shirt in frustration. He arched his back and let her push it over his shoulders and down his arms.

She went for his belt buckle next, and she heard his smothered laugh against her neck as she fumbled eagerly at it. She gave it a vicious tug.

"Ow!" he howled.

"Sorry," she muttered, tugging more gently.

"All right, all right. *I'll* do it," he said hastily.

"I'll get it—just hold still."

He tried to hold still, but his hips kept moving involuntarily under her inefficient hands. Having succeeded at last with removing his belt, Marla yanked impatiently on his zipper.

He gasped. "Be gentle with me," he pleaded.

"That's my line." She yanked again and then looked at his moon-streaked face in exasperation. "What do you people at Ventura base your clothing designs on—chastity belts?"

"Marla, I can't stand much more of this," he said significantly, his voice strained with laughter and mounting passion. "Put one hand here, the other one there. Good. Stop shaking."

"I can't help it."

His hot, tongue-thrusting kiss didn't help any. "Now pull. *Very* gently," he added between clenched teeth.

She did. "Oh, my," she said a moment later.

She pulled his pants down his hips and let him kick them off impatiently along with his shoes and underwear while she watched with mute fascination. She resisted his effort to pull her down into the pillows. Full of admiration and awe for this magnificent male creature, Marla stroked one palm slowly up his tense, well-muscled thigh.

His legs were long and beautifully contoured, tanned and lightly covered with dark hair. His chest, pumping in and out with his excited breath, was sculpted like a Michelangelo masterpiece. The dark, curly hair covering it trickled in a thin line down his flat stomach, over his hard abdomen to his groin.

"Oh, my," she said again. If she didn't trust him so much, she might have been a little afraid.

"Come here," he insisted. He reached out and drew her to him.

His arms were around her, and she could feel him stroking her body with urgent hands, searching for the fastenings on her clothes. He tugged impatiently at her skirt.

"How does it come off?" he demanded.

"The buttons..." She sighed incoherently and closed her eyes, loving the feel of his lips on her neck.

"Where are they?" he growled.

"On the side. Here, I'll—"

"Oh, no. You tortured me, now it's my turn."

He pushed her underneath him and then rose to his knees above her. She lay back in the pillows feeling wonderfully womanly and sexy. The moonlight flowed over his shoulders, obscuring his expression but making his hair and skin glow. He rubbed her abdomen gently with a firm palm, teasing her with a subtle massage as he explored lower and lower. She lay pliant and willing, watching him with enraptured eyes. He slid his hand down and gently cupped her feminine mound.

Marla gasped and reached for him. Her seeking hand fell across his thigh, and she clutched him, squeezing her eyes shut. Brent stopped his teasing and followed the waistband of her skirt around to her right side, where he found the fastenings and undid them with careless disregard for the material. Marla heard something rip but didn't care. He tugged the skirt off her hips, lifting the lower half of her body as easily as if she were a rag doll.

He pulled off her panty house, panties and shoes, smoothing his hands down her thighs, murmuring words she had longed to hear, telling her how beautiful he found her. Then his hands were moving over her blouse, seeking the fastenings.

"Just pull it over my head," she whispered with difficulty.

"Where do you find these ridiculous clothes?" He eased her to a kneeling position and pulled her blouse over her head before she could respond. Then his arms slid around her, and a moment later he tossed her bra over his shoulder.

"Just come naked next time," Brent whispered.

"You, too," she murmured. She rose up higher on her knees and slid into his embrace.

Every sensation was rich and stunning. She could feel the hard muscles of his chest and the rough hair tickling her as she pressed her breasts against him. She sighed at the way his smooth arms felt against her naked back, at the way their bare legs felt as they pushed and brushed against each other, trying to get closer.

They exchanged long, drugging kisses, lips rubbing moistly, tongues dueling and caressing, hands stroking and exploring. Marla had never wanted a man this much, had never needed anyone this desperately or shared this uninhibitedly. She buried her face against his neck and nuzzled him, concentrating on how good his touch felt to every cell in her body.

He hugged her tightly for a moment, a mixture of affection and ardor, then she felt the smooth bulge of his muscles an instant before he lifted her and lowered his head to her breasts.

Her back arched and her hand came up to tunnel into his hair and pull his head even closer. She could no more have tamed her eager response than she could have stopped breathing.

He nuzzled her breasts gently, touching them with one hand as his other arm supported her, caressing them with his lips. She could feel his fingers probing and exploring, shaping and smoothing, teasing and soothing. He kissed a tender, aching nipple. Marla reacted uncontrollably, pulling his hair and pushing herself closer. She heard incoherent sounds of pleasure and realized vaguely they were coming from her own throat.

She felt his faint smile against her skin. Then she felt his tongue on her nipple, hot and wet, agile and velvety. He licked lazily, again and again, and then tasted the other one, as slowly and thoroughly as if he had all eternity to explore her body. Marla's breath was coming in harsh gusts, hurting her lungs, pushing her breasts up and down provocatively.

He stilled one creamy breast in his palm and brought his mouth to the nipple again. Marla went suddenly still, too consumed by pleasure to move restlessly anymore, though she could feel sobs of delight tear through her throat to emerge as hoarse groans.

He nibbled and licked and sucked, making her quiver and beg incoherently. Pleasure scorched her senses, and she dug her nails into his back, tugged on his hair, pleaded shamelessly with him. She writhed against him, still held prisoner by his arms as he brought his mouth up to hers and they kissed wildly. Her shifting thighs felt his hot, hard manhood, and she pressed ruthlessly against him, rubbing and tormenting. The next thing she knew, the world had tipped over and she was on her back, lying beneath him, and his strong hands were under her hips, squeezing her soft bottom and lifting her to him.

"Marla," he whispered.

"Yes, yes." She stroked her hands up and down his sides, urging him not to hesitate.

Brent took a steadying breath. He pushed her thighs apart and slid his narrow hips between them with predatory grace. She could feel him at the hot entrance to her body, and her moan was one of pure exultation.

He was gentle, as she had known he would be, but his power and his size were still a shock to her body. He thrust once, and Marla gasped in mingled pleasure and pain.

"Marla?" he whispered again, his ragged voice laced with concern.

She made a small, inarticulate sound to reassure him. His hand touched hers. Their fingers interlaced for a moment, and then she let him guide her hand down to where their bodies joined.

"Help me," he murmured, his lips hovering over her mouth.

She nodded, her blood roaring through her ears, her whole body strung taut with anticipation. Almost, she thought, they were almost one.

She guided him by instinct, and he pushed gently again. She took a deep breath and opened her eyes. His face was only inches from her own, looking down at her with mingled tenderness and raw desire. They whispered to each other, frank and unashamed. She could feel her body tingling with impatience, and she lifted her hips tentatively against him. He trembled.

She did it again, and this time she urged him with her hands. He thrust again, without gentleness now, and she didn't ask for any. And then she felt him deep inside her, hot, hard, welcome, spreading delight through her, pushing her closer and closer to the edge of sanity.

He stroked her thigh. She responded and wrapped her legs around his hips. He arched his back and clasped her tightly to him, moving against her, in and out, in nature's pulsing, erotic rhythm. She heard his harsh breath, saw the sheen of moonlight around his head, felt every inch of her body stimulated by his hot skin.

Their hips glided together and apart, faster and faster. She could feel the fullness, the pressure, the growing tension, the almost-pain of his unleashed strength inside her, and she called his name, sobbing as she caught fire beneath his moving body and burst into flames.

"Brent, oh, *Brent*." Her head thrashed on the pillow, and she cried out as pleasure burned every nerve ending to cinders, showered her with sparks, exploded inside her and engulfed her in its inferno.

And then she felt his powerful body stiffen on one final, forceful thrust before he sank against her, trembling and groaning.

She felt his arms tighten around her, and she clung to him until long after the bonfire had died to smoldering embers. And she knew that from now on he would be able to ignite those embers within her at will.

Chapter Nine

It took Brent a long time to pull his senses together enough to push himself to Marla's side and relieve her of his weight. She lay still as he shifted, with her eyes closed, her lovely face flushed with pleasure and a contented smile curving her full mouth. He leaned over and kissed her tenderly.

"Mmm," she said on a sigh. "I don't think you've forgotten *anything*."

"You reminded me pretty well," he murmured. He put a hand on her waist, and she rolled toward him, nestling in his embrace. He buried his face in her silky hair, aware that he was shaky and trembling in the aftermath.

He lay still, savoring the feel of her warm body pressed against him, savoring the sweetness of their intimacy. Tonight had confirmed what he had believed for all those lonely months before Marla had entered his life. Having sex wasn't enough for him. It had to be making love, like this, like now. He had been waiting for her.

Now he knew why her previous rejections had hurt him all out of proportion to the apparent situation. Some part of him had known how deeply they would sink inside each other when they finally joined.

Marla sighed again. She turned her head, pulling her hair out from under his cheek, and sought his mouth for a quick kiss. They smiled at each other with half-closed eyes.

"I have to ask," Brent said at last. "Why tonight?"

She rested her head against his shoulder. It was a fair question. "Because after the way we argued the other day, and after the way I felt when I saw you today, I knew I was all tangled up with you despite my best intentions. Since we were acting like quarreling lovers anyhow, I wanted us to really *be* lovers."

"We were getting all of the sting and none of the honey," he said wryly.

"Exactly." She rubbed a hand across his chest. "It was my fault—"

He covered her hand with his own. "No blaming. It's done now."

"Yes." She had known from the moment she made her decision to make love with him that he wouldn't gloat or admonish her.

"Now what?" he asked. "I suppose you still want to keep this a secret."

She raised her head to meet his eyes. "We have to. I may have redeemed myself at the agency, but that doesn't change company policy. I could still be in hot water for this."

He frowned. "I know that other people have done this, Marla. There's that woman who owns one of the big agencies in New York. She even married her own client."

"She *owns* the agency, Brent. She can do whatever she wants. I'm still quite a few years away from anything like that."

"But there are others," he protested.

"Have you been reading up on this or something?"

"I asked Nigel about it."

Marla sat bolt upright and looked down at him. "You *asked* Nigel? So much for keeping it secret."

Brent folded his hands behind his head and studied her naked body with bold appreciation. "Nigel already knew, Marla. He noticed the way I was looking at you even before I realized I was doing it."

Marla looked uneasy. "Who else knows?"

He shrugged. "Felice, I'm sure. Maybe a few others. I'm not very good at hiding my feelings."

"I've noticed," she agreed wryly.

"Look, I thought it was *your* colleagues who weren't supposed to know," he said.

"It is, but if everyone on your staff knows I'm sleeping with you, it's likely to get back to the agency sooner or later."

"Not *everyone*—"

"Besides, it can't do my credibility any good at Ventura."

"Why not?" He looked puzzled.

"Oh, Brent," she said with mingled affection and exasperation. She let him pull her back down into the pillows so they lay face-to-face.

"You didn't get the job because we were sleeping together," he said. "You didn't even get the job because I wanted to sleep with you." He paused for a moment. "At least, I don't think that's why I hired you. I'm just not sure anymore. And you proved today that you're not keeping the job because of how I feel about you personally. So why should this affect your professional credibility?"

"Look, *you* know that and *I* know that—"

"And that's all that counts as far as I'm concerned. Anyhow, my company isn't full of jealous, back-stabbing vultures. I think anyone who either knows or figures it out will be happy for me and will realize you must be pretty special for me to be so crazy about you."

She couldn't help smiling, even though she suspected his assessment of the situation was naive and overly optimistic.

Brent wasn't fooled by her fond smile. He suspected that her negative experiences had clouded her views of human nature; she was always prepared for adversity rather than moral support. He also suspected that there were a number of experiences, besides those she had already described to him, that had shaped her that way.

He was about to pursue the subject when she kissed him with warm intent, gently kneading the muscles of his back while her tongue brushed his lips with tantalizing delicacy.

Every cell in his body responded. Desire shimmered through him as furiously as if they hadn't just made love twenty minutes ago.

"I'm not a kid, Marla," he said sternly.

"Oh?" She squirmed when he stroked her thighs.

"I'm thirty-eight years old, and there are just some things that take—"

"Uh-huh." She laughed softly as she felt his body stir with arousal. "Not bad. Must be all that outdoor exercise you get."

"Must be," he muttered, shuddering as his hands traveled over her slim, willing body.

They made love again with slow, lingering enjoyment, giving and taking without reserve, tasting the full delight of being together at last. Afterward, they fell into a deep, dreamless slumber, wrapped in each other's arms.

"Hey, wake up," Brent whispered the following morning.

Climbing from the depths of the most peaceful sleep she had enjoyed in longer than she could remember, Marla rolled toward the source of delicious warmth lying a few inches away. She bumped into a hard, hairy chest. She opened her eyes and blinked sleepily.

"Good morning," Brent said. He kissed Marla softly on the mouth, and memories of their night together came rushing into her consciousness in bold, vivid detail.

She smiled and rubbed her cheek against the smooth arm beneath her head. "It's still dark out."

"It's just before dawn. We forgot dinner last night. Are you hungry?"

"I'm not sure," she mumbled. "It takes a while for my responses to kick in."

"Really?" He touched her with knowing hands.

Marla drew in a sharp breath, and her eyes flew open. "Oh, that's nice."

"You were saying?" he teased.

"You jump-started that response," she chided lazily.

"Well, I'm starved. I'll shower first and then make breakfast while you get ready. Okay?"

"Mmm."

He woke her again a few minutes later, glistening wet from his shower. He looked so gorgeous she let him envelop her in a sodden embrace. When she took her own shower, she was pleased to note that his bathroom was a lot cleaner and more orderly than most men's. A half hour later she had finished dressing and was toweling her hair dry when the delicious aromas coming from the kitchen made her realize she was as hungry as Brent. She put down her towel and went in search of food.

"Wow! You don't take breakfast lightly, do you?" she said in astonishment.

Brent turned away from the stove and grinned at her. "You've got to eat serious food at breakfast if you want to climb mountains and surf and swim and kayak."

The table was covered with a tempting and daunting selection of juice, coffee, milk, cereal, muffins, eggs, fruit and yogurt. Brent finished frying some sausage and bacon and put a huge portion of each on his and Marla's plates.

"Since I'm sitting at a desk instead of climbing Mount Cuyamaca today, I think I'd better stick to toast and coffee," she said.

"There are other strenuous physical activities besides sports," he reminded her with a gleam in his eye. "Eat up."

The eggs looked fluffy and the bacon looked crispy. It all smelled divine. "Well . . . maybe just a bite or two."

She didn't wind up eating as much as Brent, but she certainly did justice to his excellent cooking. "A few more meals like that and I'll go up a dress size," she said ruefully as she pushed her plate away.

"Honey, I like a woman who likes her food," he said in a broad Montana accent.

"You won't like it so well when my hips expand to fill the doorway."

He grinned. "We'll find some way to burn off those calories." His eyes glittered like emeralds, and he added softly, "I usually exercise in the mornings, but maybe we could..." He rolled his eyes toward the bedroom.

"I'd love to," she admitted, "but I've got to go home. I can't wear these clothes to work. You ripped my skirt and my blouse looks like we used it to dust the furniture."

"Sorry about that." Then he looked smug. "*My* clothes held up all right."

"That's because I'm gentler than you." She rose reluctantly to her feet. "I'd better get going."

He walked her to the door. By the time Marla finally left, she figured they might as well have gone to the bedroom and made love again for all the time they spent kissing and cuddling and whispering at the door. A rush of pure happiness flooded her when she settled into the driver's seat of her car.

Although Brent had woken her an hour and a half before her normal rising time, her trip to her apartment in Pacific Beach made her late for work. Luckily there was no pressure on her that day, although Warren sneered at her when he saw her arrive late.

In one sense the day seemed interminable, since she kept looking at the clock and counting the hours until Brent would meet her at her apartment that evening. On the other hand, she felt so buoyantly happy that her daily tasks flowed by, and even some of the more tedious paperwork couldn't dampen her spirits.

Everyone seemed to notice the change in her that day. She laughed easily and smiled more times in one day than she had in the whole previous month. Vernon commented on her carefree state of mind. Since she had no intention of telling anyone, even colleagues she trusted, how personal her relationship with Brent Ventura had become, she simply insisted that her mood was the result of yesterday's successful presentation.

Vernon clearly didn't believe her, but he was too miserably sick and congested to argue. He finally took her advice and went home at noon to recuperate.

Marla and Brent had vaguely planned a romantic evening together, a quiet dinner in some out-of-the-way candlelit restaurant with an ocean view. However, as soon as she showed him into her simple, modern apartment in Pacific Beach, they wound up tumbling urgently into bed together and raiding the refrigerator afterward so they wouldn't have to bother getting dressed again.

"We'll go somewhere nice tomorrow night," Brent assured her.

"Promises, promises," she said, sitting curled up on his lap in her living room while they ate cold chicken and left-over pizza.

The following night wound up being as torrid as the previous two nights. It wasn't actually until the weekend that they finally got around to going out for the evening.

Considering how much food Marla consumed around him, she decided to cooperate wholeheartedly when Brent insisted they had to find a sport they both enjoyed.

"After Katie made it clear to me that she hated climbing," Brent explained, "I took up sailing so we could do that together."

"But didn't you both like kayaking already?" Marla asked, leaning against him on his terrace as they watched the sun set over Windansea Beach.

"We liked it, but not together," he said wryly. "She was so much faster at it than I was that she felt I slowed her down. I, on the other hand, wanted to strangle her the whole time for not taking proper precautions. Out of respect for our marriage, we wound up agreeing not to go kayaking with each other."

"Well, I definitely don't want to race down white-water rapids or dangle over gorges," Marla said emphatically.

"Sailing was important in my marriage. It helped bind us together." He squeezed Marla's shoulders with one arm. "We'll find things we like to do together. Besides this, I mean," he added, and kissed her briefly.

The calm certainty in his voice sent a small flicker of unease through Marla. She certainly wanted to make the most of this relationship while it lasted, but she didn't want Brent to mistake their love affair for something permanent.

Marla never felt that Brent wanted her to be like Katie, or even that Katie overshadowed their relationship. He seemed to have comfortably reconciled his life with Katie as being irrevocably part of the past. He spoke of her with fond remembrance rather than with longing. Those had obviously been happy years for Brent, and since he mentioned Katie's name infrequently—and usually only when Marla invited the subject—she would have to be both petulant and insensitive to object.

However, there was one big difference between Katie and herself that she was afraid Brent didn't fully grasp. Katie had apparently decided to marry him within days of meeting him and had cheerfully uprooted and overturned her entire life to be with him.

Marla wasn't made that way. She had built her whole life around being autonomous, independent and completely self-sufficient, and she regarded even being Brent's lover as a dangerous compromise of her principles. By sleeping with him, she was risking her professional stability and financial security.

But Brent's comments, with increasing frequency, were forcing Marla to realize that he was prepared to make changes in his life for her, just as he had made changes in his life for Katie. And he clearly assumed—so inherently that he hadn't even brought it up for discussion—that Marla was prepared to make changes in her life for him.

She shivered, sadly aware that she had just identified the basic character differences that would eventually end her blissful relationship with this extraordinary man. If only things could have been different.

"Cold?" he murmured, feeling her shiver against him.

"No. Yes." She hid her face against his sturdy shoulder and said, "Hold me."

It was a request she had made often since their first night together, but Marla's desolate tone surprised Brent. He tried to question her, but she pressed her warm, eager lips against his with such fervent passion that all other thoughts were swept away by the sudden flood of his desire.

As he scooped her up into his arms and carried her inside his house, he wondered vaguely why making love only seemed to intensify his need for her rather than slake it. Every time he wanted her, he felt it more deeply and more urgently than the time before. And every loving was, incredibly, even better than the last time.

He smiled slightly against her lips, feeling her fumble at his clothes as he lowered her onto the couch in his living room.

"We didn't even make it to the bedroom this time," he whispered, tugging her shirt over her head.

Her answer was incoherent but emphatic.

The days that followed were so full of joy and adventure that Marla pushed her forebodings aside with firm resolve. She'd be happy until she no longer could, she decided.

She took Brent to all her favorite places: the Museum of Man, the San Diego Museum of Art, the Organ Pavilion in Balboa Park, the Embarcadero and San Diego's Old Town. When she took him to an excellent production of *Much Ado About Nothing* at San Diego's famous Old Globe Theatre, she was scandalized to learn he hadn't been to a play in nearly fifteen years.

"How can you be such a heathen?" she exclaimed. Then she added virtuously, "*I* have season tickets."

"The play was pretty good," he conceded mildly. "You could even talk me into coming again if you'd get that self-righteous look off your face."

When it was Brent's turn to decide what they would do together, it was always something exhausting. And intimidating.

"Surfing?" she croaked one weekend morning when he cheerfully told her how they would spend the day.

"You loved the surf simulator," he said coaxingly.

"That's because I knew I couldn't get hurt."

"I won't let you get hurt out there, either." He waved vaguely toward the Pacific Ocean and voiced his statement with the air of one delivering an obvious, self-evident fact.

Marla didn't even choke on her coffee, having grown accustomed to his naive belief that the world was a safe and friendly place if you just took a few basic precautions.

She resignedly donned her Ventura swimming gear—she was acquiring quite a large stock of free Ventura clothing—and followed him down to the beach. They spent the day paddling around the ocean while Brent patiently explained and demonstrated the basic techniques of surfing, then urged her to try.

She found that, contrary to her trepidation and expectations, she enjoyed it so much she was reluctant to paddle back into shore when Brent decided she had done enough for one day. She also learned that he was serious about safety and sensible precautions. For the first time since meeting him, she started to believe he would come to no harm while pursuing the dangerous sports he favored.

Inevitably, tension began to creep into their relationship the following week. Marla didn't exactly come down from the fluffy pink cloud she was living on; she had a feeling that Brent would influence her that way for as long as they stayed together. But it wasn't in her nature to ignore the real problems of daily living.

That week Marla visited the Ventura offices for the first time since becoming Brent's lover, and she discovered he was just as incapable of subterfuge as she had feared. He remembered not to kiss her when she showed up, but as she was studying some papers with Felice, he put his arm around her when he asked if she wanted more coffee. Then he was gone before she could tell him, by her expression, that his behavior was compromising her.

A half hour later, she said something that made both him and Nigel laugh, and Brent stroked her hair in an absent caress as he teased Nigel. The unconscious casualness of the gesture made it clear how accustomed Brent had become to touching her. She saw by the look in Nigel's eyes that he had noticed and was not surprised. In fact, the private smile he exchanged with her supported Brent's continual insistence that Nigel was happy for them and didn't feel less professional respect for Marla because of their romantic involvement.

Nevertheless, she brought the subject up with Brent as soon as they were alone that evening.

"What did I do?" he asked innocently.

She explained her objections.

"You're upset because I touched you?" he asked, looking hurt.

"Because you touched me familiarly at work, in front of your colleagues," she corrected.

He prowled restlessly around his living room while she sat watching him. "I didn't even realize it," he said at last. "It just seems unnatural *not* to touch you now. I'd have to be thinking every moment you were at the company, 'Don't touch Marla. Don't touch Marla.' I can't do that."

"*You're* the one who kept insisting you weren't going to compromise my job if I got involved with you."

He plopped down next to her and searched her face with worried eyes. "Did I compromise your job today?"

"No," she admitted. "But if anyone from the agency had seen us together, they would have suspicions about us now."

"'Have suspicions'?" he repeated. "I hate this! We're two healthy, unattached, independent adults, yet you're talking like we have to hide the way we feel about each other from the whole world, as if we were cheating on our spouses and meeting on the sly."

"Now you're exaggerating. I'm just asking you to exercise a little discretion at work. That can't be so much to ask."

In the end, he agreed he would try harder. Marla let it go at that and changed the subject, since he obviously felt bad about upsetting her but still didn't accept her reasoning.

Later in the week, he inadvertently let the cat out of the bag in front of his entire staff.

Marla showed up at Ventura on Friday to discuss business with Brent, Nigel and Felice. It was a beautiful day, and they were all tired from a busy week. Since it quickly became apparent that none of them really had their minds on the discussion, Nigel proposed a rousing game of volleyball. Felice found some shorts and a T-shirt for Marla to wear, and they led a company exodus out to the volleyball net on the beach.

After the second match, Nigel called a conference.

"We've got to change the teams a bit," he explained to Brent.

"Why?"

Nigel grabbed Marla and started dragging her to his side of the net. "I only let you have her on your team because I didn't think she knew how to play."

"I was captain of my high school volleyball team," Marla said smugly, shaking sand out of her hair.

"And now that we've clobbered you twice in a row, you want her on your team?" Brent said. "Forget it!"

He grabbed Marla's other arm, and the two men played tug-of-war with her while the raucous staff took sides. After a brief struggle, Brent, Marla, Nigel and a number of other people all fell down and rolled across the sand.

Brent was still laughing when he stood up. He hauled Marla to her feet, pulled her into his arms to brush the sand off, then kissed her soundly.

Marla had lost her inhibitions in the general atmosphere of hilarity, and for a moment she responded. She heard someone whistle at the same moment that she realized Brent was kissing her very familiarly in front of his entire staff.

The second Brent felt Marla go rigid in his arms and clamp her lips together, he realized he had just made a big mistake. He opened his eyes and searched her face as she pulled stiffly away from him. She wouldn't even look at him. Most of the staff were already arguing with Nigel about how to divide the teams, but Brent knew that Marla considered the damage done.

Marla joined Nigel's team on the other side of the net. The game that followed was as enthusiastic and unorthodox as the previous two matches, but Brent paid no attention. Marla didn't even look in his direction. She participated in the game without any of the high spirits she had shown before. As soon as it was over, she excused herself and deserted them.

Brent tossed the ball to the company accountant and followed her. As soon as he caught up with her and took her arm, she jerked away from him. Her gaze flashed up to his face. He had never seen her expression look so cold. It shook him to think she could look at him that way.

"Don't follow me—that only makes it worse," she said in a low, furious voice.

"Worse than what?" he demanded.

"Dammit, just go back to your staff. We'll discuss this later."

"No, let's discuss it now." He was getting a little angry himself. It had been an honest mistake, and it had only happened because he cared so much about her.

"Don't push me," she snapped.

She was walking fast, and they were nearing the Ventura buildings. He tried to sound calm, aware that she was about to erupt. "Look, let's go inside and—"

"Oh, that would look just great."

"I don't care how it would look!" He forgot his intention to stay calm. "I care more about settling an argument with you than I care about what my staff thinks of my personal life."

She stopped in her tracks, closed her eyes and appeared to be counting to ten. When she spoke again, he sensed the enormous effort it took her to sound reasonable. "This isn't an appropriate time to have a personal argument. I would rather we discuss this when we can be sure of not being interrupted."

"Let's go home, then."

"I don't think we should go home together."

Her tone sounded as if she were talking to a dull-witted child. He ground his teeth together and resisted the impulse to shake her. "I'll meet you there later. My house?"

"No," she said quickly. "I'll be at my apartment."

He watched her walk away, then went back to the volleyball game. His heart wasn't in it, and he was relieved when everyone decided to call it quits an hour later.

He had originally intended to rush right over to Marla's house after work but decided against it that evening, wanting to give them both time to cool off. He had a feeling that tonight could be the end of their relationship if he didn't handle it carefully.

He went home, showered, changed, read his mail and started his laundry. When he finally thought he'd given her enough time to recover her equilibrium, he got in his Jeep and drove to Pacific Beach.

For almost two weeks Marla's eyes had sparked with happiness every time they met. Brent felt chilled by the guarded expression on her face when she let him into her apartment that night.

He paced around as he always did in stressful moments. "I'm sorry. I don't have to tell you I didn't think first. It just happened."

"I know," she said wearily.

He looked at her sharply. "You must have more to say about it than that."

She shrugged. "It's been less than two weeks, and already your entire staff knows." She swallowed painfully. "How much longer before my superiors find out I'm sleeping with my client?"

"Do you have to make it sound so sordid?" He was stung by her tone. "I feel good about you, I feel good about us, and that's why I keep forgetting to hide it."

"I feel good about you, too," she said irritably, "but that doesn't alter my professional situation."

He gave an exasperated sigh. "Then maybe you should change your professional situation."

She shot out of her chair like a bullet and confronted him. "I knew it! As soon as push comes to shove, you want me to give up *my* job and *my* security for *you*. How the hell am I supposed to make a living if I let my career depend on every man who waltzes into my life?"

He stared at her in shocked silence, stunned by the vehemence of her outburst. He had never seen her look so hostile. After a moment, the astonished look on his face penetrated her anger, and she sank back into her chair in a defeated slump.

"I'm sorry, Brent. I . . . um . . ."

He sat down, too, trying to think of what to say. He groped for some means of reassuring her. "I didn't mean you should throw your whole life overboard for me, Marla. I just meant that now that I've spilled the beans in front of my staff, for which I'm very sorry, maybe we should consider other options besides keeping our relationship a big secret."

She heard the word "we" and realized she had misjudged him again. He still expected their adjustments to each other to be mutual, rather than a lot of sacrifice on her part and a lot of complacency on his.

Feeling drained by the anger and panic she had been battling for the past few hours, Marla said tiredly, "There are no other options for me, Brent."

"Of course there are," he said calmly, trying not to sound pedantic.

"You don't understand," she said brokenly.

He realized with another sensation of shock that she was trying not to cry. He had never seen her close to tears before, and her vulnerability brought all his protective instincts to the fore. He forgot their argument. He forgot his own hurt and confusion, and he went to her, wanting to comfort her, needing to be needed.

Marla felt Brent's warmth near her a second before his strong arms slid around her and picked her up. He sat down with her in his lap and she drew in deep gulps of air, fighting tears, shocked that she was once again so close to crying because of Brent, after years and years of never letting her emotions get the best of her. How could knowing him make her so happy *and* so miserable? How could he be the source of her pain at the same time that he provided all her comfort?

The mysteries of her heart suddenly seemed too exhausting and overwhelming to deal with, and she clung to him gratefully. He stroked and petted her, smoothed her hair, kissed her brow and murmured soft, soothing words. He rocked her gently, comforting her as no one ever had.

She took an enormous step then, knowing he probably didn't even realize it. She let herself drift off to sleep, trusting him to undress her and tuck her in, turn out the lights and lock up the apartment. It was the first time since she was very young that she had willingly surrendered control of her life to someone else, even for a few hours.

Brent put Marla to bed, closed up the apartment, then sat brooding in the dark for a long time. He had thought they were growing closer. Now he realized with a feeling of self-exasperation that he had taken advantage of Marla's being such a good listener to pour out all the thoughts and feelings he had been keeping inside for such a long time. She, on the other hand, had revealed relatively little about herself during the past two weeks.

He didn't know anything about her childhood or family. He didn't know if she had ever been in love or felt betrayed. He had yet to learn what she wanted out of life besides the career that obviously meant so much to her.

Katie had been easy to get to know. Before her, he had never been concerned about intimately understanding any of the women he had known. He realized that he would have to learn to be more exacting with Marla or she would keep evading him. He knew better than to think he could extract information from her subtly, particularly not when she was obviously unaccustomed to sharing herself in that way. He would have to simply start asking her about herself, straightforwardly and directly. And he wouldn't let her get away with vague and evasive answers, either.

Chapter Ten

When Marla awoke the next morning, the first thing she saw was Brent, lying on his side next to her and studying her with troubled green eyes. She remembered her outburst of the night before and closed her eyes again, wishing she could call back those angry, accusing, revealing words.

"Are you okay?" he whispered.

"Yes," she said. She tried to smile reassuringly. She could tell by his expression that it was a failed attempt. "Don't worry. I'm not going to start ranting at you again."

"I don't mind ranting, as long as I know what's behind it," he said candidly. "What was last night really about?"

Marla sat up and slid out of bed. "If I know you, you're probably starved. I'll see what's in the fridge." She slipped on her robe and hurried out of the bedroom.

Brent sighed. He folded his hands behind his head and stared at the ceiling. Last night was the first time they had slept together without making love. It made him feel closer to her, as if their relationship still included but had now transcended their sexual chemistry. This was also the first morning she had jumped out of bed as if she were afraid he would bite her.

"Well, I knew it wouldn't be easy," he muttered. He got out of bed and headed for the shower.

Marla wasn't a chatterer, but she certainly knew how to steer a conversation. As they picked at the huge breakfast she had cooked for him, she made sure he didn't find another obvious opportunity to ask probing questions.

He waited until after they were dressed and had washed the breakfast dishes to confront her about their most immediate problem. "How do you want to handle what happened yesterday at the company?"

She frowned, avoiding his eyes. "If anyone asks, just say you got carried away in the heat of the moment. Don't admit to anything more serious."

"How long," he said carefully, "do you expect to keep up this illusion that we're not together?"

She looked at him in genuine surprise. "Until it's over."

He stared at her, feeling betrayed and hurt. His voice sounded strange to his own ears when he said, "It's barely begun between us and you're already thinking about it ending?"

"No, of course not," she said quickly, immediately picking up on his reaction to her statement.

He spread his hands wide, wordlessly asking her to explain.

"Well Brent..." She shrugged, trying to find a tactful way to phrase it. "I mean, nothing lasts forever, does it? Sooner or later we'll have one fight too many, or you'll lose interest, or..." She shrugged again, aware that her awkward speech wasn't producing a look of reasonable agreement in his expression.

"Or *you'll* lose interest. Is that what you're saying?" he demanded, trying to keep his voice even.

"No, not at all. I mean... people just grow apart, relationships end. These things are natural and to be expected.... My God, I sound like some hackneyed Hollywood divorcée." She gave him a weak smile, trying to quell the storm she sensed was brewing between them. "How can you make me resort to such clichés?" she joked feebly.

He folded his arms across his chest and scowled at her. "I freely admit that I don't know much about the theater, and I hadn't been to an art museum since high school before you took me to one, and I definitely don't share your passionate commitment to the business world—"

"Brent, I don't—"

"But I think I'm not entirely lacking in worthwhile qualities, Marla, and I had the impression that you thought so, too."

"I do!"

"No." He shook his head vigorously. "I know you think you're risking a lot by sleeping with me, but you haven't really ventured anything yet that's hard to lose." His voice roughened when he continued, "I know, because I once lost a hell of a lot."

She shook her head, mutely denying the accusation she could hear in his voice. Of *course* she was risking a lot.

His scowl deepened. "As much as I've cared about you, I don't think I would have gotten involved with you if I had known you were already looking for the end of it when we started."

"Will you please—"

"That's why you don't make any effort to open up to me."

"Yes, I do!" She was stung by his assertion.

"Oh, Marla." He looked at her almost pityingly. "No wonder you care more about my business than about me. You don't want anything really worthwhile from me."

She felt as if he had slugged her in the chest. She strained to breathe. Her throat burned. "Yes, I do." Her voice was a hoarse whisper.

"Like what?" he challenged.

"You . . . I, uh . . ." She grunted incoherently and looked at her feet.

He sighed. "I'm going home."

Her eyes flashed up to his face. "You're walking out because I can't describe what I want from this relationship in twenty-five words or less?" she accused.

"I'm not walking out on you. I'm going home for a while. I need to think." There was no mistaking the exasperation in his voice.

"Oh."

He looked at her peculiarly. "You always expect me to leave you holding the bag, don't you?"

She made a feeble sound of denial. His green eyes narrowed. She looked away, flushing.

"Why is that, Marla?" he persisted.

"You're exaggerating again," she said dismissively.

"Am I?"

She didn't respond.

After a heavy silence, he came over to where she stood in a hunched, defensive posture. "We've both got a lot to think about," he said quietly. "I'll talk to you in a day or two."

She nodded. Then she felt him rest one hand on her shoulder. His breath brushed her hair a moment before he gently kissed her forehead. She thought she would shatter. She looked up at him with pleading eyes. His face softened for a moment, but he left anyhow.

The fact that he could kiss her after the things they had said to each other during the past twenty-four hours was the only thing that kept Marla from falling apart. During the rest of her haunted, desolate weekend alone, she recalled that brief but tender touch of his lips against her brow every time she felt misery welling up to unbearable proportions inside her.

She tried to reach him twice on Sunday, but he wasn't in. She felt resentful after the second try and resolved not to call him again. He was probably off playing at something, as if that were a reasonable solution to life's serious problems.

Monday was a stressful day at work, primarily because she was being included in a number of meetings now that she was back in favor. Her cheeks ached by midafternoon from the effort of maintaining her polite social smile.

It was even an effort to listen to Nathan's latest ideas for the Ventura ads. Yvonne had gone against his express wishes and informed his parents that he was in jail two days after his arrest. They had bailed him out and—he claimed—nearly made his fillings fall out of his mouth with the sheer volume of their criticism.

He got his revenge on Yvonne in what Marla considered a particularly underhanded manner.

"What is that noise?" Marla demanded irritably, stalking out of her office late that afternoon. Her gaze lighted on the psychedelic pop art radio on Yvonne's desk. Gloria Estefan was loudly urging some boy to say he loved her seven times. "Oh, no," Marla groaned.

Yvonne looked at her with a martyred expression. "Nathan gave it to me."

"Figures," Marla muttered. "What do you see in that man?"

Yvonne shrugged, then looked doubtfully at the radio. "I know it's wrong to give away a gift, but..."

Marla stared at the obnoxious little radio. The impulse that seized her was crazy, but she gave in to it. What an ice-breaker that little radio was. "I'll take it off your hands." She scooped it off Yvonne's desk and cradled it in her arms.

Yvonne stared at her as if she were indeed crazy. "Are you sure?"

"Yes." Marla carried the radio into her office.

Yvonne followed her. "You know, you've been acting awfully strange lately."

"Strange how?" Marla asked sharply.

"Oh, more emotional."

"Oh." Marla frowned. "Sorry."

"I didn't mean it to sound critical," Yvonne said quickly. "You've been here three years. It's good to see you loosen up a little, laugh now and then, get mad at people."

Marla put down the radio and stared at Yvonne. "Did you think I was uptight before?"

"No, not you. Always cool as a cucumber. It's just good to see the real you, if you know what I mean."

"Mmm." Marla sat down and stared out the window for a few minutes after Yvonne left the room. She had always thought she *was* acting like "the real her" all those years. She regarded her behavior since meeting Brent as an unusual, and usually unfortunate, aberration. It was disturbing to realize that her colleagues were fully conscious of a change in her manner, and even more disturbing to realize some of them considered her recent erratic moods more genuine than her accustomed behavior.

And all of it was unsettling in light of Brent's accusations that she didn't open up to him and had never intended to share anything worthwhile with him.

She had to see him. She didn't care how they settled their recent fight or even *if* they settled it right away. She was just too lonely for him to cut off her nose to spite her face tonight.

"Good Lord, that sounds like something Nigel would say," she muttered. The phone rang. She picked it up. It was Brent.

"I was just going to call you," she admitted candidly.

"Really?" He sounded wary.

"Uh-huh." She glanced at the radio. "I have a present for you. A peace offering."

"We're not at war, Marla."

"All the same..."

"What is it?"

"It's a surprise."

"When can I have it?"

She could hear the smile in his voice. "Tonight. My place."

"I've missed you," he said huskily.

"Me, too."

They were silent for a moment, savoring each other's presence across miles of telephone cable. Finally he said, "What's that racket in the background?"

"I don't hear anything. Must be a bad connection," she said innocently.

"What have you got there?" He sounded suspicious.

"You'll find out tonight," she said mysteriously. "Come alone."

"I wasn't planning on bringing the volleyball team," he said dryly.

If she was resigned to losing Brent eventually, in the natural course of events, she was a least comforted to know he obviously didn't want it to end tonight any more than she did. With that thought lending her courage, she went home after work and prepared a nice dinner for him.

She heard the doorbell chime at seven o'clock and dropped what she was doing to answer it. He looked wonderful, standing there in the light of the dying sun, smiling faintly. He looked as strong as an oak tree, but deep in his eyes she could see a hint of the vulnerability that made him so endearing.

"What's that?" she asked, nodding at the box he carried under his arm.

"Well...I don't believe in killing flowers just for a romantic gesture, and I didn't think you'd appreciate chocolate since you keep worrying about eating so much when I'm with you, so—" he opened the box and showed her the contents "—I brought you some hiking boots."

Marla laughed. "Oh, Brent." She slid her arms around his neck and hugged him in a natural, comfortable embrace. He participated enthusiastically.

"Come inside," she urged after a few moments.

"So where's my present?" he demanded.

"You're worse than a kid," she chided. She handed him the hideous, colorful abstract radio and chuckled at his look of consternation.

"How do you turn it off?" he asked immediately. Whitesnake was crooning about love and desire. Brent grimaced at the loudness of the music.

"I'm not sure," Marla said. "It'll give you something to strive for."

"*This* is my peace offering?" He looked crestfallen. "I want my boots back."

"Too late."

They smiled at each other again. He put down the radio. "Come here," he murmured. His kiss was thorough and lingering. "Something smells great. Am I invited for dinner?"

"And for whatever you want to do after dinner."

"So I'm not in the doghouse?"

"Am I?"

He kissed her again, more urgently this time. She responded without reserve, hungry for him. She pressed her breasts against his hard chest, teased his lips with her tongue, ran her hands over his shoulders. His mouth slanted fiercely across hers, and his arms tightened ruthlessly around her waist, pulling her hips against him.

She could hear the quickening of his breath and feel the hardening of his body. She moaned and nuzzled his neck, inhaling his masculine smell and warmth. She felt his mouth move moistly down her cheek. He muttered something indistinct and traced hot kisses along her neck.

Liquid heat rushed through her. Her breasts ached for his touch. She quivered in his arms. A few days without him was lonelier than years without other people. She wanted him to touch every part of her, to heal every inch of her body and soul with his affection.

He buried his face in her hair. "At least we can always count on this." His wry voice was slightly hoarse with emotion.

"Mmm." Marla stood wrapped in his arms, hovering between hot passion and warm contentment. She rested her cheek against his chest and listened to the steady beat of his heart.

Brent finally loosened his hold and leaned back to look down into Marla's face. "I've been doing a lot of thinking," he said carefully. "And the bottom line for me is that I can't sleep with you, worry about you, care about you and work at getting to know you, all the while assuming we'll eventually split up. I'm not made that way."

"Is that an ultimatum?" Marla asked quietly.

"No. I just want you to know where I stand, and I want to know where you stand."

Marla glanced at the noisy radio, which was so incongruous in the midst of their discussion. "Brent, I appreciate what you're saying, but I can't rearrange my life for someone else. *I'm* not made that way."

"Define 'rearrange.'"

She took a breath. "I can't risk my security, stability or independence for you."

"Why?"

She gave him an exasperated look. "That's like asking me why I don't take every penny I have and bet it on one spin of a roulette wheel."

He released her and sat down on the couch, stretched out his legs and looked at her with a puzzled frown. "I'm not even remotely like a roulette wheel, Marla. I'm a thinking, feeling person who keeps making choices to be with you. I'm not some high-risk, irresponsible gamble."

"All relationships are a gamble."

"Don't you think some relationships have a good enough chance of succeeding that it makes sense to take a risk?" he pressed.

"I'm already risking my job—"

"I know, I know," he said tiredly. They had been over that argument so many times he couldn't bear to hear it again. He looked at her for another long moment, wishing he could understand what she was so afraid of. Finally he sighed and said, "I don't want you to risk everything in your life for me, but . . . Oh, let's let it go tonight. I didn't come over here to argue again. I just wanted to be with you."

She crossed the room and sat next to him. "I'm glad you came," she said softly. Her eyes were filled with tenderness and anticipation.

Brent's arms slid around her and pulled her closer. "Let's make love," he whispered. "Now."

"I'm afraid dinner's ready."

He sniffed the air. "Mmm." He looked back at her and grinned. "Decisions, decisions."

"Let's eat first," she said, laughing. "You'll need all your strength tonight."

"While you put supper on the table, I'm going to go put that radio out in the Jeep. It's driving me crazy."

They had a wonderful evening together, laughing over their dinner conversation and avoiding any further references to the conflicts Brent knew were still brewing between them. They cleaned up the kitchen and went to bed at a scandalously early hour, too eager to wait any longer.

Afterward, they rolled across the sheets together, touching and stroking each other's bodies with lazy delight. Marla's skin was flushed and damp with perspiration. Brent had made a messy tangle of her hair, and her lips were slightly swollen from his demanding kisses.

"You look so beautiful," he said with a sigh.

His frank, ingenuous comments always thrilled Marla more than the most practiced, elegant compliments she had ever heard. She smiled, basking in the open admiration of his gaze.

"I can't decide which part of your body I like best," he confessed drowsily.

Marla raised her slanted brows in silent query.

Brent lightly stroked one soft, roseate nipple. "You must have noticed I'm kind of partial to your breasts."

"I noticed," she murmured. They were still tingling.

"But I have to admit that your ankles drive me nuts."

"My ankles?" She laughed.

"I guess your thighs were the first thing I really noticed about you. Sexually, I mean."

Marla glanced down at the thighs she was certain had suffered from the outsize breakfasts she had been eating with Brent lately. "Is that good or bad?"

Brent grinned and ran his hands around and across her thighs in a smooth, teasing caress. His fingers slid into the dark tangle of hair between her legs. "But there are moments when this is my favorite part," he whispered.

With skilled, knowing hands, he demonstrated his appreciation of that portion of her anatomy. Marla moaned, becoming aroused all over again. Brent gently urged her onto her back so he could continue his delicate exploration more easily. Only the sound of the telephone cooled their play.

Brent glanced at her. "Do you have to get it?"

Marla tried to steady her breathing. "I should."

He sighed and rolled onto his back so she could reach past him for the phone. Marla sat up and tried to calm her senses while the phone rang three more times. As soon as she leaned across Brent to answer it, he discovered another favorite part of her body that he just had to taste.

Marla gasped and clapped a hand over the receiver before even saying hello. She tugged at Brent's hair, laughing and whispering incoherently at the same time. Finally she scolded, "Stop that. This could be one of my other boyfriends."

She gasped once more when he pinched her and then spoke into the receiver. "Hello?"

"Marla? Did I wake you, honey?"

As soon as Marla recognized her mother's voice, she sat bolt upright and scooted away from Brent. He looked at her curiously.

She mouthed silently, "It's my mother." Brent sat up quickly, too. Marla smirked at him. What was it about parents that made you suddenly develop a teenage sense of embarrassment again?

"Marla?" her mother prodded.

"Oh, sorry, Mom.... No, I was awake." She wondered why her mother was calling and then realized she had been so absorbed in her thoughts about Brent this weekend that she hadn't made her habitual Sunday night phone call home.

Brent was torn between giving Marla some privacy while she talked to her mother and openly listening to the conversation. Marla had never offered information about her family, and she had evaded his attempts to learn more. Since she didn't seem to mind his presence, he decided to stay where he was.

At first, the conversation seemed full of banalities. Brent could tell by Marla's friendly but vague answers about her work and her daily life that she wasn't accustomed to confiding in her mother. It was also obvious that Marla's mother didn't know about him. Brent hadn't told his own parents anything specific about Marla during their last phone call, but he had admitted he was seeing someone, knowing it would make them happy.

It was when Marla started asking her mother about her own life that the conversation became revealing.

"You got the check all right? ... Good," she said. There was a lengthy silence, then Marla said, "No, Mom. I'm not going to send her money. She's young and healthy, and her church provides excellent day-care services. She can go get a job if she needs more money."

Brent frowned, realizing for the first time that Marla was evidently not the only person who relied on her salary. He could tell by the expression on Marla's face that her mother was disagreeing with her. After a few more minutes, Marla gave an exasperated snort. "I'm not lucky, for Pete's sake. I worked my butt off for everything I've got. Don't—"

She lowered her head and listened again, apparently having been interrupted. A moment later she glanced up at

Brent. She must have noticed the intent look in his eyes, because she put her hand over the receiver and said, "You don't want to listen to family squabbles. Why don't you go see what's on TV?"

Brent wrestled with his conscience for a moment. Marla's suggestion was a blatant request for privacy, and she had every right to make it. Finally he said, "I'd rather stay with you."

For a moment Marla looked as though she would argue, and then she seemed to change her mind. Her expression was one of pure resignation when she said, "Suit yourself."

After a few more moments, Marla said, "Look, why don't you tell me what the lawyer said. You met with him again last week, didn't you?"

Marla's face grew more and more strained as she listened to her mother. Apparently the lawyer's news had been bad, whatever it concerned. Finally she said, "John's that determined not to pay alimony? ... Oh, Mom." Marla rubbed her fingers across her forehead and closed her eyes. She looked suddenly weary.

"No, I think it sounds like your lawyer knows what he's talking about.... Yes. Did you do what I told you to about your health insurance? ... And have you considered what you're going to do about the house?"

Her mother must have started crying at that point, because Marla spent the next few minutes repeating soothing words and phrases. The calm, comforting tone of her voice was at odds with the haggard look on her face. The conversation ended with Marla apologizing and promising not to forget to call the following week.

She hung up the phone and stared at it bleakly.

"Need a hug?" Brent said quietly.

She shot him a grateful look but shook her head. "No, I'm used to it." She stood up and slipped into her bathrobe. Brent pulled on his trousers and followed her out of the room. She went into the kitchen and started brewing a pot of coffee.

"You'll have trouble sleeping if you drink that," he murmured.

"It's decaf. And I'll have trouble sleeping anyhow."

He came closer to her. He wanted to hold her, but something about her body language told him she didn't want to be touched. He wished once again that she would trust him more. "Is your mom getting divorced?" he asked sympathetically. He knew from friends how that could traumatize a family.

"Yes," Marla said on a gust of air, "she's getting divorced. Again."

His brows rose questioningly. "She divorced your father?"

Marla nodded. "And two men after him. This will be her fourth divorce." She shook her head. "You'd think she would get better at it."

He had never heard Marla sound bitter before. "Is that... Marla, is that why you don't like to talk about your family?"

"To say I don't like to talk about them is a gross understatement." She pushed her hair away from her face and then noticed her hand was shaking. "Sorry. That call upset me more than usual."

He reached for her hand. "It's natural. We were both so relaxed after making love. Things like that hit you harder when all your usual defenses are down."

"I guess so," Marla conceded. "I hadn't counted on that." She gave him a weak smile. "You bring about all kinds of things I hadn't counted on."

"I know I've sort of destabilized your life," he said carefully, "but the advantage is that I'm here to help you weather the changes." His eyes pleaded with her. "So why don't you tell me what your mom said to upset you so much?"

Marla shook her head. "It's okay. I'm used to handling it alone, Brent."

"But you don't have to now. That's the whole point."

This was also the kind of stability and security she was afraid of risking. She could grow too accustomed to sheltering in his arms. But suddenly the urge to share some of the burdens of her private life was too strong. Her face crumpled and she gave in.

"My mom is a sweet woman, Brent. But she's always trusted other people to run her life, especially to earn the money. Consequently, she's always been totally helpless. When she hasn't got a husband to pay her way and run things, she needs me to do it."

"She's had four husbands?" he asked, sliding into one of the kitchen chairs.

Marla nodded. "My father was just plain irresponsible. He was never around when you needed him, and he never kept his word. She divorced him when I was ten, thinking we'd be better off without him. Unfortunately, she had no understanding of the cost of living, and she had never worked before. She married my father right out of high school and just figured he would look after her the way her father always had."

Marla poured two mugs of coffee and sat down across from Brent. "It was a shock to her to find out that she, my sister and I couldn't live on the wages she made running the cash register in a coffee shop. She also didn't like working, so she quit and wound up moving in with my grandparents for three years."

"Did you understand what was going on?" he asked. She had been just a child.

"Only in a limited way. But I understood enough to realize we had no money and no security. My mother was pretty free about explaining all her problems to me, and I overheard her talking with my grandparents sometimes."

Brent's jaw tightened. "I don't believe in hiding the truth from children, but why would she share all her economic troubles with a little girl?"

"She's a weak woman, Brent." There was no anger or condemnation in Marla's voice, only time-worn acceptance. "Anyhow, instead of learning basic survival and job skills, Mom just fretted for three years. Then she met her second husband."

"And you moved back out of your grandparents' house?"

"Yes. I was thirteen by that time, and I never became at all close to her second husband, although the marriage lasted until I was seventeen. But I was seldom in the house. I had a paper route, I was involved in athletics, and I studied hard. As soon as I was old enough, I always had a job of some kind."

"So you were an overachiever even then?"

Marla smiled wryly. "By the time I was sixteen, I could see the writing on the wall. My mother was headed for another divorce, and she was no more prepared for this one than she had been for the first one. I already knew I wanted to go to college and make something of my life so I wouldn't have to depend on anybody else for my food and shelter." She studied her coffee with a frown. "There was just too much instability in my life then."

"That's for sure," Brent said sympathetically. "It's so different from my family. I was really lucky. My mom and dad were always there, always sensible, reliable, trustworthy. I always knew I had a safe place and someone who would take care of me."

"I envy that," Marla admitted. "We were broke my senior year of high school, after the divorce. My mom, my little sister and I all moved into a tiny, one-bedroom apartment. I had to change schools. My mom needed some of the money I had saved for college." She shook her head. "I was determined to get into a state university on scholarship."

"Did you?"

Marla's lips twisted. "My real father popped back into the picture briefly. He said he was very proud of my good grades and all my accomplishments. He had made some money in the intervening years, and he wanted to help me go to a prestigious private university." She met Brent's gaze. "I was young enough to believe him."

"Why shouldn't you? It sounds like he was trying to make up for your hardships."

"I think that believing my father about that was the last naive thing I ever did. Halfway through my freshman year at college, he told me he wouldn't be contributing to my tuition and living expenses anymore. I wound up having to make a hasty transfer to the state university I had intended to attend in the first place."

Brent made a stifled sound of disgust. He was becoming painfully aware of why Marla was so committed to her job and her self-sufficiency and why she kept expecting him to let her down the way she had been let down by all the other important people in her life.

"Anyhow, my mom remarried again. Within two years her new husband left her for another woman. I only saw that husband twice, since I seldom went home once I had moved out."

"I can understand why."

"Luckily, she married John two years later." Marla gave a heavy sigh. "And now they're getting divorced. She's fifty years old, and she can't support herself. She just keeps trusting other people to look after her. Every time her husbands let her down, she calls on me to clean up the mess. I feel resentful, then I feel guilty for feeling resentful. It just never stops."

"Why doesn't your sister help you carry some of the weight?" he demanded.

"My sister is just like my mother, Brent. She's another grown woman who can't look after herself. She refused my offer to help put her through college because she was getting married and wouldn't need to make a living." Marla rolled her eyes. "But her husband's not doing so well, so she keeps begging me to send her money because I'm so 'lucky.'"

Brent propped his elbows on the table and considered everything Marla had just told him. He respected her more than ever now, knowing how hard she had worked all her life, realizing how much she had had to overcome. Brent's own family had always scraped by when he was growing up, but he hadn't known anything like the financial difficulties Marla had faced from an early age.

However, he considered the emotional hardships she had suffered a far harsher deprivation. His head was reeling with how much it explained about her. So many of her puzzling phrases and attitudes now fell into place.

He felt a heavy weight in his chest as he met her eyes. He wanted her; he wanted them to live together and be part of each other. But that kind of commitment and intimacy inevitably meant giving up some of the autonomy that meant so much to her.

Realizing that she believed she had already jeopardized her job for him gave him heart. Maybe he was becoming important enough to her that she could learn to trust him, to believe in him, to accept that he would always be there for her.

Because he suddenly knew that he *did* want to always be there for her. For better or worse, he loved her.

The weariness in her expression convinced him that she needed to rest before he could press her any further. He led her into the bedroom, slipped her robe off her shoulders and cradled her in his arms until she finally slept.

"Thank you, Brent," was the last thing she murmured before she fell asleep.

He wasn't quite sure what she was thanking him for, but he intended to continue encouraging her to rely on him in any way possible. He drifted off to sleep once he finally thought of the obvious solution to some of their immediate problems.

He brought the subject up over breakfast the next morning. "We need to get away together," he said.

She smiled at him. She looked exhausted but noticeably less tense than she had for a while. He hoped that sharing her family troubles with him had helped her. He wanted to help her deal with all her problems from now on—if she'd let him.

"Get away? What did you have in mind?" she asked.

"Your boss said you should clear your desk and take a few days off, didn't he?"

Her eyes widened. "Yes, he did. I had completely forgotten."

"Do you think you could finish things up today and take the rest of the week off?"

She considered his question for a moment. "Yes, I think I could." She glanced at him hesitantly. "Could you just make sure—"

"I know. You want me to make sure no one guesses we're going away together."

She nodded. "If we leave tomorrow, we could have five whole days. Six, if I can get Monday off, too."

"Good. Let's do it."

"Where will we go, though?"

"Someplace where no one in advertising will see me touch you. Someplace far away from telephones and relatives and pressure."

"Is there such a place?" Marla asked wistfully.

"Plenty of them. Trust me."

Chapter Eleven

The following day, they drove east from San Diego together. Turning off the interstate and onto State Highway 79, Brent steered his Jeep toward the heart of the Laguna Mountain range.

"Cuyamaca," Brent said.

"Gesundheit," Marla responded.

He grinned. "It means 'the place where it rains.' The Kumeyay Indians who lived here before the arrival of white settlers named it."

"Is that where we're camping?" she asked.

"Unless it's crowded. Then we'll try the Cleveland National Forest."

"Crowded?" she said skeptically. "If Cuyamaca Rancho State Park has more than twenty-four thousand acres—which I know because of the state park campaigns I worked on—how can it be crowded?"

He frowned. "I'd really like to take you someplace quiet, like Great Basin National Park in Nevada, but since we only have six days..."

"Believe me, Brent, this seems plenty quiet to a city girl like me." All she could see were trees and mountains.

"Well, one of the things I like about the San Diego area is that we're near to the good things in life. There are lots of places like this to camp and hike and climb within a few hours' drive."

Marla plucked at the sturdy Ventura clothing she was wearing. Brent had thrust a bundle of it at her early this morning, as well as a backpack full of the more lightweight supplies they would need for six days of wilderness camping and hiking.

He saw her fiddling with her clothing and frowned as he drove. "What's the matter? Isn't it comfortable?"

"Oh, it's very comfortable. And sturdy and durable." She rolled her eyes at him. "When you said we'd get away to someplace quiet together, I thought I'd get to wear sexy underwear and low-cut dresses for you."

"Hmm." He considered the idea, then asked hopefully, "Did you bring some of the underwear?"

Marla laughed at his expression. "No. I jettisoned it after you handed me two pairs of waffle-weave long underwear."

"Oh." He shrugged. "Well, it can still get cold at night out here. I'd rather have you bundled up and warm than slinky and shivering."

Marla leaned across the front seat of the Jeep and impulsively kissed his cheek. "Thank you." It was nice to let someone else think of the details for a change.

As soon as she had agreed to go out of town with him the previous morning, he had sent her off to work and assured her he would make all the arrangements. Marla had once again experienced a brief internal struggle over relying on someone else to organize things, but she had given in to the unaccustomed luxury of trusting Brent to take care of everything.

He had not only planned where they would go and what they would do, he had also bought and packed all the necessary supplies. He had even chosen the clothing she would need, since she was inexperienced at packing for this sort of trip. All she'd had to do in the end was fit a few toiletries and personal possessions into the small, lightweight backpack he had chosen for her.

When they arrived at the visitors' center, they parked and unpacked the Jeep. Brent's backpack was twice the size of Marla's, and she was convinced it weighed at least three times as much.

"No wonder you've got muscles on top of your muscles," she said as he hoisted it easily and positioned it comfortably on his back.

He helped her into her pack, shifting it and adjusting various straps until she said it felt comfortable. "I think I could carry more," she said. "Why don't you shift some of the stuff from yours to mine?" She felt guilty about him carrying such a large majority of their supplies.

He brushed a kiss across her lips. "You're too nice to be in advertising," he teased.

"Well?" she prodded.

He shook his head. "You're not used to this. Believe me, in a few hours that little pack on your back will feel like it's made of lead."

She grabbed his arm as he started to turn away. "A few hours? Just how far are we walking?"

"Now, Marla," he chided, "if you think of it in terms of miles it will sound like a long trudge instead of a relaxing hike."

"How far?" she persisted.

He shrugged. "We'll walk west from here until I find a spot where I think we can spend the night without being disturbed by other people."

"I never knew you were such a misanthrope," she muttered.

"I'm not. But we're here to get away from the rest of the world. Anyhow," he added enticingly, "if there's no one else around for miles, we can make all the noise we want."

Marla considered this. "Well, maybe a little isolation wouldn't hurt," she conceded.

He grinned and took her hand. "Come on. We'll just go into the visitors' center, tell them we're here, where we're going and when we plan to come back."

"Well, that makes sense," she said, pleased to know the park ranger might notice if they failed to come back the following week.

"I've told you I believe in sensible precautions."

It turned out that a couple of people who worked in the park knew Brent, so he and Marla were only able to get away after a cup of coffee and a friendly chat. When she and Brent finally disappeared into the forest, she felt a rush of excitement. This was the beginning of an adventure.

They walked through beautiful forests and glades for the rest of the afternoon. They spoke very little. Marla was content to follow him, accepting his helping hand over difficult parts of terrain and admiring the natural beauty around them. She realized with a feeling of surprise just how stifling her way of life could be. She never took time out to simply enjoy being alive for its own sake. Not until she had met Brent, anyhow.

She realized that he was purposely setting a slow pace for her, and she was grateful for his thoughtfulness. They stopped to rest often, and they would talk then. He pointed out plants, trees, insects and animals to her, explaining their habits and their life cycles.

"There's a lot to know out here," she murmured, sitting with her back against a log during their third rest stop.

"There's at least as much to know out here as in the city. Maybe more, because you're on your own out here."

"Does that ever frighten you, to know that you're miles from help if you get hurt or go hungry?"

He lay back in the grass and gazed at her thoughtfully. "No. I'm aware of the dangers, but I believe nature looks after us if we respect it and take the time to understand it. Anyhow, you could be run over by a truck or mugged in the middle of a city, and statistics show you couldn't necessarily count on anyone rushing to help you."

"That's true," she admitted ruefully.

"Everything here matters. Everything has a reason, plays a part. You can't really say that about society. We've invented and abstracted most of our rules and goals and relationships. But out here, everything is exactly what it needs to be."

"Including man?"

"Man's an intruder if he violates the wilderness." He rolled toward her and laced his fingers with hers. "But you and I can be in harmony with these mountains if we respect them."

Marla brushed her fingertips along his smooth cheek. "I'm glad I came here with you."

Brent kissed her lingeringly, then pulled her to her feet and suggested they press on. She started getting very tired by late afternoon and was grateful for the pouch of high-energy munchies he had insisted she carry. She wolfed down several handfuls of nuts and dried fruit after climbing one particularly steep slope. She considered devouring a chocolate bar, too, but decided to save it for a more desperate moment.

"Tired?" Brent asked in concern.

"No," she said stoically.

She suspected he didn't believe her hardy insistence that she could continue walking for hours yet. Her backpack did indeed feel as if it were made of lead, and her legs were starting to feel rubbery. She was just about to swallow her pride and ask if they could stop soon when Brent found a spot he decided they could camp at that night.

"You held up well for your first day out," he said encouragingly as he removed her backpack. "I'm proud of you."

"Thanks," Marla said, basking in his praise. A moment later she collapsed to the ground in a weary heap.

"Don't quit now," he admonished. "We still have to make camp."

Marla groaned theatrically and lay facedown in the grass.

Brent laughed and sat down beside her. He scooped her up in his arms and cuddled and kissed her affectionately.

"It will take more than that to make me get up again," she said repressively. A moment later her eyes widened. She gasped and squirmed in his arms. "Oh . . . Do that again."

"I thought that would revive you," he said smugly. Marla wiggled enticingly in his embrace. He held her still and said sternly, "Stop it. That's all you get until the tent is up."

Marla pouted but let him haul her to her aching feet. "How come you still have so much energy?" she demanded grumpily.

"I'm used to it. I've spent years training my body to do this." He crouched by their packs and began unpacking equipment. He selected the exact spot for their tent and started directing her, telling her how to help him pitch it.

After a few slapstick attempts, Marla said, "Have I mentioned that I've never done this before?"

"Could've fooled me," he said dryly, untangling her.

With a combination of ruthlessness and patience on Brent's part, they finally got the tent up. Most of the other supplies he had brought looked foreign and mysterious to Marla. By the time he had explained and demonstrated their uses, her head was spinning and her weariness was complete.

When Brent noticed how her eyes had glazed over, he laughed. "Now you know how *I* felt when you were shoving all those strategy analyses and target-market breakdowns in front of me."

"Touché," she said wryly. She was all set to plop down on the ground again when he dragged her off to find firewood and water. Once that task was completed, he showed her how to build a fire and purify the water.

She finally got to rest, leaning against his backpack in exhaustion while he prepared their dinner without her help. She had insisted that a cooking lesson could wait until tomorrow. By the time they were done eating and Brent had cleaned up the area, it was dark out. They sat companionably together in front of the camp fire for another hour. Marla listened to Brent recount memorable camping trips with his father and with various friends through the years. She felt very close to him and was glad that now they were going to spend a few days making similar memories together.

She felt glad, that was, until a howl pierced the peaceful night. Marla nearly jumped out of her skin. "What is that?" she croaked.

"Coyote." He noticed her fear and gave her hand a reassuring squeeze. "Don't worry about it. He's not going to come around us. He's more afraid of you than you are of him."

There was another howl, eerie and wild. "You're sure about that, are you?" she asked nervously.

He grinned. "I'm sure. But if it'll make you feel better, creep a little closer to me."

She scrambled into his lap without waiting for a second invitation. "As long as we're on the subject, what else are we likely to encounter out here?"

"This park isn't that big, and it's pretty close to civilization," Brent said. "There's nothing else out here that might scare you." He paused. "Unless you're afraid of snakes."

"Brent!" Marla started looking around as if she expected them to be attacked by a horde of reptiles at that very moment.

He sighed. "Maybe I shouldn't have mentioned that."

"No, no, I'm a responsible adult. It's better to be prepared." She searched his face in the camp fire's glow. "Did you bring snakebite medicine?"

"I brought everything," he assured her. "Don't worry. You're in good hands."

She curled up against him, enjoying once again that unusual sensation of trusting someone else to look after her. It was a seductive feeling, one that she was always on guard against in her normal life. But out here, normal rules didn't seem to apply. Particularly since she knew nothing about the outdoors, and it was Brent's way of life.

They continued talking for a while. When a bird shrieked in the night, not far from them, Marla tensed again. Brent realized how worn-out she was and suggested they turn in.

"Okay." She brushed his lips with a kiss and stood up. At the flap of their tent, she looked questioningly at him. "Aren't you coming?"

"I'm going to douse the fire and double-check everything."

"Okay. I'll be waiting in my synthetic fiber sleeping bag, wearing the sexiest long underwear you've ever seen," she said, imitating the voice of a popular television vamp.

He grinned. "I'll be right there."

When he crawled into their tent five minutes later, he found her shifting impatiently from side to side. She sat up and looked at him accusingly. "The ground here is like rock! How can you expect me to sleep on it?"

Brent crept onto his half of their zipped-together sleeping bags. He cocked a brow at her. "Nigel says an honest man's pillow is his peace of mind."

"Nigel would," she muttered. "I'll bet he has a water bed. A *heated* water bed."

"How did you know?"

Marla rolled her eyes and shifted again. "No wonder they always had camp cots in all those old safari movies." She plumped up the corner of her sleeping bag and rolled on top of it. "I thought it was fear of bugs and snakes." She squirmed and rolled over. "Or maybe pure elitist snob-bery." She sat up and tried to make a little mound where the small of her back would lie. "But now I know." She lay back down and squirmed again. "It's because the ground is so damned uncomfortable!"

Brent was sitting cross-legged on top of the sleeping bag, his chin propped in his hand, watching her contortions with a bland expression. Finally she sat up and looked at him resentfully.

"Take your clothes off and get in bed," she ordered.

"Why, Marla, I'm flattered."

She scowled. "I want to see if you make a good cush-ion."

He laughed at that and obligingly started to undress. When he had stripped off everything but his long-underwear bottoms, he turned off their small lantern and slipped into the sleeping bag. He slid an arm under Marla's head when she rolled toward him.

"Oof! Get your elbow out of my stomach," he re-quested.

"Sorry." She ran her hand over his bare chest. "Won't you be cold in the morning?"

"No. I make a lot of body heat."

She shifted around for a few more minute before finally finding a position in which she felt comfortable. Three-quarters of her body rested on top of him by the time she was through.

"What if I have to go out in the middle of the night?" he murmured.

"You're a big boy. Wait till morning," she said unsym-pathetically. A piercing shriek made her strangle on her next words. With her heart thudding, she asked at last, "What the devil is that?"

"Raccoons. They're disagreeing about something," he said, massaging her back soothingly. He kissed her brow. "It's been a rough day for you, hasn't it, honey?"

Marla smiled drowsily. "It's been exciting," she admitted. "I just hope I can make it through five more days."

"You're doing fine," he whispered.

"You sure are nice and warm." She nuzzled him sleepily.

Within minutes he could tell she had drifted off to sleep. He rubbed his cheek against her silken hair, feeling more contented than he had in a long time. He hadn't yet told her what it meant to him, her being here with him, sharing this experience with him. He hoped it wouldn't be the last time, but it would always be special to him, because it was the first time.

He felt her body relax even more, sliding slightly off of him and onto the hard ground beneath him. He had pushed her a little too hard today because he had wanted to find a good campground where they could stay for a couple of days without being disturbed. She had pushed herself with the same determination she brought to all activities, and he could tell that she was proud of herself, too. He felt happiness wrap around his heart like a physical force as he drifted off to sleep.

He woke up before her the next morning. One look at her peaceful face made him decide to let her keep sleeping. He got dressed and left the tent to start breakfast.

Marla crawled out of the tent an hour later. Her Ventura clothing was wrinkled and some of it was only half-fastened. Her hair was a rat's nest and her face was bare of makeup. He thought she looked beautiful. When he told her so, she squinted suspiciously at him.

"Have some coffee," he ordered. She accepted it silently. After drinking half a cup, she stretched and yawned. She inhaled a few deep breaths of pure mountain air.

"Sleep well?" Brent ventured to ask.

"Like a rock," she admitted. Then she rubbed her back. "I also feel like I slept *on* rocks. Some cushion you turned out to be."

He scooted behind her and started massaging her back. "Eat up," he urged.

Marla devoured her breakfast, then leaned back and made little moaning noises while Brent's big hands soothed her back and shoulders and eased the kinks out of her tired, cramped muscles.

"Thanks," she said. His arms slid around her, and she felt him rub his cheek against her hair. "My hair!" She jumped away from him as if she'd been burned.

He looked at her in bewilderment. "What about your hair?"

She scrambled to her feet. "I accept that I can't have my blow-dryer and my curling rod out here, but I should at least brush it out before you—"

He laughed and pulled her onto his lap. "I never knew you were so vain."

"I'm not, but there's no point in looking like Frankenstein's bride."

"I told you you look beautiful. Anyhow, I like it when it's messy. It's another sign that you're not perfect, after all."

She rolled her eyes, but she let him run his hands through her hair and kiss her. She slid her arms around his neck and pulled her mouth away from his to look into his eyes. "I conked out on you last night, didn't I?" she said apologetically.

"I figured you'd be pretty tired after that hike. Don't worry, I'll see that you make up for it tonight," he promised.

Brent also promised they would have a leisurely day today, so Marla could build up strength for another long trek the following day. However, Brent's idea of leisurely had Marla panting with exhaustion at various moments. They packed a light day pack of food and water and explored the area around their campsite.

Despite their earlier conversation, Marla had brushed her hair till it crackled and had braided it neatly. She had also smoothed and buttoned her clothes into some kind of order and was pleased to notice Brent ogling her legs—at least the part that stuck out of her practical hiking shorts.

The breadth and depth of his knowledge about the natural world continued to amaze her. Her head started to reel with the accumulation of information he was sharing with her. Her own ordered mind had to classify the various facts as botany, geology, zoology and meteorology. To Brent it was just the world as he knew it.

Later that afternoon, when she breathlessly reminded him of his promise that they would have an easy day, he looked sheepish.

"I'm sorry," he apologized. "You keep up like such a veteran that I keep forgetting this is new to you. You should learn to complain more."

To her relief, he found a clearing where they could sit quietly and watch wildlife for a few hours. By the time they returned to their campsite, Marla was feeling better. By the time they had eaten dinner and turned in, she was feeling positively energetic and did everything she could to make up for her lethargy the night before.

They packed up and set out early the next morning. Marla was pleased to find her legs and shoulders were already getting stronger, and she meant it when she told Brent they could press on until they found the perfect spot to settle down for the rest of their vacation. They found it in the late afternoon, a sheltered, grassy area near a small stream.

When he had originally told her they were going camping for a week, Marla hadn't actually pictured what they would do with their days. She thought it would be a good opportunity to be alone with Brent, away from the pressures of her life. She had also expected it to be a little monotonous at times, though she hadn't admitted that to him. By the fifth day of their adventure, she wondered how she could have been so ignorant.

The days were filled with discovery and satisfaction. Once Marla started learning to identify basic plant and animal groups, Brent turned her attention to more practical matters. He began showing her edible and medicinal plants, and they made some of their meals primarily out of wild edibles they had found together.

Although she had initially enjoyed trusting everything to him, self-sufficiency out here was a practical goal, and she insisted he teach her what she needed to know to take care of herself. She felt pride in her own accomplishments. When she built a fire without a match, she felt as thrilled as she had when she'd received her undergraduate diploma.

As her strength, stamina and skills increased, she began to wonder how much she could learn and accomplish if they could go away for a long time together, to one of the really wild places Brent waxed eloquent about during their evenings in front of the camp fire.

The hard walks and long silences gave Marla an opportunity to do serious, reflective thinking, which her life didn't often provide the time or atmosphere for. She thought about her own plans and values, and she considered bigger moral and social concerns as she trailed quietly behind Brent or sat watching the sunset, wrapped in his strong arms.

On their fifth afternoon together, they found a beautiful glade and decided to sit there and relax for a while.

"I wish we weren't going back tomorrow." Marla sighed wistfully.

"There'll be other trips," Brent assured her. "Plenty of them."

She smiled and linked her fingers with his. "Everything seems stripped down to basics here. Even you and me." Her eyes caressed his rugged features. "If I hadn't know before what a fine man you were, I would certainly know it now."

He raised her hand to his lips and kissed her fingers. "I hoped you would love all this."

Marla lay on her side in the grass and looked at him. "I have to admit that I was wrong about a lot of things."

"Oh?"

"Until we came here, I thought all your sports and activities were frivolous and just playing."

"And now?"

"Now I know better. Everything here is hard and challenging and rewarding. You come face-to-face with yourself every moment of the day, and there's no escaping your own thoughts or your own character. You have to do everything thoroughly and competently."

She rolled onto her back and looked up at the vast expanse of sky. "And you realize how small you are, how ephemeral your concerns are. It puts things into perspective." She paused. "It's a very maturing experience."

"That's why I need the things I do," he admitted quietly. "If I just stayed home and made money and conformed, I'd become petty and neurotic."

She rolled onto her stomach and looked at him again. "No," she said with certainty. "Not you."

"Yes. I know what I need." And now he needed her. He wondered what would happen when they went back, as they had to. Would this solid feeling remain? Would she be ready for the commitment he needed from her? Or would her customary worries and defenses move back into her heart as soon as she reached San Diego? He shifted restlessly.

"What's wrong?" she asked immediately, so closely attuned to him that she had noticed the flicker of worry in his eyes.

He smiled. "Just wishing we didn't have to go back so soon. I haven't been this happy in a long, long time, Marla."

Her whole expression softened, and a smile lighted her face. "So what else can we try together?" she asked. He arched his brows inquisitively. "Besides camping and hiking, I mean," she elaborated.

"I thought you said you liked surfing."

"That's true." She rested her cheek against her fist. "Do you find the same challenges and rewards in that as you do here?"

"It's different. So are climbing and kayaking and sailing. But the end result is pretty similar. You know yourself and the world better, and you usually like both better."

She touched his face as he lay down near her, then tunneled her fingers into his curly dark hair. It gleamed after their freezing cold bath in the stream this morning. His skin was smooth and bronzed, and his eyes glittered emerald green. Every movement he made was powerful and graceful, every muscle rippled with perfect masculine beauty. He had never been more sensuous and irresistible than out here, where he felt most content.

"When will we leave tomorrow?" she whispered, her belly tightening with a combination of desire and sadness.

He brushed his fingers along the smooth, silky column of her throat and then traced the shape of her full lower lip. "It'll be a long hike back and a couple hours' drive once we reach the Jeep. We'd better leave at dawn."

He touched his lips to her cheek, then leaned back to look at her. Her dark blond hair was streaked by the sun, her tan had deepened to a healthy glow and the peaceful contentment of the past few days had cleared her face of the strain that was so often evident in her expression. She didn't look younger so much as completely ageless, as if nature had made her fully grown and perfect, just the way she was.

He had marveled at the quick increase in her strength and stamina, at the way she had thrilled to every new experience and risen to every new challenge. It was as if these few days had released all her potential for intimacy and daring, and he was nearly bowled over by the force of the emotions rushing out from her to greet him. The mystery and intensity that had so intrigued him now blossomed into the remarkable, giving qualities he had sensed from the beginning.

He moved his hand down to her shirtfront and started unbuttoning it. He felt her tremble with anticipation. Her responses always excited him. Her body thrilled him more and more every time they made love. She was sleek and smooth and graceful, soft and silky and feminine, warm and hot and giving.

He unbuttoned her blouse to the point where it disappeared into the waistband of her hiking shorts. Rather than pulling it out, he shifted closer to her, unbuckled her belt and unfastened her shorts. As his hand explored lower, she made a sound of choked amusement.

"We'll shock the squirrels," she said.

"It's spring," he reminded her. "Everything around here is doing it. We'll blend right in."

He was starting to pull her clothes off when she sat up suddenly and said, "Let me take my hiking boots off, or I'll look ridiculous."

He laughed at the image of the two of them making love, stark naked except for their bright socks and heavy boots. He rolled away from her, sat up and started untying his own boots while she took hers off. While he was at it, he started taking off his own clothes. He glanced up and saw her watching him. She was always frank about her admiration for his body, and he could feel her gaze burning on every inch of skin he revealed while he stripped. He slowed his movements, enjoying her interested stare, enjoying the anticipation.

"You're such a tease," she murmured when he took an extra long time with his belt buckle.

He grinned and stood up to push down his now-tight trousers and kick them away. Marla's gaze moved slowly over his body, lingering at his groin.

"All ready for spring, I see," she said huskily.

He looked as wild as the creatures of the forest, standing there, lean and well muscled, gloriously naked and uninhibited. He stalked forward gracefully, like a predatory cat, and crouched beside her.

She felt his hot gaze move over her, admiring the bare expanses of skin exposed by the clothing he had unfastened. He reached for her again, and with slow, steady strength, he pushed her shirt off her shoulders and over her arms, removed her bra and pulled her sturdy shorts down her hips, over her thighs and along the smooth length of her legs.

Marla's body was pliant and limp as he undressed her silently. She watched him with heavy-lidded eyes, feeling as if she were being seduced by one of the woodland spirits of pagan legends. He looked too wild and untamed to be the man she had met in a business meeting in San Diego all those weeks ago. As she stretched out naked in the grass and beckoned to him with her eyes, she suddenly wondered at the changes in herself since then.

That Marla Foster wouldn't have dreamed of taking a few days off work in her competitive profession to run off to the mountains with one of her clients. That woman wouldn't have been content to spend the past five days living for the moment and enjoying simple pleasures.

And that woman certainly wouldn't have avidly watched a man strip in the open air or have stretched out naked in the grass for her lover and invited him to study every inch of her body under the brilliant sun.

She lay beneath the heat of Brent's gaze and marveled at the changes in herself—changes wrought by her relationship with him, she realized. She had tried so hard to remain the woman she was, but he made her care about him so much that stagnation had become impossible.

Brent touched her with sure hands, placing his palms on her shoulders and then gliding them down and around her body with firm caresses. He stroked the rising mounds of her breasts, teased their pink nipples into aching peaks, then explored farther, tracing intricate patterns over her smooth sides and across her flat belly.

"Roll over," he ordered huskily.

She rolled over onto her stomach without hesitation, intending to fully enjoy whatever he did next. All forethought and inhibitions seemed foreign and foolish. This man was linked to her, body and soul. She and Brent were female and male in creation, and everything they did together was good and right.

She felt his big, warm hands on her back, gentle and massaging. He lovingly soothed and kneaded the muscles she had been developing all week long. Marla groaned luxuriously after a few minutes and wriggled slightly, contentedly basking in his care.

When he had finished with her back, he started massaging her arms, gently relaxing her overworked biceps and murmuring over new scratches on her wrists. Marla continued to lie facedown on the grass, making sleepy little noises of delight as he worked.

When he was done with her arms, she mumbled, "Mmm, thanks, Brent."

"Oh, I'm enjoying it, too," he murmured wryly. She could hear the smile in his voice as he drew one of her hands to his body to prove his point.

As soon as her fingers touched the hot, bold proof that Brent did indeed enjoy massaging her body, Marla made a throaty sound of mingled amusement and desire. "I take it we're done playing?" she said, starting to roll toward him.

His hands on her back stilled her. "No hurry," he said easily. "Hold still."

He stroked her lower back with hypnotic effect, then spoiled it by pinching her bottom. Marla yelped, then sighed when his strong, skillful hands began kneading the tension out of her calves. After he had made them warm and throbbing, he moved down to her abused feet and worked magic there, too.

"You've got blisters. Don't those boots fit you well?"

"Yes," Marla answered groggily. She moaned when he rubbed the arch of her left foot. "But my feet aren't used to being used so relentlessly."

When she felt his hands on her outer thighs, her mood started to change. By the time he began gently rubbing the flesh of her inner thighs, Marla felt a hot, liquid throbbing in her loins. She was ready to stop playing, even if he wasn't. She rolled over without warning, knocking him off balance.

"Something wrong?" he asked knowingly.

"Come here," she insisted, stretching out her arms to him.

He shook his head. "Got to get those quadriceps. They've taken a beating this week."

She made an involuntary sound of desire when Brent started rubbing the tops of her thighs with firm, rhythmic strokes. Their eyes held as her skin grew hotter and his hands grew bolder. When he finally pushed her thighs apart, she spread them willingly, waiting for him.

He lowered his head and planted a kiss on her soft belly. "You're so beautiful," he whispered. His mouth moved to the lowest curve of her abdomen. "You look like a wood nymph." His lips moved even lower.

Marla moved her arm at last and touched his shiny hair. He pressed a kiss against her palm and firmly laid her arm back by her side. A moment later she felt his hot, wet tongue trace the crease of her thigh. Marla gasped and shifted her legs suddenly. Brent grunted when her knee struck him in the ribs, and his hands gripped her legs firmly to move them to a comfortable position. She could feel his hard, muscled torso slide between her legs, his chest hair tickling her soft skin and his body heat burning her with excitement.

Surprised again at her total lack of inhibitions, Marla propped herself up on her elbows to look at him. The sight of his dark head lowered between her thighs made her arms shake.

He was gentle and exploring, releasing all her inhibitions.

The sound of Marla's strangled moan could have left Brent in no doubt about how he was affecting her. His breath escaped him in a soft puff of amusement and sweetly caressed her thighs.

"Okay?" he whispered.

"Mmm." She didn't trust herself to say more.

She felt the sun beating down on her naked body, the grass beneath her tickling her with its healthy resilience, and the cool mountain air caressing her as tenderly as Brent did. She felt the heat of his body between her legs, his hands urgently stroking her bottom.

She could smell every flower, tree and blade of grass in nature's pageant under the sun, but those scents faded into insignificance compared to the heady smell of their mutual desire, which had a special, unforgettable fragrance all its own, musky, warm and earthy. She had been missing so much until he entered her life.

She made soft sounds of delight as her passion mounted, and she heard Brent's husky, pleased murmurs in response.

Marla's whole body arched as climax shimmered through her body, flooded her being and deluged her senses. She shredded grass with wildly seeking hands and sobbed again and again as pleasure soared inside her, long and hot and scalding. The earth turned over and over. The sun went black and the sky swirled around her, and Brent was the only thing she was still sure of, holding her tightly and murmuring intimately to her.

And then Brent slid up the length of her body to wrap his arms around her and kiss her, a hot, lingering, possessive kiss, followed by another and another. She wrapped her arms around him, returning his kisses with ardor, loving him until her heart hurt, shifting her hips against his hot, hard manhood in a way she knew would drive him crazy.

"Look at me," he growled.

She opened her eyes and drowned in his glittering green gaze, feeling preyed upon and protected at the same time, as he entered her body with one fierce, aggressive thrust. She held his gaze and arched upward, lifting her hips against him, drawing him in even deeper, welcoming him home. If any one moment in her life was perfect, this was it. Nothing could be more right than the two of them joined together like this, in total harmony with each other and with their surroundings.

"I love you," she said without thinking. She covered his passion-tense face with adoring kisses. "I love you."

That finally broke through what was left of his self-control. He shuddered violently and buried his face against her neck. His mouth was hot and rough, and his thrusts were deep and savage. He muttered words she couldn't understand, repeating her name often, but his tone was loving, ardent and urgent.

They mated like two healthy wild creatures, rough and greedy, demanding and intimate, needy and giving. In the vast expanse of the lonely universe, she became one with him at last, transcending ordinary physical barriers. They melded together, in spirit and intent, at the same moment that their bodies shuddered and writhed against each other, inundated by the most shattering, soul-searing pleasure Marla had ever known.

They fell into exhausted slumber immediately afterward, still lying with their limbs entangled, as natural and innocent as the wildlife around them. They slept in the grass, naked and serene, until the sun started going down and the first chill of evening crept into the air.

Brent woke up first. One glance at the sky told him how much time had passed, and he realized they'd have to hurry to get back to camp before the sun went down. He didn't want Marla hiking through the dark, no matter how confident she was becoming. He stood and grabbed his pants, then allowed himself a moment to watch her as she slept sprawled out in total abandon, her hair a glorious tangle of dark gold flecked with blades of grass. She frowned in her sleep and started to curl into a little ball, feeling the cold now that he had moved away from her.

He gently shook her awake, feeling so tender he thought he would shatter in another moment. She opened her eyes and blinked sleepily at him. She looked around in confusion for a moment and then appeared to recognize their surroundings. When she looked at him again, her whole expression flooded with warm emotion.

He had intended to turn her attention to practical matters immediately, for her own safety, so he was surprised when the first words out of his mouth were, "Do you remember what you said?" He smiled sheepishly but didn't retract the question. He needed to know.

He had learned to expect caution and self-protection from her, so he braced himself for some sort of denial. In the hesitation that followed his blunt question, he felt his heart aching despite his firm resolve to be patient with her. Don't expect miracles in just a few days, he reminded himself.

Then, to his surprise, she slowly rose to her feet and her face took on a look of tenderness and confidence. "I remember," she said simply. She stood on tiptoe to kiss him lightly. Then she smiled. "And if you get some food into my stomach real soon, I might even tell you again."

He dropped the pants he had been about to put on and pulled her into his arms. He held her closely against him for a moment, shuddering with his need and his relief. Then he looked down into her face, smoothed her hair back and held her chin in his hand.

"I love you," he said. It was the greatest gift he could give anybody, the most profound emotion he had felt since losing the only other woman he had ever wanted to marry.

Marla closed her slender fingers around his wrist and met his candid, trusting gaze with a similar expression. When she shivered after a moment, Brent ran a hand over the goose bumps on her arm and decided they had better get dressed, get back to camp and build a fire.

"You're a cruel taskmaster," she grumbled as he hustled her lethargic body over the hills and through the woods. His concern touched her, though, and she had to admit that he practically carried her over the most difficult stretches of terrain.

She had confessed her feelings to him in the height of passion, but they had been growing inside her all along. She realized now that love, more than anything else, accounted for her severe mood swings around him and for so much of her unreasonable behavior in recent weeks. She could finally admit that she *had* been unreasonable and demanding, and she knew that a lesser man than Brent would probably have washed his hands of the whole thing several times before now.

However, she supposed she loved him because most men *were* lesser men. He was extraordinary, special, one-of-a-kind. She smiled to herself. He was a unique combination of adult perception and childlike naïveté. Since coming to these woods with him, she had started to realize that a lot of his naïveté was simply optimism and confidence, just as a lot of her own so-called realism and common sense were really cynicism and insecurity. However, the two of them were a good balance for each other.

It was like him to avoid mentioning his own feelings until he was sure it wouldn't scare her away, just as it was like him to make an honest declaration to her as soon as he thought it was safe. Brent wouldn't hold out on her, leaving her to wonder about his intentions. Nor would he gloat over having finally gotten her to recognize and admit that she was in love with him.

She had resisted because she was afraid. Out here there seemed to be nothing to be afraid of, so she could examine her insecurities from an almost impartial standpoint. Being in love meant giving up emotional autonomy, which she identified with self-preservation. Look where love and marriage had got the other women in her family, after all.

Love also meant compromises and commitments, all of which Brent would make and would expect her to make in return. Above all, being in love with him meant she needed to make some difficult professional decisions. And soon.

But when he reached for her hand to help her over a tricky section of rock, when he smiled lovingly and trustingly into her eyes, Marla resolved not to worry about anything while they were here together. This time was special; these hours belonged to them alone. Trouble would come looking for her soon enough.

Although Brent did get food into Marla's belly relatively fast, he didn't remind her of her joking promise. He was a confident man. Since she had told him she loved him in a vulnerable moment and then confirmed it in a calm moment, he believed her. He didn't need reassurance. All the confusing pieces of his existence fell into place again for the first time in years.

He knew what counted most in life. He and this woman would build something solid and fulfilling together, something that permeated every aspect of their lives. Their marriage would be very different from his first marriage, and he looked forward to the new challenges and discoveries. His life would always be wound up with hers now, and he knew it would include things he had never expected in his life.

He could help her bear the weight of her needy family; she could give him the intimacy he desired. He could take her hiking and surfing; she could advise him about business. The perfect union and balance of their differing characters pleased him. Everything, even her professional problems, could be worked out easily, he decided. Because they already had what counted most.

He knew how precious love was, how important it was to take what you wanted and to get the best out of it. Not a minute of time or a second of happiness should be allowed to slip by. He wanted to marry Marla—and soon, before another precious moment of life passed by.

Chapter Twelve

It seemed strange to Marla to return to her daily routine at the Freemont agency two days later. It felt as if she had been away much longer than a week. But then, she had undergone many changes during the six days she had spent in the mountains with Brent.

Vernon noticed the difference in her right away. He had finally recovered from his nasty cold and was bright eyed and bushy tailed when he popped into her office that Tuesday. "Wow!" he said as soon as he saw her. "You look great! What kind of vitamins are you taking?"

Marla gave him a broad, unrestrained grin. "It's the effect that relaxation has on me."

"Well, it's quite an effect. Where did you go, anyhow?"

"The country," she said evasively.

"Alone?" he prodded.

She didn't intend to give him a straight answer, but to her chagrin, her expression gave her away. Vernon hooted, declaring all along that he had known she must be in love to be acting so erratically. Marla sighed. Until Brent, she had always been able to control her feelings and her expression. But Vernon's genuine happiness for her made her natural sense of privacy and caution seem petty. She was happy, and it was hardly a crime to fall in love.

"Who is he?" Vernon demanded.

"Oh, no one you know. I met him a couple of months ago."

"I might have guessed!"

Vernon made a few attempts to get Marla to reveal her sweetheart's identity, but she resisted. She couldn't risk anyone at the agency knowing about Brent, even now. After Vernon left her office, she toyed with her misshapen little horseshoe and acknowledged that she would have to make some important decisions before long.

A rueful smile played around her mouth. This was a peculiar romance, she admitted wryly. Her mementos of her lover were a pathetic handmade horseshoe and a trunk full of rugged outdoor gear. Brent didn't give her sexy negligees and costly jewelry. It was always hiking books and lightweight, water-resistant sporting clothes. She clutched her horseshoe to her chest with fondness for a moment, then got back to work.

Brent called her a few hours later to say he couldn't see her that night, contrary to their plans. His father had been injured, and Brent was flying to Montana to be with his mother during her vigil at the local hospital.

"Oh, Brent, I hope he's all right," Marla said sincerely. She knew how much he loved his father.

"I don't know how serious it is," he admitted in a troubled voice. "I'll call you tomorrow from Montana."

"Have a safe trip," she said, wishing the words from her heart didn't sound so banal.

"I love you," he said, and the words didn't sound banal at all. "We have a lot of plans to make," he added.

She didn't pursue that intriguing comment but let him hang up and make his preparations to leave.

The week that followed was extremely hectic. There was plenty of work to do on the Ventura account, the Rawlins Pocketknives account required considerable attention and she was being included in a number of meetings with prospective clients.

She spent two long evenings on the phone with her mother, feeling depressed and emotionally drained after each conversation. In addition to her own troubles, her mother was now worried about Marla's sister, Leila, who seemed unhappy.

Normally, Marla would have called Leila, found out what the trouble was and tried to help straighten it out. This time, however, she resolved that her sister was an adult and should be left to sort out her own problems. She and her mother weren't doing Leila any favors by assuming she couldn't run her own life. Actually, Marla suspected she really couldn't, but since Leila was only twenty-six years old, there was still plenty of time for her to learn.

Brent called to tell her his father had been injured while working. Although the injury was serious, his father was healthy and had a positive attitude. The doctors expected to release him from the hospital by the end of the week, and he'd probably be able to return to work within a month.

"I'm staying until early next week," Brent told her. "My mom is going crazy with him in the hospital, but it'll be even worse when he gets home."

"Is he in such bad condition?" Marla asked.

Brent chuckled. "No, but he can be a cantankerous old goat. He'll be cranky and bored after a few days of confinement. I just thought I'd give my mom some relief."

Marla smiled faintly. "I get it." She knew about family responsibilities only too well. She envied the fact that Brent enjoyed his.

"I miss you like crazy," he said huskily.

"I miss you, too."

They talked a little while longer, and Marla cradled the phone in her hands after they said goodbye, wishing she could hold him for just a few moments. His absence made her feel like a part of her was missing.

She met with Nigel that week out at the Ventura offices. As she made herself comfortable in the alcove by Nigel's and Brent's desks, she noticed her gift to Brent—the well-traveled pop art radio—sitting on his desk in total, blessed, blissful silence.

She made an exclamation of surprise and picked it up. She caught Nigel eyeing her with mingled curiosity and amusement. She started smiling sheepishly.

"Brent said that was a gift from you." Nigel arched his blond brows curiously. When Marla admitted it was, he laughed and said, "Then it must be love. Nothing short of undying devotion could make Brent keep that hideous thing on his desk, where he has to look at it every day."

Marla agreed with Nigel's evaluation of the radio and was touched to learn Brent kept this peculiar memento so close at hand. She was surprised to find she didn't even mind Nigel referring to their relationship so openly. He was Brent's friend, after all.

"But how on earth did he finally turn it off?" she asked.

Nigel scowled. "He didn't. I spent two days after you guys left town trying to figure out how to make the damn thing shut up. What kind of batteries has it got? I thought it would never stop!"

"Did it finally run down?"

"No. Felice turned it off. She saw me fiddling with it, took it away from me and turned it off faster than you can blink."

"How'd she do that?"

He grimaced. "She's got one, too. Hers came with an instruction booklet."

Marla laughed, thinking she would have to tell Vernon about the radio's fate. Then, since she realized Felice wasn't joining them, she asked, "Where is Felice, by the way?"

"She's up north participating in one of those suicidal contests she loves so much," Nigel said in disgust.

"What kind of contest?"

"One of those things where you swim about a hundred miles, jog until your shoes burn up and then bicycle till you're hauled off to an intensive care unit. It's just her cuppa tea."

Marla laughed as Nigel shuddered with horror. "It doesn't exactly sound like a pleasure pursuit," she agreed. She steered the conversation toward business.

"By the way," Nigel said after a while, "I love the photo contest idea and also some of the other promotions you've outlined since then. But it's going to make a lot of extra work around here. I told Brent before he left that he's got to stop dallying and finally hire a full-time marketing director. Got any suggestions?"

"No. I would think you'd know better than I what kind of qualifications you're looking for in someone," she said in surprise.

Nigel studied her speculatively for a moment, then shrugged. "Well, no harm in asking."

Brent called her at work early the following Tuesday to tell her he'd be flying home that afternoon, since everything in his parents' lives seemed to be running smoothly. She missed him so much her whole body shook when she realized she could touch him in just a few hours. He agreed to meet her at her apartment right after work.

"I'll be there by four o'clock," he promised.

"I'll see if I can leave work early today," Marla said, consumed by eagerness.

Fate seemed determined to keep her away from Brent for a little longer, however. That afternoon she was taking one last look at a final layout the agency would submit to Ventura for approval that week when she noticed a printing mistake that gave the copy an embarrassing connotation. That would mean staying late to make a lot of extra phone calls and pull a few strings, she realized disappointedly.

Marla showed the mistake to Warren, expecting him to blow up at her even though the error wasn't her fault. She was surprised when he not only failed to include her in his general outburst of criticism, but actually asked if she was busy and offered to do the necessary work when she admitted she was.

Marla gaped at him in astonishment for a full ten seconds before saying, "That's very kind, Warren."

"It's all right. I have to stay late for a meeting with the company's most senior officers, anyhow." Marla tried not to notice how pompous he sounded, since he was doing her a favor. "I don't have anything pressing to do between now and the meeting, anyway, and my telephoning will have more impact than if you do it."

Marla thanked him sweetly and left his office, thinking wryly that even when he was trying to be nice he had to play at one-upmanship. She worked like a demon for the next hour so she could still get home to Brent at a reasonable time, even if it was much later than she had hoped. As she was preparing to leave at five-thirty, she mentioned Warren's unexpected kindness to Vernon.

"He's been told by the powers that be to get off your back," Vernon said with satisfaction.

Marla paused with her hand on the doorknob of her office and stared at him. "How do you know that?"

Vernon smirked. "I have my sources."

Marla shook her head, knowing he wouldn't tell her any more. "Well, I'm glad for the change." She left the office in a hurry, knowing that Brent was already waiting for her.

An hour later, Brent pushed himself up on trembling arms and rolled away from Marla. His naked body was covered with a fine sheen of perspiration. "Now that's what I call a tempestuous reunion," he said with a sigh.

Flat on her back, lying on the carpet just inside the front door of her apartment, Marla laughed softly. "Is that what that was? I thought I'd been hit by a low-flying jetliner."

He propped himself up on an elbow and looked down at her. "Sorry about your clothes," he said sheepishly.

Marla glanced at the heap of wrinkled, battered clothing lying near them. "Well, I was tired of that skirt, anyhow. And I can sew new buttons on the blouse." She laughed again and touched his cheek. "You're so impetuous."

"I was starving for you," he murmured. He kissed her again, gently this time. Then he traced his fingers over her swollen lips and brushed her hair off her flushed face.

Marla closed her eyes contentedly and waited for the tingling in her loins to subside. It was a long time before her blood stopped hammering excitedly through her veins and she thought she could get up off the floor with some semblance of grace.

Brent hopped up and declared he would start gnawing on the table if they didn't get something to eat. Knowing his appetite, Marla half feared he meant it.

"There's nothing in the fridge," she said apologetically. "Why don't you order some carryout food while I take a shower? Get them to deliver it so you don't have to get dressed," she added, giving him her best come-hither look.

Brent watched Marla gather up her clothes and walk naked into the bedroom. Not wanting to be any farther away from her than he had to after a week of separation, he grabbed her stash of carryout menus and also went into the bedroom. They agreed on what they wanted to order, and he sat down on the bed to make the phone call while Marla disappeared into the bathroom.

A moment later he heard the shower spray. He grinned when Marla started humming to herself. He gave their carryout dinner order to the boy who answered the telephone. Brent assumed the boy was new at the job, since he had to patiently repeat each item at least twice. The kid got it wrong, anyhow, and they wound up starting over from the beginning. When Brent said he wanted the food delivered, the boy took Marla's phone number and said goodbye.

"Don't you want the address?" Brent asked. He rolled his eyes when he realized the line had gone dead. When he tried the restaurant again, the line was busy.

He hung up the phone and stared at it. Maybe the kid would call back in a minute. Thirty seconds later, the phone rang shrilly.

Brent picked it up on the first ring. "Hello?"

There was a slight pause. Then a man's thin voice said, "Is this Marla Foster's number?"

"Yeah." Brent frowned, realizing with disappointment that it wasn't the carryout service. He was starved.

"May I speak to her?"

"She can't come to the phone right now. Can I take a message?" Brent said politely. Get off the phone so I can make sure my dinner gets here, he added silently.

"This is rather important. Why can't she come to the phone?" the speaker said impatiently.

The querulous tone made Brent wonder if the speaker was Marla's stepfather. "She's in the shower. Can I help you?"

"Who is this?"

"Brent Ventura. I'm a good friend of hers. Who's this?"

There was something palpable in the long silence that followed, something heavy and unpleasant. Brent started to get a sick feeling, as if he had just made a very stupid mistake. He thought he knew the answer before it came.

"This is Warren Tallman. Please tell Marla I want to see her in my office at nine o'clock sharp tomorrow morning."

Warren hung up before Brent could say anything in response. He stared dumbly at the receiver for a full minute afterward. Finally, he placed it back in the cradle and took a deep breath. Another sick sensation shook him when he realized how much malice had been contained in Warren's last two simple sentences. The man really hated Marla and was clearly delighted to have found a weapon he could use against her.

And I'm the one who gave it to him, Brent thought bleakly. The sound of Marla's cheerful humming in the bathroom cut through him like a knife. He was still sitting on the bed, trying to work up the courage to tell her what he had just done, when she came into the bedroom, dripping wet and wrapped in a towel.

"Aren't you going to offer to dry me?" she asked with a grin.

His only response was a somber, worried look. Her eyes widened and she sat down next to him.

"What is it? What's wrong?" she asked immediately.

He gestured inarticulately.

Her gaze flew to the phone. "Who called? Brent!"

He sighed. She was going to be furious and upset no matter how he phrased it. "Warren Tallman."

She gave him a puzzled frown. "Warren? But why? He never phones me at home." Then her eyes widened as realization dawned.

"I . . . He asked who I was, and I told him without thinking, before I realized who he was. I'm sorry, Marla."

"Was he . . . ?" She licked her lips nervously. "Did he seem upset?"

Brent's mouth twisted in anger. "He said he wants to see you in his office at nine o'clock tomorrow morning."

Marla's face crumpled. "Oh, no," she said despairingly. "I should have realized today was just the calm before the storm. Now that he has something to use against me, he'll do his best to get me fired."

"Marla." Brent put his arm around her, relieved that she didn't shake him off. "Why don't you just hand in your resignation tomorrow? That company treats you like mud."

"They don't really, Brent. It's just Warren."

"That's not true. They let him get away with it. You said yourself that you fell into disfavor over one error, *his* error."

"It was my mistake, too," she insisted irritably.

"What's more, they want to run your personal life," he continued.

"They just don't want me dating my clients. We've been over this before."

"I don't want you to have to go in there and take a load of crap from someone who doesn't deserve to clean your boots," he said earnestly.

"And how do you suggest I support myself and my mother if I quit my job tomorrow?" she snapped.

"Come to work for Ventura."

"Sure," she said sarcastically. "As what?"

"Our marketing director."

Marla's jaw dropped when she realized he was serious. "You mean that, don't you?"

"Of course I do. You have the background, you already know the company well, you're becoming a sportswoman, it's a great place to work, I'll at least match what Freemont pays you and we could work together all the time."

"Brent, this is a crazy impulse. You don't know—"

"Nigel thinks it's a good idea."

"You've discussed this with Nigel?" she said incredulously.

"Yes. When he told me that we would definitely have to hire someone before long, we both agreed that you would be the perfect choice. *If* you were interested."

"So that's why he . . ." She sighed, touched and tempted by Brent's offer but knowing how impractical it was. "It's impossible, Brent. Don't think I'm not grateful—"

"I don't want your gratitude," he said irritably. "I want your expertise."

"Not only would it be unethical to leave my company for a better offer from my client—"

"Why?" he challenged.

"But there is still the chance that I can salvage my career at Freemont."

"Why do you want to?" he demanded.

"I think we have discussed why my career is important to me enough times, and Freemont is still the biggest, most prestigious agency in town. My career and my security matter too much for me to recklessly quit the job I've worked so hard at just because my lover offers me another job on impulse after we've had a wonderful vacation together.''

He started to respond when the phone rang again. They both stared at it for a moment. Finally Marla said, "If it's Warren, I might as well get this over with now." When she picked up the receiver, however, it turned out to be the carryout restaurant. Brent heard her giving her address to the boy, correcting him several times as he read the information back to her.

As soon as she hung up, Brent was prepared to continue the argument. "Look—"

"I don't want to talk about it anymore," she said tersely.

"I do."

"I have enough to worry about without your nagging me tonight!"

That stopped him. He gave in. "All right. I'm offering the job to you seriously, but I won't pressure you any more tonight. I just want you to think about it."

"Brent—"

"That's all I ask. For now."

The rest of the evening was far from pleasant. Marla was tense and restless and picked at her food. Brent felt guilty and hurt by turns. When she finally suggested he go home and relax, he exploded again.

"No! What kind of a person do you think I am?"

She stared at him in bewilderment. "What are you talking about?"

"Even disregarding the fact that *I* got you into this mess tonight—"

"I knew it would happen sooner or later," she said wearily.

Her fatalistic tone of voice surprised him and made him calm down. "Marla, I love you. I can't just trot home and get a good night's sleep when you've got a problem. I want to be here for you, even if only so you'll have someone to snap at."

Marla felt a rush of gratitude and affection so strong it filled her eyes with unexpected moistness. She pushed her plate away, stood up and rounded the table to slide onto Brent's lap.

"Thank you," she said inadequately.

"You don't have to thank me," he mumbled into her hair.

"Yes, I do. I've been taken for granted by my family long enough that I know it's wrong to assume it's someone's ordained duty to help you out all the time."

"You're wrong. From now on it *is* my duty and my privilege to help you out all the time. Your family is . . . That's different. Your mother is . . ."

"Unhealthily dependent," Marla finished for him, recognizing his reluctance to criticize her family to her. She kissed his cheek. "I'm sorry I've been snapping at you since Warren's call," she added.

"It's okay. I feel guilty, honey. I'm sorry."

Brent tried to help Marla work out what she would say to Warren the next morning, but she finally snapped at him again, telling him to leave it to her. Brent just didn't have any understanding of how a businesswoman had to address a hostile superior.

She slept very little that night, unable to relax no matter how much Brent soothed her. She was grateful for his presence, though, and started thinking about how many other bad nights in her life would have been easier if he had been there with her. That she slept at all was only due to his loving, comforting presence beside her all night.

By the time she faced Warren in his office the following morning, it took all her strength of will to speak to him with her once-customary calm control.

Warren began by explaining curtly that he had telephoned her at home the previous evening to tell her about some further complications with the Ventura ad layout that had the embarrassing printing error in it. When he outlined the situation, Marla realized it was an annoying but common problem and sensed that Warren had panicked because he didn't know how to deal with it. She assured him she would take care of it. He suggested she might no longer be in a position to do that. She calmly asked him to explain what he meant.

"When you said you were busy yesterday, I had no idea you meant you were just in a rush to get home," Warren began scathingly.

"I *was* busy. And I left the office late," she said reasonably.

He ignored her. "I also didn't realize you were rushing home to your *client*, Marla."

She remained silent. She wouldn't stumble through denials before he had even made an accusation. Instead she looked at him with polite interest. It seemed to enrage him.

"Well, are you going to deny that Brent Ventura was in your apartment last night? While you were *showering*?"

He made it sound as though she had been engaged in some obscene, immoral ritual. "He was there," she agreed steadily.

"Have you nothing more to say?" he demanded furiously.

"You called this meeting," she reminded him politely. "Surely you must have something more to say."

"I do! You must realize that by becoming good friends with Ventura—as he so coyly put it last night—you jeopardize an important account, the agency's respectability and several people's jobs. How can you have committed such an irresponsible breach of professional ethics?"

She could tell by the way he had phrased the question that he had prepared it in advance. What's more, he obviously enjoyed delivering it. "Mr. Ventura has assured me daily that our personal association will not jeopardize the account, no matter what happens between us."

"Of all the—"

"Furthermore, I take full responsibility for my actions, and he knows this. My behavior after working hours does not reflect on the agency and never has. What's more, you and I both know that *my* job is the *only* job in jeopardy on this particular occasion.''

Warren obviously resented Marla's self-control, but her calm manner prevented the meeting from descending into a hysterical shouting match of swapped insults and name-calling, which was what she had most dreaded with him. He ended the meeting by announcing he would have to report this incident to the board. The glee with which he told Marla that he had ''grave doubts'' about her continued employment at Freemont made her want to punch him. Instead, she rose from her seat and left the room with dignity.

Since the best defense was undoubtedly a good offense in this case, Marla went immediately to a senior vice president whom she knew respected her work and liked her personally. As calmly and objectively as possible, without making excuses for herself or violating Brent's privacy, she explained the situation. She could tell by the expression on the man's face that she had dropped a real bombshell.

He said he could probably keep the board from firing her immediately but admitted cynically that that was only because they would want to wait long enough to ensure they could keep Ventura's business if they got rid of her.

Knowing Brent so well, Marla knew Freemont would definitely lose the account for firing a friend or lover of his. But she also knew that those weren't the terms under which she wanted to be retained at Freemont. She knew this senior officer wasn't contemptuous of her, but he did point out that she wasn't yet in a firm enough position at the agency to have committed an error like this without repercussions.

Marla walked wearily to her own office after that inconclusive meeting. She had known all along that this could happen. Indeed, she had resisted Brent's overtures for so long because she had been *convinced* it would happen. Now that her job really was at stake, hanging by a tattered thread, she felt a curious sense of anticlimax, as if it didn't really matter that much in the scheme of things. She shook herself mentally and irritably reminded herself of her long-held priorities.

Marla was only able to interest herself in her work that afternoon because she was concentrating on Ventura, the account that had come to mean so much to her personally. By the time she left work that evening, she felt too numb and exhausted to think clearly about her future.

She reflected bitterly on the irony of her situation. She might well wind up penniless and out of work because she had wanted a man too much to behave with her customary good sense. The fact that she didn't even seem to care very much at the moment was only further proof in her mind that her feelings for Brent distorted all her values. And yet she still loved him.

Marla realized, with a growing sense of unease, that for all her hard work and determination, she wasn't really so different from her mother, after all. And she was frightened by the wreck that that woman's life had become.

Chapter Thirteen

Marla's numbness was shattered by the telephone call she received when she got home that evening. The phone was ringing when she walked through the front door. Since Brent had called her twice that day and insisted they still needed to talk some more, she assumed it was him. He wanted to confront the situation, and she wanted to curl up and hide from it for a few hours. All the same, she suddenly missed him. She hoped he was calling to tell her he was on his way over.

She picked up the receiver. "Hello?"

"Marla, it's Leila. I thought you would never get home!"

The broken, frantic tone of her sister's voice alarmed Marla. She put down her small bag of groceries and immediately asked what was wrong.

When Brent arrived an hour later, she was finishing her conversation with Leila. She let him in the door, continued talking for a few minutes, then finally hung up.

"Was that your mother?" he asked. He had noticed Marla's soothing tone and caught her references to a divorce.

She shook her head and sat down. "My sister," she said bleakly.

He came to sit near her on the couch. "She's worried about your mom?" he asked sympathetically. Marla looked terrible; her face was drawn and pale, her eyes haunted. He tried to put his arms around her and felt pain stab through him when she shook her head and scooted away from him.

"She's not worried about my mother. I doubt if she's spared a thought for my mother in weeks and weeks." She met his confused stare. "She's getting divorced, too."

"Oh, Marla. That's too bad," he said, knowing the words were inadequate.

Her dry laugh was bitter. "It's not too bad. In my family, it's merely inevitable. That's how we live."

He frowned. He didn't like it when she included herself in her family's self-generated problems. She was vastly different from the two kind, weak-willed, helpless women he had learned about through their phone calls and her own descriptions.

"She needs financial and moral support from you?" he guessed.

Marla nodded and ran her hands through her hair. "Yes. I promised her money. What else could I do? I told her that this won't be like what I send Mom, though. Leila can put her daughter in day care—or get my mom to baby-sit—and go get a job. She's too young to spend the rest of her life relying on me." Then she took a deep breath. "I promised her money, and I'm probably going to be out of work soon. Oh, God."

The broken tone of her voice tore through him. "How can I help you?" he asked desperately.

"It's sweet of you to want to comfort me, but I—"

"I don't want to comfort you, dammit. I want to *help* you."

"There's nothing you can do."

"Of course there is! You're out of a job, and I can offer you a good one. You need money for two women in your family, and my money is yours."

"I'm not out of a job yet, and I can't take the one you're offering me!"

"Why the hell not?" he said through gritted teeth.

"Where will I be when we break up? What will I do then? Go out and look for *another* job, telling all my prospective employers that my ex-boyfriend threw me out of work?" she snapped.

"I don't want to be your boyfriend! God, that's a ridiculous word to apply to a thirty-eight-year-old man. I want to be your husband, so I think we can safely say you won't have to worry about me throwing you out of work."

"Until we get divorced, you mean."

"We *won't* get divorced."

"*Everybody* in my family gets divorced."

Brent stared at her in shocked silence, finally realizing the root of the problem. He took a steadying breath and said, "This is crazy, Marla. We're fighting because your sister's getting a divorce."

She shook her head. "No. We're fighting because I've finally come to my senses and realized how impossible this is."

He felt as if the floor had bottomed out. "What do you mean by that?"

"Oh, Brent. I know you have the best intentions, I know you always believe everything will work out—"

"No, I believe *we* can work things out. I'm not naive enough to believe it happens by itself. Maybe that's why no one in your family can stay married. Marriage requires hard work."

"Don't lecture me about marriage," she pleaded.

"It happens to be a subject I know something about. Because I had a good marriage. So, unlike you, I know that it's possible, and I know how to recognize the signs of a good partner." His voice became intense, and he continued, "You and I would make great partners if you could just give up this idea that it's natural for us to split up and an aberration for us to stay together the rest of our lives."

"Maybe you did have a marriage that would have lasted forever. Maybe you're capable of that," she said shrilly. "But I was raised without that example, and I don't believe in it enough to risk my security."

"I'm not asking you to stop working, forget how to drive or become illiterate. I just want us to be together!"

"If I worked for you in your company, I would be reliant on you for my income."

"Is it somehow preferable to rely on Freemont for your income?"

"Yes! Of course it is!"

"That's got to be the dumbest thing you've ever said to me," Brent said critically. "At least *I* care what happens to you. Don't kid yourself that you're ever completely secure and self-sufficient in this world, Marla. Your security depends on Freemont right now, on a board of directors who don't give a damn about you and just treat you like a cog in their machine. Your security depends on a creep like Warren Tallman, who has the clout to make you lose your job. And I resent your preferring to rely on *him* for security rather than on *me*. I happen to love you."

"You *will* not understand, will you?"

"No! I won't understand crazy, convoluted thinking that makes you trust them more than you trust me. I won't understand why you think two mature, experienced adults like us, who are in love with each other, can't make a successful marriage together. And I won't understand why you insist I would willfully fire you and throw you out in the cold, no matter what happens between us personally."

Her hands clenched with fury, and she said in a low voice, "Then you have conveniently forgotten the pressure you put me under a few weeks ago at work just because I wouldn't sleep with you!"

He didn't back down, but he modified his tone. "I haven't forgotten. May I point out that I didn't fire you, but gave you a chance. And I wasn't even in love with you then. Or if I was, I didn't know it." He sighed and rumpled his dark hair. "And I knew it was wrong at the time, and I would never put you under pressure like that again. I couldn't do anything to hurt you, not on purpose, not the way I feel about you."

Marla's throat burned with the tears she knew she would forbid herself to ever shed. Her heart pounded as if it wanted to escape from her, and her stomach churned with her tumultuous emotions.

"Please go, Brent," she whispered.

He shot out of his seat and grabbed her by the shoulders. "No! I've told you before—"

"Please," she said, backing away from him. "I'm sorry. I never should have gotten involved with you in the first place. This can't work out, and you deserve someone who believes in happily ever after. Please go."

He released her. His gaze took in her haggard, beaten expression, and he knew that nothing and no one could get through to her that night. He finally relented, understanding that he couldn't force her to accept his permanent commitment until she was willing to believe in it.

"Okay. I'll go, and I'll wait for you to call me." He went to the front door and paused. "But I'm not giving up, Marla. I don't love lightly. There was only one other woman in my life I wanted to marry, and I lost her. I won't lose you, too. Not if there's anything I can do about it."

Those words haunted Marla during the days that followed. True to his word, Brent didn't call her. She knew what an effort of will that was on his part, but she also knew it was for the best. The deeper their relationship got, the more it would hurt them both when it ended—particularly Brent, who had believed they could marry and be together till they were old and gray. She wished she could believe, as he did, that love lasted forever, but her little sister's sudden announcement of divorce had shaken her to the core.

Brent had grown up in the midst of a secure, happy marriage, and he had followed that example with his first wife. Marla had never even entertained the hope of a lifetime marriage, having grown up as she did. And if Brent had started to sow new dreams in her mind, the realization of continuing patterns in her family—like mother, like daughter—had smashed those dreams to bits.

She might have continued the relationship anyhow under different circumstances, because she loved him so much. But once Brent had fallen in love with her, he wasn't able to accept anything less than the same total commitment he was prepared to give. And despite his best efforts to be phlegmatic, Marla had seen the hurt in his eyes every time she couldn't give him that total, unconditional commitment. Now that her family's past had caught up with her, that failure on her part would grow and fester between them. He might even hate her by the time their relationship ended.

The next few days passed in such a vacuum of lonely misery that Marla could only survive by living through them one moment at a time. If she thought even an hour ahead, she would start to crumble, knowing that the succeeding hours and days and months would be as lonely and as barren as the present. How long, she wondered desperately, would it take to get over Brent's absence? She couldn't think that far ahead, or she would break down.

Vernon had informed her that her superior's guess had been correct: she wasn't going to lose her job because Freemont was afraid she would take the Ventura account with her. She also wasn't being considered for any new business anymore. Although most staff members and some senior people continued to treat her normally, Warren and his cronies radiated hostile disapproval in her presence.

She had too much self-respect to continue in that atmosphere, but too much common sense to simply walk out. She decided to look for a new job, letting it be known at the agency that she planned to leave. For the first time in her life, she couldn't work up any interest whatsoever in her career. Revising her résumé seemed meaningless and empty, but she did it anyhow to fill up her lonely hours.

She found her time at home agonizing, since her apartment was full of memories of Brent. She remembered him eating gargantuan breakfasts in her kitchen, sleeping in innocent abandon on her bed, hesitantly offering her a gift of hiking boots at her front door, making love to her everywhere: in the bed, on the floor, in the shower, on the couch.... She wondered if she should move before she went crazy.

But moving also seemed pointless, and she had no energy to pursue the idea. The only thing that could rouse her interest was the Ventura account. She worked harder than ever, coming up with new ideas, checking several times a day on the creative team, phoning Nigel daily with questions and suggestions. She asked after Brent every time she phoned, unable to resist, and always got vague, troubled answers. When Nigel finally inquired bluntly what had happened between her and Brent, she stopped asking about him.

The account was at least something she could do for Brent. She couldn't give him any of the other things he wanted and deserved, but she could give him her very best work. She came in early and worked late, she supervised everything to do with the account, she went the last mile for him on every occasion—because it was all she could give him ultimately.

She struggled through the following week in total despair, wondering how she was ever going to get her life back in gear. It had been eight days since she had seen Brent, and she guiltily wondered if he was suffering this much because of her and her inadequacies. She was considering calling him from her apartment one night, just to make sure he was all right, when her sister, Leila, phoned again.

Marla listened apathetically for a while, then something her sister said started niggling away at her subconscious.

After a few more minutes of hearing Leila drone on about how hard her life was and how awful her marriage had been, Marla started listening and responding alertly for the first time since she had last seen Brent.

"Wait a minute, wait a minute," Marla said suddenly. "You left him because you had nothing to *talk* about?" Leila confirmed this emphatically. "How is that possible? You were madly in love with him at your wedding, and you lived in the same house with the man for seven years. You bore him a daughter. How could you possibly not have anything to talk about?" she demanded.

"I don't know," Leila said casually. "I guess we just grew apart."

"No, that's the kind of thing Mom says, Leila, but it's not good enough to explain throwing seven years down the drain. You must have a better reason than that."

What it came down to, after another hour of tearful conversation, was that Leila really didn't have a better answer. She had simply been bored, tired of the marriage, sick of her husband's habits, annoyed by his company. There was nothing in the marriage to compensate for those failings, so she'd ended it.

Marla decided she had better finish the conversation before she said something devastatingly rude to Leila. She stared at the phone in exasperation. She would bring more effort to a dinner party than her sister had brought to her own marriage. After seven years, Leila didn't even know what her husband's interests, fears, plans or politics were. She didn't know what his finest character traits were or where his weak spots were.

As near as Marla could tell, Leila had married him because he was "so cute and such a good dancer" and because he had asked her. Not very serious criteria on which to build a life together, Marla mused.

She ironed her clothes that night, thinking furiously the whole time. Leila did indeed take after their mother, who had married and divorced four men with—Marla now consciously realized for the first time—equally insubstantial reasons. She lowered her hand as a freedom-giving, confidence-building awareness dawned inside her. No wonder those two women didn't have successful marriages!

Brent had said that marriage took hard work, and as he had pointed out, having had a good marriage, he certainly ought to know what he was talking about. Her mother had never applied herself to marriage with any real commitment or effort, just as she had never applied herself to any other aspect of life—work, child rearing, practical matters—with any commitment or effort. Marla's sister appeared to be turning out the same way.

Marla didn't need Brent to tell her she wasn't like that at all. She had run her whole life with steely determination and unwavering commitment to her goals. Even in the throes of her insecurities, she had brought more effort and commitment to her relationship with Brent in a few weeks than her family members had brought to years of marriage. In only a short time she and Brent had found activities they could share, things they could teach each other, subjects they enjoyed talking about. She knew his strengths and vulnerabilities, and she knew why she loved him. She knew almost as much about him as she knew about herself, and she looked forward to filling in the gaps.

She ran to the phone and dialed his home number with shaking fingers. She didn't know what would happen or how they would work it out, but she had to see him. Right now.

When he answered the phone, she said, "This is Marla. I have to talk to you. I'm coming right over."

There was a long silence, and then he said in a strangled voice, "For the love of God, don't have an accident on the way here."

She was nearly out the front door when she smelled something burning. She looked around the living room in frantic haste, then cursed when she realized she had left the iron sitting facedown on her favorite linen skirt. She picked it up, turned it off and regarded the damage fatalistically.

"Oh, well," she muttered. "I won't be wearing many skirts at my new job, anyhow."

The drive to Brent's house seemed to take forever. She gripped the wheel, forcing herself to drive carefully. He'd never forgive her if she got herself killed now. He had even once told her that he liked her cautious nature because he had lost his first wife due to recklessness and couldn't bear the pain of living with another reckless woman.

With that heartfelt admission of Brent's in mind, Marla stoically forced herself to obey the speed limits and come to a full stop at every stop sign, even though every part of her body was shaking with the need to see and touch Brent *now*. When she finally arrived at his house, his front door flew open as soon as she pulled into his driveway.

She had planned to apologize for her stupidity and lack of faith and to discuss everything coherently. But the look on his face got to her, and she flung herself wordlessly into his arms and kissed him again and again. She felt his strong arms wrap around her waist and lifted her off the ground so he could carry her inside and shut the door while they plundered each other's mouths with hungry passion.

She smiled and laughed and babbled incoherently while he brushed rough, greedy kisses across her face and down her neck. It was a long time before he pulled back to study her face. When he looked into her eyes, he made a choked sound of surprise.

"You're crying," he whispered. "I've never seen you cry."

"Oh, Brent," she sobbed, and buried her face against his neck.

He picked her up and carried her to the couch, where they settled down comfortably together. "What's wrong, honey?" he asked gently.

"Nothing's wrong," she told him joyfully, wiping at the tears that streamed down her face. "I've just been...tense."

"Oh, Marla." He hugged her to him again and then gave her a pained smile. "Tense? I've been a bear. I've been mean, snappish, miserable.... I can't stand this anymore." He looked at her hopefully.

"You won't have to," she assured him. "I've finally figured out that I'm perfect marriage material. If your proposal's still open, that is."

"If it's still open?" he said incredulously. "Let's go get our license tomorrow morning before you can change your mind."

"Oh, I won't change my mind about marrying you," she said. "Not for the rest of my life."

He brushed her hair away from her face. "Not that I'm not thrilled, but how did this happen?"

She told him at length about her sister's phone call. "I didn't choose you the way Leila and my mother chose their husbands, and I'm certainly not going to run my marriage the way they ran theirs," she concluded. "If anybody knows about commitment to a goal, it's me. And my most important goal is to spend the rest of my life with you. From now on, you're an irrevocable part of my security and stability."

She paused briefly, then added, "I'm still a realist, Brent, and I know there's always the outside chance that any relationship won't last forever. But I believe in ours. Anyhow, as Nigel would say—"

"Nothing ventured, nothing gained."

She looked at him in surprise. "How did you know what I was going to say?"

"I didn't. I knew what Nigel would say. He's so predictable," Brent said dryly.

She smiled. "Well, I'm ready to venture everything with you."

He held her tightly and rested his cheek against her hair. "I'm so glad you realized you're not like the rest of your family. I tried to tell you a number of times, but I guess it's one of those things you have to learn for yourself. And," he added, "I doubt that I'm remotely like their husbands. It takes two people to make a marriage work. It takes maturity and strength to love honestly and to give unselfishly."

"And we've got that," she agreed. How could she have ever thought he was immature, irresponsible or unreliable? She knew without a doubt he would be there for her for the rest of their lives, giving her support, stability and unconditional love. As for his naïveté—well, it was one of the things that made him so endearing, and he obviously wasn't too naive to be a successful businessman. Which reminded her.

"Now, about my desk," she said. "I don't want it too close to Nigel's because he's so sloppy. And I don't want it near Felice, because just seeing her wears me out."

Brent sat bolt upright, letting her fall back against the couch cushions. "You're coming to work for me?" he asked in astonishment.

"Yes. I haven't actually given my notice yet, but I think two weeks is all Freemont deserves, don't you?"

"Marla, I..." He gaped at her speechlessly for a moment. Then he tried—unsuccessfully—to hide his pleasure at her statement. "Listen," he said seriously. "I was out of line about your job. I mean, I want you to join the company for good reasons, not all of them personal, and so does Nigel. But you might prefer to work at another ad agency, and I never even discussed that with you."

Marla smiled gratefully at him. Then she continued, "And I don't want one of those awful posture chairs half the people at Ventura have. It'd make my knees—"

He cut her off with a hard, possessive kiss. Then he said, "I'm the boss so I don't have to think about details like that. That's someone else's responsibility." He frowned. "I wonder if I should keep my account with Freemont, since they've treated my wife so shabbily."

"Oh, you must Brent! You're getting some great advertising there, thanks to me. And I wouldn't dream of taking the account away from Vernon and Nathan. Besides," she added with a grin, "it'll be a pleasure to see Warren being deferential to me now that I'm the client. I'll bet you he never comes near the account again as soon as I start working for you."

"Well, that won't be for a while. At least two months," Brent said.

She frowned at him. "Why not?"

"Because we're going on a nice, long honeymoon as soon as you're done at Freemont. Six weeks or so."

"How can you be away for that long?"

"I founded a whole company just so I could be gone whenever I feel like it," he reminded her complacently.

Marla's eyes sparkled. "Where are we going?"

He shrugged. "Nevada, Wyoming, Arizona . . . wherever we decide. A big park—one we can wander around in together for weeks."

"Mmm." She nuzzled his neck. "It sounds perfect."

"In the meantime . . ." he said suggestively, starting to unbutton her blouse.

"Yes?" She shifted to make it easier for him.

"Maybe we could start moving your stuff in here."

She nodded. "We'll have to decide which pieces of my furniture will fit." Brent touched her bare skin longingly, and she lost interest in talking.

His lips explored hers with infinite gentleness, despite the hunger riding them both. This was a special night, the night Marla had chased away the last of her ghosts and married Brent in her heart. The ceremony would be a mere formality. And so they touched each other with slow, burning passion, wanting to capture each moment, wanting to make each sensation and expression linger in their minds through all the shared years to come.

When they were both naked, he carried her into the bedroom and laid her lovingly on the bed they would sleep in together from now on, as man and wife. They explored and adored each other with the frank tenderness their bodies had craved during their painful separation, heightening and drawing out each shimmering sensation.

"I love you," Marla moaned when he thrust into her body at last with such a combination of strength and gentleness it made her helpless with emotion.

He answered her with his body, and their passion fulfilled and completed them both. Afterward, they lay wrapped in each other's arms, warm and drowsy and totally content.

"It'll always be like this," he promised softly.

"I know," she answered. Just before she drifted off to sleep, she murmured, "Brent?"

"Yes?"

"About our honeymoon?"

"What about it, honey?"

"Unless you bring a thick mat to put on the ground under my sleeping bag, I'm not going."

He chuckled. "Well, marriage is full of these little compromises." He was still smiling slightly when he fell asleep with his cheek resting against her hair.

* * * * *

Back by popular demand, some of Diana Palmer's earliest published books are available again!

Several years ago, Diana Palmer began her writing career. Sweet, compelling and totally unforgettable, these are the love stories that enchanted readers everywhere.

Next month, six more of these wonderful stories will be available in DIANA PALMER DUETS—Books 4, 5 and 6. Each DUET contains two powerful stories plus an introduction by Diana Palmer. Don't miss:

Book Four	**AFTER THE MUSIC** **DREAM'S END**
Book Five	**BOUND BY A PROMISE** **PASSION FLOWER**
Book Six	**TO HAVE AND TO HOLD** **THE COWBOY AND THE LADY**

Be sure to look for these titles next month at your favorite retail outlet. If you missed DIANA PALMER DUETS, Books 1, 2 or 3, order them by sending your name, address, zip or postal code, along with a check or money order for $3.25 for each book ordered, plus 75¢ postage and handling, payable to Silhouette Reader Service to:

In the U.S.
901 Fuhrmann Blvd.
Box 1396
Buffalo, NY 14269-1396

In Canada
P.O. Box 609
Fort Erie, Ontario
L2A 5X3

Please specify book title(s) with your order.

DPD-1

SILHOUETTE'S "BIG WIN"
SWEEPSTAKES RULES & REGULATIONS
NO PURCHASE NECESSARY TO ENTER OR RECEIVE A PRIZE